PASSING THROUGH

Guida Jackson

SIMON AND SCHUSTER

NEW YORK

Published by Simon and Schuster
A Division of Gulf & Western Corporation
Simon & Schuster Building
Rockefeller Center
1230 Avenue of the Americas
New York, New York 10020
Designed by Irving Perkins
Manufactured in the United States of America
Printed and bound by Fairfield Graphics, Inc.
1 2 3 4 5 6 7 8 9 10

Library of Congress Cataloging in Publication Data

Jackson, Guida.
  Passing through.

  I. Title.
PZ4.J1336Pas   [PS3560.A2155]   813'.5'4   79-12878

ISBN 0-671-24865-0

For my parents, Jimmie and Ina Miller

With special gratitude to Ronald S. Joseph

Author's Note

Emancipation Day, "Juneteenth," celebrated in the South on June 19, commemorates the date slaves first learned of Lincoln's Proclamation.

Part 1

Leah's Journey

1

June 18, 1960, Eve of Emancipation Day

IN HER haste to get out, Leah forgot about the catch on the
screen door. She met the screen full force, and it didn't give.
The tiny steel fibers cut crosshatch patterns on her knee and
forearm, patterns she wouldn't notice until the next day and
would wonder about. The impact hardly jarred her and only
slowed her an instant. The man had told her, "Get out of
here!" as if an instant was all she had left.

Outside, the midmorning heat hit her like a furnace blast,
but for once she took no notice. Clattering down the back
steps onto the gentle green slope which ended at the pier, she
fought the urge just to keep on going, to run splat into the
placid chill of the lake and sink out of sight. The scratch on
her cheek burned, and her chest ached where Doris Jean's
knee had been. And just before she reached the car, hidden in
the shadow of a small knoll just out of sight of the house, she

stumbled and skinned the other knee. She was panting now, and salty tears slid into the corner of her mouth. When she reached for the car door handle, she realized that her sleeve was partially torn off and was binding her left arm. She ripped the sleeve free and skinned it off.

The interior of the car was steaming, and the steering wheel was too hot to grip. She fingered it gingerly. She didn't look back at the lake house, didn't think at all as she threw the old Chrysler into gear and went jouncing off along the washboard road. She was an inexperienced driver; she had her first lesson a year before on her twenty-fifth birthday, and it didn't include back-country driving. She had never driven this road before today. Still, she did miraculously seem to be heading in the right direction.

The road, like all East Texas back roads, was hilly and winding. It was hardly more than a car's width across, and its convex surface sloped off into stagnant, mossy, spongy ditches on each side. When Leah saw the old Chevy coupé veer around the bend ahead, she looked for a wide place to pull over. A side trail split off some thirty yards ahead. She jammed the gas pedal to the floor and made for it. The Chrysler gave a cough then leaped ahead. The Chevy was bearing down fast—didn't he see her? She beat on the horn in a frenzy; he may have been trying to stop, but his slick old tires got no traction on the pebbly road. She slung the Chrysler onto the rutted side trail as a black Chevy with a silver streak barreled past. A dark figure hunched low over the wheel never looked her way. The other occupant was slumped against the outside door. Too much Juneteenth, she supposed vaguely, shaking from the extra surge of unused adrenaline. At any rate, they would never recognize her, she was sure.

When her weakness passed, she whipped onto the meandering dirt lane again, not as sure, now, that she was heading toward town. Except for a plot here and there that had been painfully scraped clean, the land was a luxuriant mesh of steeping green, the short-needle and slash pine, the chinquapin, sweet gum and wild plum all wound together with a tangled web of ripe vine. She couldn't even see the sun, although by now it must be well overhead. In the dappled light of the road, everything looked the same. Perhaps she wasn't heading west at all. The road snaked so crazily that she may well have doubled back.

Then around the next bend hove up the old house where she had stopped to ask directions thirty minutes before. It looked like any one of a dozen other gray frame shotguns along this way, except for the tree. Same long plank porch across the front. Same lean-to on the back. The usual daybed and washing machine and rocker on the porch. Same old tires and other auto parts strewn in the hard dirt yard. But the tree set this house apart. A tremendous shaggy oak sat smack against the ancient house, nudging it so that the whole house leaned. And a large branch threatened to push the porch roof clean off the house. Still, it wasn't a very healthy tree; the top third was dead, and the rest looked ragged and sketchy, a specter of a tree. This was the house, make no mistake.

Now it was the dogs' wails that drew her to a temporary stop. Several long-legged hounds ran from the house to an object in the yard and back again to the house, alternately yowling and then hacking in frantic staccato, until Leah's car slowed in front of the house. Then—strange!—they tucked tail and tore under the porch. Shrugging at their strange behavior, she ground the Chrysler into gear and caught only a glance at the thing in the yard as she pulled away. Then, heart pounding in apprehension, she pulled up sharply and backed up for another stunned look. The dogs barked and whimpered, but none came out to challenge her.

The cacophony of cicadas buzzing swelled in unison and added to Leah's dazed sensation that she might be hallucinating. She tried to deal with conflicting impressions exploding in her head. Underlying her initial horror, there was something kin to glee: a morbid elation, release even, at a sight so revolting. She dug her nails deep into the armrest and shivered with loathing of the awkward remains of a corpse whose head had been battered to the pith. The hideousness of the human form so mutilated filled her with hatred for the dead woman who dared to be so flagrantly grotesque. The body lay facedown, the spindly legs drawn under it, the blood-covered hands clutching at the mushy nub that had once been its head, around which several great green flies now swarmed. It was several long seconds before Leah could comprehend that this could be the same woman she'd asked for directions a scant half hour before. Now she wondered why the crude creature, so rude in life, couldn't at least have been more discreet in death. The wretched thing was still kicking, twitching!

Just as the burning bile welled up in her throat, she flung open the car door and retched wildly. The vomitus splattered crazily on the hard clay road, exciting the dogs—or maybe they heard something else—so that they leaped from their shelter and lunged toward the car, enraged. She slammed the door and gunned off, spraying pebbles behind her.

So that's what murder is like? she thought. Is this fate, some kind of universal justice at work? If I kill someone in absentia, I still must view a corpse, if not my own victim, then someone else's. Maybe it's karma. Or maybe I have the Midas touch.

Unconsciously she made a sign of the cross and thought ruefully that at least Sister Fain would approve of that.

Her Chrysler swerved around the last curve, leaving behind the tangle of marshwood, and she was on the blacktop headed for town. Oleander big enough to conceal a patrol car lined the highway. She eased up on the gas.

Got to slow down. Can't get stopped. Got to make it home, change clothes. Get back before Jennings gets home from the hospital. . . . Almost noon. Never make it. Got to make it.

She sped up cautiously, eyes darting down side roads watching for speed traps. No one in sight. At length she reached the crepe myrtle boulevard at the city limits.

Traffic was heavy all over town. Typical Saturday. No, worse. Eve of Juneteenth. They've started already.

Miss town. Skirt around the park. Just get home, get this shirt off before Jennings shows up. Explain the scratch somehow, if necessary. One more lie won't matter now.

She had almost forgotten the corpse. Maybe that whole scene was imagined. She thought more about the man who had rescued her back at the lake house, had grabbed Doris Jean and held her off, giving a savage jerk of his head toward the door. Who had growled at her, but not in anger, "Get out of here!" The magnificent naked man. The quadroon.

He was always popping up. Like the time a year ago, shortly after she came to Clarington, when she was swimming in the lake, stepped in a hole and went under. He had come out of nowhere and pulled her out, while Jennings and the others looked on.

And today. If it hadn't been for him, Doris Jean probably would have killed her. Would have taken two brown wads of hair and used them for handles, would have bashed her head against the floor again and again until—

Perry; that was his name. The man who, somehow, knew all about her. Perry Johnson, the caretaker at the lake. Had a little cabin around on the other side; she remembered stopping there with Jennings that day to thank him for pulling her out of the lake. His skinny red-haired wife had come to the screen door that day—

"Good grief!" she said aloud. She turned the Chrysler into the drive, switched off the motor and let the realization soak

15

in. "Dear Jesus, I almost forgot! That corpse was his wife!"

The bloody head was too mutilated to recognize, but she knew the clothes. The same ones Mrs. Johnson had been wearing a half hour before when Leah stopped to ask directions to Tolliver's Lake. She remembered wondering what the Johnson woman was doing there, at that shanty. Still . . . she was almost positive . . .

A spastic shiver, cold and reviving, brought her back to now. She hurried to the back door and peeled off the torn shirt as she went, dropping it into the ragbag in the kitchen broom closet. She made quickly for the bedroom, shocked at the wraith who met her, wild-eyed and haggard, in the bedroom mirror. She grabbed the first blouse in the closet—wretched luck! She smiled grimly. Ironic justice again. It would be The Mistake. The blouse she bought on sale, later calling it Deathbed Puce. She put it on anyway.

"Home in plenty of time," she breathed. "Time to throw some sandwiches together for lunch. Like nothing happened. Wait to hear it all on the radio."

The shakes didn't come until she flopped in a kitchen chair. It was a delayed reaction, she supposed, folding her slender hands over her knees and drawing her elbows against her ribs, trying to hold herself together. The past two hours had been a nightmare more devastating than any of her previous ones. First that awful confrontation: caught like a common thief, breaking and entering the lake house. Just a common burglar, instead of the murderer that she was. Then the fight with Doris Jean; she felt her cheek gingerly. (Got to do something about that before Jennings gets home.) Then driving up into that dirt yard within feet of that ghastly, gruesome corpse. It was too much. Here, in the dark coolness of her air-conditioned kitchen, the sweat frothed off her like a racehorse at the finish.

It can't be real. I can't possibly hold up through this day. What will become of me? When they find the body—the other body—won't that caretaker Perry Johnson remember me and tell the police?

Leah Palmer was a slight woman of uncommon beauty, as a rule. Her thick dark hair flounced out wildly now; she felt it and began patting, smoothing it in an unconscious effort to get herself together. Her pale hands looked blotchy, and she knew that her face must be as well, must no longer be ivory-bright. Leah wasn't unaware of her attributes, her large dark eyes, the high classic cheekbones. She did, after all, have to take care of what she had. She moistened her lips and pulled herself up a little straighter, trying to compose herself before Jennings came home.

The shrill telephone startled her, and she snatched it off its hook to stop the noise. Now, worse luck, she would have to say something. Hesitantly she brought it to her ear.

"Dr. Palmer's residence." It was little more than a whisper.

"Leah? Is that you?" Her husband sounded skeptical.

"Jennings?" Silly to think that so soon the police would be calling.

"I won't be home for lunch. They're startin' to carve each other up early this year."

So damn superior. I hate you, you cocky, sarcastic son—

No. No, I love Jennings. My rescuer.

Rescuer. It reminded her again of the naked man. "Get out of here!" It wasn't a threat. It was almost as if they were in league. It was like something else that had happened a long time ago.

It was back in St. Louis when she was about seven. She had stood looking up at the counter in the corner grocery and had longed desperately to grab one candy and run. Some big boys of maybe twelve were hanging around. She turned her big wistful almond eyes on one of the boys, and when the grocer turned his back, the boy scooped up a handful of candies and thrust them into her hands.

"Get out of here!" he hissed, and she did. It worked every time.

She replaced the receiver and went back into the kitchen, poured herself a neat glass of Jennings' Scotch and gulped it down. The nasty stuff would probably kill her. Alcohol was not particularly her friend. It made her do crazy, uninhibited things. But just now she needed out, if only for an hour or so.

"I will listen to the noon news," she told the world. "I will hear the news and then I am going to bed."

But the local newscaster failed to mention the Johnson murder—any murder. She snapped off the volume and kicked off her shoes and was tottering off to the bedroom when she heard the sirens. It was impossible to distinguish the local ambulance from the fire engine. And then there was Sheriff Gunn's squad car. It could be any one of them. She froze in the bedroom doorway and tried to decide which direction the sound was coming from. It faded so gradually that she was not even sure when she could no longer hear it.

She had to know. She put on her shoes and gathered up her purse and keys. "Why the hell did I have that Scotch?" she muttered. She'd have to be especially cautious in her driving.

Past the fire station. Both trucks were inside. She wasn't surprised. Nor was she surprised when, moments later, a second siren screamed into the sweltering midday. The first must have been Malcolm Gunn's squad car; the second, the ambulance. She knew where to go now. She headed for the county hospital and wheeled into the doctors' parking lot next to Jennings' car. From there, she had a good view of the emergency room entrance and of the entrance to the small quarters designated for old Doc Grainger, who acted as the county coroner on those rare occasions when one was needed.

The wait was interminable. The car was stifling hot, even with both doors open. She felt leaden, groggy from the Scotch. Sleep overtook her in spite of her agitation, and she slumped over onto the seat and escaped into unconsciousness.

"Leah? Are you all right?"

She awakened with a start, met the steady hazel-eyed gaze of Blanche Carnes, leaning into the car. Leah sat up, feeling guilty for falling asleep. She glanced at the emergency room entrance. The ambulance was just pulling away. She had missed them, missed knowing whose body they had carted inside: the Johnson woman or her own hapless, unsuspecting victim. She mopped the perspiration from her face.

"I must have fallen asleep. I—was—waiting for Jennings to come out." She was almost afraid to ask. "Who was that they just brought in?"

The long, angular woman straightened, shuddering. "I don't know. It was a corpse, all covered up." She shook her head. "This has been the darndest day. Makes you want to go home and crawl under the bed. Have you been in to see Coy?"

So much had happened since morning. Leah had forgotten about Jennings' friend Coy, injured the night before in a knife fight. She tried to cover her surprise.

"I went in," she lied, "but they were busy with Coy, and I guess Ernestine was inside. I didn't seen anyone. Have—you been inside?"

"I'm just going in," Blanche said. "I plan to see if I can't get Ernestine to come home for a little while, get some rest."

"Good idea. Tell her—if there's anything I can do—"

"Somebody ought to try to reach Doris Jean," Blanche said.

It was like a kick in the head. Leah tried not to reel. She muttered something about having something urgent to do and started the engine, feeling the instant soothing relief as cool air shot out of the vent. The astonished Carnes woman started back from the car and waved tentatively as Leah wheeled out and left the parking lot.

If she could only undo the past forty-eight hours, erase them, just say, "King's X," the way they used to do at Saint Agnes Academy when she was a girl. If only she could go back to a year ago, relive her first year in Clarington, start fresh. She had tried, belatedly, this morning, to undo her terrible crime, to get to Doris Jean before her own scheme was accomplished, but she had failed. Now there was nothing to do but live with the consequences and her conscience.

She dared not show undue interest in today's happenings, lest suspicion point at her, dared not go into the hospital and inquire. Perhaps if she turned on the radio . . .

She cruised aimlessly around town, listening to the honey tenor of a Johnny Mathis tune, waiting for an announcement.

Circling the square, she sensed rather than saw a commotion at the far corner, around by the jailhouse. Juneteenth revelers swarmed the square, patronizing the three rummage sales, the portable barbecue cart, the snow cone peddler. She couldn't see past them, but there seemed to be a flurry of activity, people running, straining to see what had happened at the jailhouse. She crept through the traffic, past the crowd which pressed out into the street, ignoring the cars.

Fen Ledbetter, the deputy, was pushing the crowd back as Sheriff Gunn whisked his prisoner inside. Leah rolled down the window glass and hailed a tall colored man who seemed to tower over the crowd.

"What's going on? Who's been arrested?" she asked.

The tall man bowed and bobbed, grinning. "Wellum, he ain't been arrested, no ma'am. Sheriff Gunn say he only taking Mist. Perry in on protective custody. Yes ma'am."

"Perry? Perry Johnson?" She felt a certain thrill just saying his name. No. No, she denied that. "Protect him from what?"

But the tall man had turned away, pretending not to hear, hurrying away, disappearing in the crowd. Leah cast about, trying to catch someone else's eye, but no one seemed to notice her. Then, as she drew even with the jailhouse walk, a path seemed to open allowing her a glimpse of the sheriff and his handcuffed prisoner just as they reached the porch. In that moment Perry Johnson turned and looked down the walk directly into her soul. The intensity of that look so unnerved her that she almost lost control of the creeping car, almost ran it into the crowd.

"I know," the gaze said. "I know who you are."

It was the same message his look had sent her at their first meeting a year ago. After that fleeting glance, he turned and was pushed inside the small stucco building, leaving Leah shaken and full of questions.

The crowd had closed in front of her car, making it impossible to move for the time being. She scanned the square, searching for a familiar face, someone who might know. Then she saw the welcome figure of Frank Ramsey emerge from the jailhouse and head for his pickup parked at the curb. She honked and called, hailing him over to her temporarily stalled car.

A smile of recognition lit the Byronic features of Cousin Frank, and he pushed his way easily to her side.

"Leah! My God, what's happened? You look ghastly! It isn't Coy, is it? Coy isn't dead?"

She didn't know, didn't realize she looked so bad.

"No, Coy's not dead. Not that I know of. . . . Frank, what's going on here?"

The relief Frank clearly felt when he realized she didn't bear bad news about his friend was replaced instantly with a gray veil of concern. "The whole town is crazy," he said grimly. "First Coy is stabbed by Leroy Johnson and then Perry murders his wife."

21

She gasped and covered her mouth to keep from giving herself away. "No! He couldn't have!" She regretted having said it, but Frank seemed not to notice. He patted her on the shoulder.

"You look awful, Leah. You've probably been up all night, eh? Better go home and get some rest."

He backed away and she eased forward through the throng, anxious now to be far away, to think. Perry Johnson, she knew, couldn't have killed his wife; he had been at the lake house with Doris Jean at the time. She had seen him there herself. And Doris. Doris could verify it.

But then Doris—who knows? By now Doris Jean may be dead, she realized in a rush of remembrance.

"Dear Mary, Mother of God," she prayed as she hugged the curb and headed for home, "help me, Blessed Mother. Just help me get home, and save Doris. Dear Jesus, save Doris. Dear God, don't let her die, just don't let her die."

It was all too fantastic to be true, anyway. She wasn't a murderer. Doris Jean didn't deserve to die, anyway. The whole thing was a mistake. God wouldn't punish an innocent person because of a mistake. She'd never intended to kill Doris Jean, anyhow. It was a case of mistaken identity. God wouldn't let an innocent person die.

"There is justice in this world, Leah Marie," Father Richard had told her when he dumped her at boarding school.

"God will provide," Sister Fain had assured her when they turned her out, knocked her into adulthood.

Reassured, mollified, she knew it was the truth. She went back home to lie down, to put her anxieties aside, to fall into a fitful and shallow sleep while she waited for the one o'clock news.

The rest of the afternoon was a blur. Much later, she woke feeling the dusk breeze from an open window stir in her hair. She came back sullenly, reluctantly, unable to recall her dream, but knowing herself plucked from the insidious seduction of death. She felt a fleet and irrational resentment toward the man who stood there like a stone, unchanging in the gloaming light, who had brought her back, had wrenched her out of sweet oblivion back into the mire of depression. She closed her eyes and tried to make him disappear. She opened them again but Jennings was still there, his ruddy, handsome face dark with a mixture of moods that she could not read.

Something about him, some signal of catastrophe communicated itself to her with such terrible urgency that it wrung a cry from her lips. She sprang up, clutching the bed sheet as if for protection.

"What is it?" she said, not really wanting to know.

A grim, restrained smile played at the corner of his set lips, and he stiffly reached down and touched her cheek. "Now, don't take this too hard, Leah."

She held her breath and raised her arms, warding off whatever he was about to say. And then her worst fears were realized.

"Something's happened to Doris Jean," he said. "Something awful has happened to Doris Jean."

2

September 1944

SHE HAD always known she was special. Back home in St. Louis, all the women (and there were few men in her life) said so. Even when she was very young they had said it.

"She could pass," they said.

And she accepted it, but she really didn't know.

"I could pass, too," Mama used to say, "only I don't want to." And the others would nod, only they really didn't mean it.

They never said, "You are pretty, Leah," although she sometimes suspected that she was. They never said, "You are smart." Not, "You are good." Just, "Someday you could pass." And she knew it was good.

When her classmates said it, it was not always good. Some of the boys would taunt her with, "Whatcha going to do, try to pass?" and with venom the girls sometimes said, "I bet you

24

think you could pass, don't you?" And then she would shake her head vigorously and protest, "No, no!" But it did no good to protest; they shut her out anyway.

But sometimes at night Mama would come to the airless corner where they shared a cot and she would hold her close and rock back and forth and tell her, "Someday my babe's going to get out of here. Going to pass. Going to pass." And she would feel happy and content and very blessed for a time, unmindful of her urchin hungers.

If she was ever miserable, she did not know it. It was only later, looking back, that she saw her misery. It was how she had lived since she was born; it was how everybody lived. When Mama took the belt to her—and it was often—she knew that she deserved the pain, for she was often headstrong and unruly. Pain was part of the natural order of things, just as were heat and cold and mosquito bites.

Only once, on Thanksgiving Day, Mama took her to town to the parade, and she saw that there was another way to live. She loved the music, the glitter, the gaudy costumes, the hundreds of beautiful girls who knew no pain. One gleaming princess floated by and waved at her. "You can be like that someday," Mama had said, "if you'll only—"

"Only what? Tell me, Mama."

"Just stay away from boys long enough." Mama's mouth made a grim straight line and Leah knew it was the truth.

Men came around sometimes, for Mama was very pretty. Especially in her pink dress with the slit up one side and her big pink earrings to match. It took Leah's breath to see her look so pretty and she would hug her tight and say over and over, "Oh Mama, you're so fancy, so fancy!" Sometimes Mama would go off to the USO to dance with the soldiers, and Leah would sit alone in the gathering gloom of the darkening flat and wish. But she didn't know, even, what to wish for.

25

There was one man who came to stay, though, during 1944. Wounded in the war, he said. Name of Cleon. Good-looking, she supposed. "I'm tired of fighting and scratching," Mama told her. "Cleon be good to us." And Mama hummed often after that.

There was another man, too. One whom she loved, only she didn't tell anybody. His eyes were pale blue and his hair was like yellow silk and his face, not yet etched with the evidence of life's shared griefs, was so sweet she longed to reach out and touch it. She had first met him one afternoon when she was sitting out in front watching the others play, a scrawny scrap whose innocent yearnings showed in great sad almond eyes.

He stopped in front of her and spoke, only it sounded like music. "Hello there. Why aren't you playing with the others?"

She ducked her head. She couldn't look on his beauty. Couldn't admit to him her unworthiness to be included in the play.

"Do you live here?" he asked.

Suddenly she was ashamed of the ugly wooden row house, its slate-blue paint almost gone. She nodded bleakly, still unable to look up. She wanted to run up the steps into the house, up, on up to their tiny second-floor apartment, wanted to close the door and peer at him from the safety of the window—but she was certain that she was paralyzed.

"You are a very pretty little girl, did you know?"

Her courage returned, and she looked up defiantly. "I am not a little girl. I'm almost eleven!"

He didn't laugh. He looked very serious. "I'm sorry. I didn't know." He stuck out his hand. "My name is Father Richard O'Mally. What's yours?"

"Leah Marie Evangeline Boudreaux," she said, glad that she had a name that sounded so fine.

And now that she looked him over, she could tell that he

was a Father. It was just at first she could only see his blue eyes and his silky yellow hair.

"Will you come to see me sometime over at the church, Leah Marie Evangeline?"

She laughed. "Don't call me that!"

"No?"

She giggled. "Naw. Leah."

"O.K., Leah. Will you come?"

She had gone often to see him, for sometimes she felt strange, fine stirrings in her body when she was near him. He showed her books and tropical fish in a tank and told her stories about how Jesus loved her. Once or twice the Sister brought cookies or fruit and milk for them. And it would grow late, and Father would walk her home and sometimes even hold her hand crossing the street.

"God is just, Leah Marie," he would say. "There is justice in this world. All things work together for good for those who love Him." And Leah was sure that it was the truth.

One evening when she came home Cleon was there but Mama was not. She set about getting supper for them while Cleon sat in a kitchen chair and watched. Cleon always watched her, licking his lips then wiping them dry on the back of his hand. But tonight Mama came in and saw, and she sent Leah to the bedroom.

The next day Mama didn't put on her work clothes. She put on her Sunday dress—but not the pink one with the slit—and she went off. She was waiting for Leah in the schoolyard after school. She carried two paper bags, and she handed one to Leah.

"What's this?" Leah asked.

"Your things. Maybe I can bring you more later." They headed out in the wrong direction.

"Where we going?"

"To Father Richard's. Don't worry; it's something good. You going to like it." A command it was.

Mama's steps were so brisk that Leah had to skip and trot to keep up. A dark apprehension was welling up inside her.

"Like what? Where we going with all my stuff?"

"New school. New place. You going to like it."

And Mama made a thin line of her mouth and Leah knew it was futile to ask more. They walked on in silence—although Leah's heart was pounding so wildly she could hear it in her ears—until they reached the familiar black iron fence which surrounded Father Richard's place. She had never noticed before its gray and forbidding facade. There Mama stopped and looked down at her for the first time, her dark eyes pleading for understanding.

"You got a chance to be somebody, babe—get out of this place and amount to something. I guess it all turns on staying away from men for a time, else you wind up with a dark baby. Then you don't ever pass."

Leah felt herself color, and she looked away. She waited for Mama to finish.

"I can look on down the road, and I can see how you ain't ever going to know whether to pass. You going to be scared to. You not going to know how to act. Somebody got to take charge and decide for you."

The import of what was happening to her was dawning on Leah, and she thought, But I'm not ready. Not yet.

"Father Richard knows a fine school out from town at a place called Saint Agnes. All girls. All white children. The Sisters—take good care of you. Better than me."

Mama's voice trembled and she looked off quickly and reached for the gate latch. Frantic, Leah caught her arm. "Don't, Mama! Please don't!"

Mama enfolded her against her warm soft bosom and their

tears washed over them. Leah thought maybe Mama was changing her mind, but in a moment Mama held her out at arm's length and said, "We can't go on like we been, babe. I lived a long time alone just so I wouldn't have any more children so I could maybe scratch along and get us out of that place. But there never was enough money, never going to be enough. Cleon got a pension. And I get lonesome. Ain't natural to live so long without a man."

"But—I don't see—" Leah sobbed.

"And when it's your turn, I want you to have a rich one!" Mama tried to sound gay. She hesitated and then added, "Case anybody ever asks, your daddy was a Louisiana man, and his name really was Boudreaux."

She turned and headed briskly up the walk, flinging over her shoulder, "Come on now. From now on, you going to be white, and you going to love it!"

Only she didn't love it, not for a very long time. The only part she had anticipated, being with Father Richard, never materialized, for apart from the day he drove her down the Flat River Road to Saint Agnes Academy, he had never come again.

Her alarm had mounted as Father drove her farther and farther from the city. It was a long time before she even took notice of the oak-covered hills which she had only seen in books before. They looked so foreign. She began to feel frantic, trapped.

Father's pale blue eyes stared steady on the road. Father was always so at ease, so in control, but now Leah saw the white knuckles on his pale soft hands, and she knew that Father was as uncomfortable as she. This realization only served to heighten her fears.

The afternoon faded into dusk, and reluctantly Father

turned off to a small roadside café. She followed him inside and sat meekly opposite him while he ordered the Special Plate for each of them.

She longed to look up into his beautiful fair face, but she feared that he might be looking at her. And so she sat with eyes lowered and picked at her food. She was embarrassed to eat, to open her mouth and chew and swallow. Maybe she didn't do it right. She tried to take a few bites, shielding her mouth behind her napkin, but it was too awkward. Finally she put her fork down.

"Aren't you hungry, Leah Marie?"

She shook her head without looking up. A tear threatened to form in her eye. Fiercely she squinted and shook it off. His manicured and sweet-smelling hand reached out and covered hers.

"Leah, you do understand, don't you, that when you get to Saint Agnes, your mother intends that you become a—a white girl?"

She sat rigid, with her hand burning where Father's covered it. She nodded. He made it all sound dirty, somehow.

"I mean"—he hurried on—"you *look* white, of course, but you will learn to *feel* white." She had never seen Father so flustered. The pitch of his voice had risen and his Irish brogue had slipped in, the way it did when he became excited over the children's street games. Leah did not like him as much when his voice rose. He did not seem so important then. She did not care to answer him and waited patiently until he was ready to leave.

Later, when Father handed her over to the Sisters, he squeezed her hand. "You are a child of God, Leah Marie," he said. "Always remember that. Continue to love and serve Him and you will deserve the abundance of His kingdom. There is justice in this life, child. The beginnings of His justice are now."

30

She did not know what he meant. She turned to go, but he still gripped her hand.

"Leah, I feel your bitterness at this moment, dear child. But remember always that your mother gave you this chance because she loves you. Someday you will understand. Jesus' love was a sacrificial love, and so is your mother's."

Then he said good-bye, and she knew it was going to turn out bad, just like always. It was a universal law, for all she knew. Even when things were good, she knew it wouldn't last. When she had a good day, she always knew, I'll have to pay for this happiness later. So the parting from Mama, and then from Father Richard, was just more of the same. Just like always. And she began to feel her anger and her enormous grief. It built up and covered her and pressed down on her for months. She would pour it out silently, muffled into the pillow and bedclothes of the little iron bed in the room she shared with three other girls—strangers always. By day she wore her armor and carried her awful burden of bereavement like a big blue and purple bruise upon her spirit and she said to herself, You see? You see? Just like always.

Always she had thought she was special. Now she knew it was not so much special as set apart. Singled out, designated to take the knocks.

Or maybe, she was to decide much later, to give them.

3

FROM THE students at Saint Agnes, Leah gradually acquired those subtle little nuances of behavior by which members of the same class identify one another, although she remained, by habit, essentially an outsider all her days there. It was a role she knew. Old paths are known paths. There is comfort even in misery if it is accustomed misery.

From the Sisters she learned the absence of physical pain, for the whippings which had been a frequent discipline at home ceased abruptly when she reached Saint Agnes. She sometimes felt guilty not being punished, translated the lack of beatings as neglect.

The ten years she spent as a ward of the Church were not unhappy years, for she would not allow herself the pain after a while. But they were years of solitude, punctuated by only a few memories which she would later recall with difficulty. Of those few, she retained none at all of her classmates and only an occasional one of the Sisters.

Later, as she gained in critical judgment, she would come

to think of the Sisters as a mediocre lot. In the movies nuns were radiant, forbearing creatures who hid refugees and faced invading armies with indomitable spirits. They never had pimples on their cheeks like Sister Adele. They never bitched like Sister Marie, whose nasal whine was widely imitated between muffled snickers at night after bed check. Sister Andrea picked her nose surreptitiously, believing that no one took notice, and Sister Nan let off foul-smelling gas after every meal. Girls considered it high good fortune to draw mathematics at fourth period, which was just after lunch, for Sister Nan began to erupt about halfway through the period, an amusing diversion from algebraic equations.

Her favorite was Sister Fain, possibly because she never had Sister Fain for a class. Maybe Sister Fain didn't teach any classes; Leah wasn't sure. She functioned as a surrogate mother hen. Sometimes she'd pop in on a class out of nowhere, it seemed—a scrubbed, freckled pixie. She'd sit at the back of the room for a while, smiling and nodding during recitation, looking as if she might fly right off but for some concealed ballast. Then she'd slip out again when no one was looking. Sometimes she would call the girls in one at a time for counseling, and she would talk about grades and about what you liked to do, what your interests were, what you wanted to do with your life. Nobody else seemed to give a dime about those things.

It was Sister who first complimented her on her drawings and who gave her a small box of paints on her fifteenth birthday. Sister talked to her of developing her talents, repeating annually the parable of the talents, of the servant who was penalized for burying his talent to keep it safe instead of multiplying it. So that painting became a bounden duty for Leah and always remained a duty.

Sister Fain, whose small, speckled angularity had never been ripened or rounded by love, was also in charge of the

Annual Sex Lecture, which varied not at all with the years. Nothing informative, they all agreed: no "how-to"; mostly "why-not-to." Once, when news of the practice of experimenting among certain ninth graders leaked out, Sister Fain appeared, flushed and damp, at the end of choir period and held them up for half an hour to warn them about the inevitability of suffering for violating God's natural laws. Leah could credit Sister Fain for her pristine sense of propriety which never completely left her.

Sister Fain offered her whatever spiritual guidance through the years as she was able to accept. Probably, at some time, she had mentioned the Ten Commandments. Thou shalt not kill, for instance. Except for Germans and Japs. And a little later, North Koreans. But not South Koreans.

During her senior year, Leah was summoned to Sister Fain's office one day during cooking class. The little nun's green eyes lit with affection as Leah took a tentative step into the room.

"Come in, Leah! My! We're about to graduate, aren't we?" Leah nodded, eyes downcast as usual. "And do you know what you'll be doing after that?"

Leah shook her head. "I—I don't know," she said. She was thinking of Mama, wondering if Mama would want her back.

"Why, you're going to junior college, that's what!" Sister clapped her small hands in delight. She rounded the desk and caught the astonished Leah by the shoulders. "You've scraped through your exams, and I've spoken with the Sisters at Our Lady of Mercy down the road. You'll take classes there and continue to live right here! We'll send a car for you every afternoon. Now, what do you think of that?"

Leah feigned pleasure, although she really didn't care one way or the other. She was accustomed to having someone else control her life, to taking whatever came. And then quietly making the best of it on her own.

And so she struggled through two years of commuting to Our Lady of Mercy. But eventually the time came when there was nothing left that she could do, no more courses to take. And again it was Sister Fain who told her what she would do next. It was Sister who drove her to St. Louis, who paid the first month's rent on her efficiency and who folded two hundred dollars in her palm as she left her. "It's only part of God's abundance," she told Leah. "God will always provide for your needs." Then she had clasped her gingerly to her stiff front and let her go for good.

Leah had felt elation, that first few minutes alone in her own room. She whirled around the room, examining its neat shabbiness with pride, whispering softly, "Mine! Just mine! I'm free at last!"

But the mood did not last. Soon the reality of being on her own, the necessity of finding a job before her money ran out began to bear down. The whirling slowed to pacing as she fought back panic. She found it hard to think, to plan. Then she remembered the newspaper that Sister had bought for her, the Sunday edition of the *Post-Dispatch*. The classified section fairly bulged with jobs. Throwing herself upon the bed, she began to read.

"Clerk-trainee. Apply Suite C, Sixth floor . . ."

Perspiration popped out on her upper lip. She'd rarely been in an elevator, much less on a city bus. But to present herself for a job, she must first maneuver herself downtown, must locate the correct building, then find the right floor. Must offer herself without stammering, must face their critical appraisal, their rejection. She laid down the paper and rolled over, staring at the ceiling.

Why couldn't she just get married like other girls?

But that, of course, was absurd. There was no one to ask her. Even during junior college, while the other girls were making points on the weekends, Leah shied away from their offers for blind dates, because it was all she knew to do. And while the other girls explored the possibilities on Coke dates in the afternoons, Leah went home—to Saint Agnes. Nobody had followed her home, pleading for admittance and her favors. She sighed. No, there was no possibility of marriage. She would do now as she'd always done: she'd make it on her own. Besides, what was it Sister always said? "God will provide."

God provided through a variety of clerking jobs. Unfortunately for Leah, Sister Fain's counseling had never extended to practical career planning. Leah's course of study hadn't even included a single secretarial course. Eventually she switched to waiting tables because it was more profitable. But there were uniforms to buy, and she never seemed to get ahead.

Vaguely she felt uneasy that she was not planning for the future, but the present was struggle enough, what with the rent and groceries and transportation, to say nothing of clothes and the bare incidentals. After years of school uniforms, she really had little else. She might have fared better had she been able to bring herself to share an apartment with one of the other waitresses, but that was out of the question. There was no one close enough to ask. But she scrimped along, saving enough for an occasional bus trip back to Saint Agnes, for she was not yet weaned from the Sisters.

In the beginning she had tried to reestablish ties with Mama. She went across town several times those first few months, swallowing her own secret anguish, looking for the place where Mama lived. The old house had been condemned, and Mama had moved a few blocks away. At length Leah learned through the new parish priest where Mama lived. It was, if anything, a worse place than before.

They sat opposite each other on either side of the identical table where Leah had eaten so many bowls of thin stew.

Mama didn't seem the same. Or maybe she was the same. Maybe it was Leah's memory which was at fault.

Mama tried to smile. "You look good. Extra good." Leah imagined that there was rancor in her voice.

"So do you," Leah lied. She looked around the tawdry apartment. "Cleon still around?"

"At times." Mama lapsed into silence. She wasn't putting herself out to make Leah feel welcomed. Leah felt a new draft of misery welling up. She stood up.

"Well, guess I'll go. Just wanted to see how you were."

Mama gave a sarcastic sniff. "Just how you think I'd be?" She'd had other children, of course, who skittered in and out of the room, making conversation difficult. Vaguely Leah longed at least for an introduction. She was, after all, their half-sister. But Mama paid no mind. "How you think it is with all these kids to feed?"

Rage rose within Leah. It seemed to her that Mama was blaming her, somehow, for passing. For escaping. When it had been Mama's idea all along. Or maybe it was as Leah had always suspected: Mama only wanted to be shed of her.

She went away, still gnawing on the old resentment at being turned out. Still, it made Leah's heart ache to see Mama that way: dirt-poor, just like always, with the look about her of constant impoverishment. And all those other kids! Serves her right, Leah decided.

If there had ever been any doubt in her mind about whether or not to pass, it was removed that day. She never vacillated about it again, never romanticized the days past with Mama. She was chosen, chosen by God to escape, and she would never turn back again.

4

THE WINTER of '56 was bad. An unseasonal ice storm late in November paralyzed much of the state, creeping southeastward from Lake of the Ozarks and coating tree limbs, power lines and back roads with a crippling icy glacial sheet. The suburbs of the city were hardest hit, but the inner city's warmth protected it so that business slogged along as usual, even during the worst of the storm.

That was the storm that altered Leah's life, because she decided against a hazardous bus trip back to Saint Agnes for Thanksgiving.

She was working the late shift at the coffee bar at Mason's when he made his way to the counter, a strapping sandy-haired giant who reminded her vaguely of the ruddy Sister Fain. His thick, heavy features were purple-red, his face like a block of cold stone. She could see, underneath his lightweight topcoat, another long white coat like a lab technician's. He kept his big meaty hands jammed in his pockets even after he sat down. He ignored the menu which she put before him. There was a determined set to the severely square jaw as he jutted it toward her, an aristocratic bearing about him, a small flicker of hauteur in the steel-blue eyes which deigned to meet hers for the barest moment.

"Got any chili?"

Three words that summoned instant aversion, instant fear, instant suspicion. It was more than the pronunciation; it was a certain inflection. Something in the fringes of her memory clutched her, something she couldn't actually call up, some pain.

She brought him the chili without comment, not even asking for a drink order. She wrote up the ticket and moved away, never intending to notice the cold chapped hand which he reluctantly took out of his pocket. His fingers seemed stiff; he had trouble gripping the spoon. She despised her weakness. She brought him a cup of coffee. He flashed the blue eyes gratefully; they were not as steely and remote now. There was the look of Father Richard about them.

"Where are your gloves?"

Her question amused him. A smile threatened at the corners of his mouth. He shrugged and wolfed his chili, but kept his blue eyes on her.

"Don't you have any gloves? And something to go around your ears?"

Again he shrugged. She was behaving so foolishly.

"You can get frostbite, you know."

She witnessed his total capitulation. He grinned openly, showing a mouthful of even, oversized teeth.

"You're right. Pretty dumb, huh? I'll go get me some first chance I get."

She felt it was a dismissal. She pushed a basket of crackers his way and worked down to the far end of the counter. What was it Mama used to say? Big men are always the most helpless. She found herself edging her way back down the counter.

"You haven't been here long, have you?" she asked.

"Five months."

He was a resident at Barnes, he told her, seeming amused and almost delighted that she didn't know what a resident was. Internal medicine was his field. Just didn't get out of the hospital often enough to get used to the weather. Back home it snowed some, though; maybe three or four times some years. Not too different from here, that he could tell. Home? East Texas. Folks called it the Piney Woods Region. Town name of Clarington. He supposed she'd never heard of it.

"You going back there to practice medicine?"

"I might. Yeah, I guess I will." It was as if he'd just made the decision. Like she'd helped him decide.

Jennings Palmer came to the coffee bar often after that. His manner of speaking no longer intimidated her, nor did she equate it with ignorance. He was smart, she'd give him that. But neither was she awed by the difference in their stations. It was his size which was the equalizer. Big men'll have you wet-nursing in no time, Mama always said.

The holidays loomed ahead, desolate and endless. The Christmas season had never been an easy time, although the years at Saint Agnes were pleasant enough. The Sisters taxed themselves to imbue the old halls with cheer for the few girls who had noplace else to go for Christmas. Surely those were the best Christmases she ever spent.

As a small child she had heard about Santa Claus, and she asked Mama what Santa Claus was.

"Something invented by the Devil to make poor folks more miserable," she said. Mama always said things like that. Later it would set Leah to wondering if talking negative was a sin, but she was powerless to do anything about it, anyhow. Especially during the holiday season.

Christmas week Jennings asked her out, as if he had come to a momentous decision. With a courtly gravity he helped her into his old Chrysler, adjusted the heating ducts for her. Offered her his arm going down the aisle at the movie. She was touched by his gentlemanliness. She found herself, at the end of the evening, wishing he would kiss her good night. But he merely opened her apartment door for her, backed off a respectable distance and thanked her for the evening. Maybe there was something wrong with her.

"Are you going home for Christmas?" she asked, just to delay his leaving.

He looked genuinely pained. "I have to work Christmas Eve," he said. "Besides, we haven't had a traditional Christmas since my dad died."

She had an inspiration. "Look: why don't you come over and have Christmas dinner with me? I—really will have too much food to eat alone."

Maybe it was a mistake. Jennings came, but he never went home.

He'd brought a bottle of wine for a gift, and they had drunk it all. He was lonely, she could tell. He needed comfort, and she had left her half-finished plate to weave around to his side of the table and kiss him—although later she couldn't remember why.

He pulled her down on his lap and held her hungrily, and she burst into flame. On and on it went, this eager and passionate and arousing kiss, until she felt she could stand it no longer. She broke it off and held him close, whispering in his ear, "Jennings, don't you want me?"

"Oh yes!" he breathed, but he only held her close.

She wrapped her arms tightly around his neck. "Then why don't you take me to the bed?" And only then had he lifted her and carried her into the bedroom.

It was Christmas, after all, and they were both alone. It

41

seemed so natural to her at the time. She was even willing to do most of the work, make most of the preparation, even to undressing him. But the next morning she was devastated, stricken with shame to find him lying beside her. Sister Fain would be so ashamed. How could she ever face them at Saint Agnes again? It was the ultimate degradation.

Jennings was genuinely sorry and took most of the blame upon himself. "I didn't realize it was your first time, Leah," he said, standing big and helpless beside the bed where she lay sobbing. "Oh, not that I ever thought you were that kind of girl. No, not at all. I respect you very much, Leah. I guess I just had too much to drink, just like you. Otherwise, I would never have . . ."

In the end he did the gallant thing and proposed, but it wasn't gallantry which prompted it, and she knew it. And in the end she accepted, for the same reason. Because she had so little to offer the world and he had taken her ace card. Because justice demanded it. And because it hadn't been half bad.

It had happened the following week. He had spent the whole week trying to make it up to her; she had driven herself through the week with a dispirited, resigned discipline. He was the first good thing that had happened to her, and she had blown it. Just like always.

He was walking her home after a movie, and she was feeling dull, dead, not caring much what happened next. At the entrance to her apartment building, he stopped her, picking at her sleeve.

"Leah? Can't we talk?"

She shrugged, not looking up. "What about?"

"Leah, I've made you miserable, and I never meant to. Wait!" He held her as she tried to leave him. "Leah, it's hap-

42

pening again, what happened on Christmas. I don't want to go home. Marry me, Leah."

That was all. He just held her there at the open apartment door. Listless tears sprang up in her eyes. She leaned against him and sighed and nodded. Is this all there is to it? she wondered.

There were no arrangements to make. He didn't know about Mama, and she didn't know about his family. Maybe he was ashamed of her; she always suspected it. They were married by a justice of the peace. To her, that was no marriage at all, but she never even mentioned going to a priest.

It bothered her sometimes, remembering Mama and Father Richard, and especially Sister Fain. But she never went home to see Mama anymore, anyway; Mama didn't seem anxious to acknowledge a grown daughter. And Father Richard had long since moved on, she supposed. As for Sister Fain and the other gentle folk at Saint Agnes, she blocked them from her mind. That wasn't the real world. In the real world, God didn't provide, the way Sister Fain believed. In the real world, it was, "Get in there and fight for yours." Mama had known that, even.

Jennings seemed content to be hers, in his distant way. She could have wished for a deeper relationship, shared intimacies, feelings. But a deep relationship was beyond Leah's ken. She settled for companionship, trips to the zoo, pizza for two, warm feet, shared rent. It was really more than she'd ever dared hope for, anyway.

They never talked about family. He never asked about hers, and she was careful never to ask him about his lest he ask her. Didn't matter, it turned out. His mother, a widow, had moved to Arizona and quite probably had entered into a liaison which Jennings didn't want to know about, didn't even want to suspect. She surmised all this from a single postcard which

43

she discovered one day while cleaning the bureau. It was signed "Mom" and postmarked Sunshine Retirement Village. Leah scanned it casually but didn't even actually read it. Maybe she should have cared more. She even felt guilty, sometimes, for not caring.

She felt guilty, too, because he called her an incredible luxury, and she knew it was the truth.

His residency ended in June of 1959. She had never thought beyond that. Never considered what would happen to them when it was time for him to move on. Nothing had ever been permanent in her life before; she scarcely dared expect this to last.

"We'll have to move soon," he told her one night.

That moment she began putting down roots in her marriage. He was so matter-of-fact about it that she wondered why she ever doubted. Now there was so much to catch up on. So much thinking, so much planning that she had never dared do. She had never thought, before, about leaving St. Louis. About setting up house in some remote little Texas town and being a doctor's wife. Never even considered it.

Too long she had directed her energies toward just getting through the day, the week, to the next paycheck. Always looking for a better job, a better place to stay, a way to pay the bills. Never making friends, but rather economic arrangements. Never making long-range plans or lasting commitments to anything. She halfheartedly considered bowing out.

"Jennings, if we go to Clarington, just remember: I don't want to have any children," she said. She was giving him an out. If he wanted children badly, he could leave her behind.

Jennings shrugged, as usual. "You may change your mind someday," he said. But she knew she never would; she was terrified of having a black baby.

She didn't like change, never had, not since the first big one that had wrenched her from her home. And yet she had failed

44

to accept this arrangement with Jennings as permanent, for fear of disappointment. Now the change of location didn't concern her; she certainly wasn't tied to St. Louis. Change of status intimidated her, for being the wife of a resident was a far cry from being the wife of the town doctor. It was like going to Saint Agnes all over again.

But there would come a time when she would come to cherish this change, would defend it against all peril, would protect it unto death.

Someone else's death, of course.

5

Summer 1959

THE WINNOWING of her ways spanned more than a decade. By the time Leah reached Clarington, she was as adaptable as a cockroach, with a shell as crusty. She could make a right-angle turn at the bat of an eyelid. At the slightest hint of a furrow of the brow she could recognize the danger, back off, cover her tracks. She had no fear of meeting new situations. But she had this one figured wrong.

She didn't reckon with Jennings' image in his hometown. He wasn't Dr. Palmer; he was Weslay and Mamie's boy, come home with a strange little bride. Town folk wished him well. They sent him pot plants tied in bows to decorate his new office. But they stayed away. Took their ailments to old Doc Grainger or up to Dallas to the medical school. A few of the country people wandered in, and a few crocks, but building a practice was painfully slow.

For the first few weeks Leah helped in the office until Jennings could hire an office nurse. She wanted to work permanently, but Jennings Palmer's wife didn't work. They had to keep up appearances, after all.

Setting up housekeeping posed no challenge. The house, Leah's first ever, was where Jennings grew up. It was a roomy old place, all soft worn chintz throughout, and shadowed all around by twenty-year-old chinaberry trees. When Mamie picked up and moved to Arizona, she took only her personal things to make the small retirement village apartment seem like home. She left furniture, linens, canned goods, a partially filled freezer. The long-unused rooms were heavy with dust, but it took a scant week to put them in order. Then Leah began to prowl the house, looking for something to do.

She got out her watercolors, the ones Sister Fain had given her so long ago, and turned out paintings as if she were trying to meet a deadline. Sometimes she begged Jennings to let her ride along on country house calls, just to break the monotony, and she sketched rural scenes for still more paintings. In a matter of only a few weeks her feeling of helpless frustration had given her the courage to gather up a few of her better paintings and visit the local frame shop, where she talked the proprietor into taking them on consignment. At least she felt she had some small purpose.

There were callers. Ladies from the Methodist church with pecan pies. Neighbor ladies with cuttings for the yard. Friends of Jennings', like Joe Billy Tolliver and his high-toned wife, Doris Jean. Friends of Mamie's, even friends of long-gone Weslay Jennings. Relatives, like Jennings' Aunt Ida Ramsey, who promised to come back soon and bring her son Frank and his little wife. The minister. The other doctor's wife. The Avon lady.

There were invitations. To join Jennings' church. To join the choir. To join a circle. To join the Benson County Medical

47

Auxiliary. To come to dinner. Leah had never been to a dinner party before.

Jennings was enthusiastic when Doris Jean phoned, suggesting getting the old gang together for dinner. It would be a good introduction for Leah. Leah could see there was no talking him out of it. She might, after all, enjoy the experience. She could, with a little preparation, be rather dazzling to look at. She knew how to display her petite darkness to advantage. She might not be in the same league with Doris Jean, who had turned out to be a smashing blonde, but she could be exotic and quite interesting-looking. It had been apparent that Joe Billy had found her so, that time they'd dropped by. Yes, she could carry it off.

Besides, she was curious. There'd been a girl once, Joe Billy's sister. Jennings had told her so. Told her he'd been thick with Ernestine Tolliver all through high school until Coy Moseley muscled in. Leah was curious about what kind of sister that long, gangly country lawyer could have who would have turned Jennings' head so. Leah had liked Joe Billy instantly, liked the way every once in a while he'd hike up his trousers with his elbows against his belt, giving his thin shoulders a shrug in the process. It was a guileless gesture which Leah suspected was calculated to allay suspicion, suggested to her for some outlandish reason that Joe Billy was not intractable to the crackle of folding money. Perhaps liked was too strong a word for what she'd felt for Joe Billy. Suffice it to say she felt comfortable with him. She didn't anticipate having the same rapport with his sister.

Early deprivation had honed her defenses, refined her senses, so that danger never crept up on her blind side. She began to smell it that evening almost before they rang the doorbell, before Joe Billy flung open the door and pulled her over the threshold with moist, clammy hands. Momentary relief flooded her as Jennings and Joe Billy socked each other

48

and scuffled briefly as they seemingly always did. The hiatus gave her a moment to recapitulate, to try to assess where the danger was coming from.

She was standing in the immense foyer of an outlandishly elegant house. To her right yawned the archway into a lavishly decorated living room. Straight ahead she could see, through a doorway, a glittering chandelier hanging over the formally laid dining table. Past that, she could see an ornately carved sideboard strewn with heavy silver hollowware. Yes, Joe Billy, had done all right for himself. She felt ill at ease amidst so much opulence. She didn't know whether the house was done in good taste; she only knew she had never before been in the presence of so much wealth.

Then Jennings remembered her and guided her into the living room to meet the two couples who waited. Now she took a deep breath, tried to remember what he'd told her about each one, tried not to believe that their conversations had revolved about Jennings' new wife before they came in. Tried to ignore the frankly appraising stare from the plump little woman on the sofa and the saturnine leer of the dark hook-nosed man who leaned against the mantel. Tried to summon again the signal of danger, to keep her head, to be on guard.

The big open-faced man who leaped up from the couch flashing a wide, bucktoothed grin posed no threat. She let him through her barriers easily. One tuft from a ginger-colored cowlick sprigged from the topmost peak of his bullet head. Leah noticed the paint under his nails and remembered that Jennings told her that Coy Moseley supplemented his bootlegging income with a job mixing paint down at the hardware store. "Hydie, Leah!" he said congenially.

Another big man, she thought. Just like Jennings, except that his big frame was beginning to run to girth. Rumor had it Coy often got back from his weekly run over the county line with a load considerably lighter than he meant to have, being forever tempted to drink up the profits en route.

But of course he would be big like Jennings. Ernestine shared her weakness for big men. Ernestine, then, would be the pudgy little lady who had jumped up from the couch, brushed aside her wispy yellow bangs and hugged Jennings at great length. Leah was mildly disappointed. She was such a dowdy little toad. No competition at all.

Belatedly, Ernestine turned her dimpled Shirley Temple smile upon Leah, confounding her and totally disarming her. "And this is Leah!" she cooed. "My God, Jennings, she's a stunner! Oh, honey, you are going to be an asset in this town. . . . Isn't she going to be an asset, Blanche?"

The tall, horse-faced woman had simply blended into the beige draperies until this moment. Now she sloped forward, a shy, lantern-jawed creature who herself needed acceptance and knew herself impotent to accept it, seeming not to know whether to offer her hand or not. Ernestine, chattering volubly, appeared not to notice her dilemma.

"Jennings, you remember Blanche Dawson? Blanche Carnes now, of course. . . . Leah, this is Blanche Carnes. She belongs to Blackie here." Ernestine skipped over to the mantel in Good Ship Lollipop fashion and tucked a plump little proprietary hand into the crook of Blackie's arm, dragging the wiry little man over to the group.

Carnes was a common name in these parts. Leah had noticed it on several country mailboxes. You could spot a Carnes by that hook nose, Jennings said. The Carnes nose.

"Hey, Jennings!" Blackie pumped Jennings' arm. "Hey, Leah." An entirely different inflection. His tone undressed her. Funny that no one else seemed to notice. She dropped her eyes, unable to meet his black agate gaze. For an instant she was so addled that her warning system failed. But only for an instant. But Blackie was not the real threat, she felt.

Blanche Carnes reached out timidly and took her hand. "I'm glad to meet you," she said simply. Leah could feel the pear-shaped rock on her finger. Must be eight carats. Of course. Blanche Dawson of the Dawson oil money. Jennings had told her. She had it figured out now, about Blanche and Blackie.

After the introductions and as if on cue, the hostess swept in, regal in flowing chiffon over swishing taffeta. A sizable corsage was pinned to her ample front. ("From my Sunday-school class, those darlings!") Her startling brassy hair was piled high in a lavish French twist. Leah mused that Doris Jean Tolliver was of the stuff of a sunbonneted pioneer who could have chopped firewood or driven a team of mules. Or maybe invaded frontier saloons armed with an ax and the intentions to set the world aright.

"I do love you all for being on time!" She planted a smeary kiss on Jennings' cheek. "That's the risk you take inviting a doctor to dinner. Joe Billy, can't you see if they want a drink? I'm certainly tolerant of anybody that wants to drink."

"Nothing for me, thanks. I might get a call." Jennings' bland smile at Leah conveyed an amused bravado. He hadn't forgotten Christmas and the wine. Maybe he never would.

"Whatever the other girls are having is fine," Leah said. She had no experience here. She wished Jennings would help her.

Joe Billy shrugged. "One more Co-Cola coming up!"

Doris Jean guided Leah to the couch and sandwiched her between Ernestine and Blanche Carnes, seating herself on the edge of the massive coffee table in front of them. Leah felt suffocated and looked past Doris Jean pleadingly to Jennings. But the glazed look in Jennings' blue eyes told her that he had forgotten all about her. He grinned at his buddies and they retreated to the far corner of the room.

Leah answered in monosyllables as the other women made several polite stabs at conversation, then they simply talked

51

around her. Leah withdrew into herself, a fixed smile on her lips, and tried hard to assess the danger.

Perhaps it was Ernestine, prattling about some vapid, frittering thing that happened to her parents, with whom she and Coy still lived. Ernestine, after all, was just about the only girl Jennings ever had. Maybe she was fed up with Coy's never making enough money to provide them with a home of their own. Maybe, seeing Jennings after all this time, handsome, virile, ambitious, had made Ernestine reconsider her choice. From what Leah could see, Coy Moseley's physique was beginning to slide, especially around the gut. He may have an aristocratic family name—according to Jennings—but he looked every inch a bumpkin. At this moment, Leah could see that Coy was getting boisterous, waving his drink in the air and slopping it onto the plush carpet. Ernestine studiously avoided looking in his direction, but Leah detected her fleeting frown as his voice rose. Yes, Leah could believe that Ernestine might be the source of her uneasiness.

Once the danger was pinpointed, Leah expected to feel easier, but she still sensed a restlessness which always before had meant that she had not yet completely resolved her problem. Perhaps there was more than one danger here.

At that point Blackie's voice joined Coy's, and it became apparent that the two of them were deep into their cups. Joe Billy excused himself and sauntered over to Doris Jean.

"Honey? Don't you think we better eat? These boys going to collapse if they don't get some food pretty soon."

Doris Jean seemed undecided. "I suppose we can. I was waiting on our other guests—"

"They ain't going to show," he said. "I told you they wouldn't."

"Who you talking about?" Ernestine addressed this to her brother.

"Frank," he said. Then he pulled Doris Jean up by the

elbow. "Get on in there and tell Luretha to put dinner on. I ain't going to wait on that beatnik sonofabitch any longer."

Doris Jean looked apologetically into Leah's eyes. "They probably didn't get the invitation," she said. "They don't have a phone, you know. I had to phone Jennings' Aunt Ida and tell her to ask them. She probably forgot."

Of course. Now Leah knew what they were talking about. She remembered Aunt Ida mentioning her son Frank.

She found herself seated at the dinner table between the two drunks, Coy and Blackie. Jennings sat opposite her, flanked by Ernestine and Blanche. Joe Billy and Doris Jean sat at either end. Two chairs had been quickly removed, and Luretha was taking up the two extra place settings as they sat down.

"You needn't have asked Frank just because of me," Jennings said.

"I thought it would be a nice reunion," said Doris Jean.

"Hell, he ain't so by God hard to take," Blackie said. "I used to like old Frank, before he went off to California and turned into a by God beatnik. Surprised me he ever came back, even if his daddy did die."

Coy belched. "Can't blame Frank for not wanting to bring his little kikette out in public," he said. Ernestine shot him a killing look.

Jennings looked surprised. "Aunt Ida didn't tell me Frank married a Jew."

"Coy doesn't know for sure she's a Jew," Ernestine said.

"The hell I don't! I got eyes, ain't I? I know one when I see one!" Coy was weaving precariously, even sitting down.

Leah's heart was thumping. Momentarily she wondered if Frank's wife were trying to pass. Maybe Jews had to pass, too.

"Joe Billy, will you ask the blessing?" Doris Jean broke in and brought them back to piety. They all bowed their heads

53

and Coy belched behind closed lips and let it escape little by little in round plumps. The pungence of his whiskey reached her nose, and Leah sensed that perhaps Coy was part of the danger she felt. Instinctively she drew away and scooted her chair to the right. She felt her elbow brush Blackie's. The hair on her arm bristled.

For a moment she was transported back to Father Richard's study, seated in Father's big leather chair, her feet dangling inches from the floor. Father had taken out a book and had read to her a long passage of meaningless words. She had tried hard to grasp just one word—anything—of what he said. It was useless. It was as if he read a foreign language. Then she heard him say something about preparing "a table before me in the presence of mine enemies." It was the only part she could remember, but she remembered it now, and the hair on the nape of her neck rose.

They raised their heads. "Now I want us all to behave," Doris Jean said. "What is Leah going to think about us? Luretha, you forgot the dressing for the salad."

They all seemed to talk at once, and Leah was excused from trying to join in. It was just as well: she needed all her concentration just to get it right, use the right fork. Out of the corner of her eye she watched Blanche Carnes, across the table to her left. Blanche would do everything just so.

It was much later, well into the evening when they were taking coffee in the living room, that the warning signal grew white-hot. Conversation was again divided across the room between men and women. Leah, listening with only half an ear to Doris Jean's description of the town's various women's organizations, was aware that Blackie had made a remark which seemed to pain Joe Billy. Almost instantly Jennings looked aggrieved and Joe Billy, in sullen reaction, leaped up and returned with the brandy bottle, in an apparent attempt

54

to avert an incident which Blackie seemed determined to provoke. Leah tried to block out Doris Jean's voice:

"Tell me this": Blackie's tone was goading, prodding. "Is it better to live off oil money or insurance money? Huh?"

Joe Billy answered Blackie's banter levelly at first, but his tone became ever more strained as Blackie bore down.

"Is one of them cleaner, hey?" he said.

What is it? Leah asked herself frantically. Why am I threatened? She shot Jennings an imploring look and he caught her signal eagerly. The women's conversation had suddenly ceased, and an uneasy tension had electrified the room. Jennings stood up.

"I'm sorry to tear us away so early," he said. "I must stop by the hospital and leave some preop orders before the nurses' shift changes."

A wave of fierce protectiveness swept over her. God love him! If only he really had a patient in the hospital! Even one!

Joe Billy followed them to the door, and the white-hot alarm signal was still stinging her brain. "I'll call you in a day or two," he was saying to Jennings. "Maybe you'll let me take you to lunch."

Jennings hesitated. "I'm not sure I can afford the time," he said. She knew what he really meant. Right now he hadn't the funds to reciprocate. Instinctively she knew that Joe Billy knew it, too. He slapped his friend on the shoulder.

"You'd be doing me a big favor if you'd make the time. I need some professional advice."

She could see that Jennings was hooked. And that underneath, Joe Billy was possessed of a serpent's cunning beneath a seraph's guilelessness. And she was afraid. Terribly, dreadfully afraid.

6

SOMETIMES JENNINGS woke up in the night and worried. About some decision he had to make. Or about decisions he'd already made. Seems he could never leave something alone, but would keep dredging it up and weighing the pros and cons far into the night over and again. For that reason, sometimes he'd marvel at how quickly he'd decided to marry Leah. Sometimes he'd wonder if he should have waited a while longer. At times he even felt a certain portent about the outcome of such a hasty action. He never talked about his difficulty in making decisions to anyone, because Weslay Palmer used to tell him, with some exasperation, "When you make a decision, stick with it, boy, no matter what! That's the mark of a real man!"

Jennings Palmer dated everything from his father's death. When Weslay Palmer died, Jennings became a "real man," for he had to begin making decisions in earnest. He was nineteen at the time and old enough to be a man—old enough to serve in the Army, only he didn't. Jennings was premed, and maybe he didn't really care so much about being a doctor as about not going to Korea. Not everyone who was premed got a deferment, but Weslay Palmer knew the right people.

Jennings was an only child, the sandy-haired, open-faced, artless product of a middle-age pregnancy. Mamie always tried to raise him like an only child; only Weslay saw to it that she didn't make a pansy out of him. Weslay made him a man's man. Or prepared him to be one. He never let him grow up, never let him make a single decision, really, until the day he died.

Mamie was always so dependent during Weslay's life she never even went to the filling station to gas up the car. Jennings figured to have a burden on his hands when his father died, but Mamie fooled him. Blossomed out. Started taking bus tours all over the country. He'd be up at A&M, and here'd come a postcard from Boston: "Am on a New England foliage tour. Wish you were here." But he knew she didn't really.

Mamie kept the house open all during his college and med school days, but when he announced plans to apply for a residency, she threw up her hands.

"I been hanging around this town for years, waiting to turn this house over to you so I can move to Arizona and start living," she said. "I just can't sit here and rot, waiting for you to decide to settle down!"

So she closed the house and moved, and Jennings only saw her once, maybe twice a year. She never suggested that he come to Arizona to visit, and he didn't even want to speculate on why. His mother would never do anything improper.

He'd never taken girls too seriously. Might have gotten serious about Ernestine Tolliver if Coy Moseley hadn't beat him out. That was probably the most traumatic experience of his life, dwarfing even his own father's death. He would always wonder if he had done the right thing that night.

He'd gone whistling up the walk to pick up Ernestine for

the junior sock hop, and he was surprised when Coy Moseley opened the door.

"Hey, Coy! You here to see Joe Billy?" he asked.

Coy looked puzzled. "You mean Ernestine didn't tell you yet? Lord, Jennings, I feel like a rat!"

Ernestine appeared in the living room doorway, her pretty face blushing to the roots of her pale hair. "I—I'm sorry, Coy. I—I meant to tell him."

Jennings looked from one to the other, feeling his face grow hot. "Tell what?" He tried to look pleasant.

"Ernestine and me have decided to go steady." Coy was beaming. He didn't look as if he felt like a rat about it. "Hey man, I hope this isn't going to affect our friendship."

"Oh gosh no!" Jennings grinned and started backing toward the porch step. "Well, guess I'll see you all at the dance."

Ernestine ran up and kissed him on the cheek. "Oh, Jennings, you are just the nicest thing! If you only knew how I worried— See, Coy? I knew Jennings would understand!"

He ought to have bashed Coy's face in, and he always told himself that if it'd been anybody but a Moseley, he would have. But after all, it was worth a lot to have everyone think he was such a good sport about it. And it was all just as well in the long run: Ernestine had gotten fat. And on that point, he was decisive: he liked them slender, like Leah. There were lots of girls like that around, but after his dad died, he didn't go out much. It was more than just a matter of economics, although he did want his inheritance to stretch as far as possible. It was just that it was so hard to decide ahead of time whether he liked a girl enough to ask her out.

Maybe he was just ready when Leah came along. Anyway, she was the first girl he ever knew whom he felt he couldn't live too long without. Three days after their first date, he could've just moved in. It became painful to think about going home and leaving her, and it was just too expensive to keep

58

taking her out. Anyhow, he knew that someday he would want to acquire a good-looking wife; she would, after all, be a good investment in the long run.

It was more than just a physical thing—although he thought her looks were perfect. She was small and dark, like his mother. Darker, even. But with incredibly long legs. Her body was lithe and wild, fluid and soft. "I never knew a girl to be so soft, to be so skinny," he told her, incredulous.

It was more than physical, but it was never very personal. They never went into feelings and attitudes and beliefs, never had heart-to-heart talks. He backed right off from all that personal stuff, and she was agreeable. Probably that was it: she was so agreeable. She expected so little. She took care of his needs, too. Saw to it that he had clean socks and ironed shirts, cooked for him.

He was such a conventional man. There is great safety, great comfort in tradition. You didn't marry the girl you slept with. Besides, he always pictured himself, if he thought about marrying at all, as marrying some girl from home. But there wasn't anybody back home like Leah. He just made the mistake of sleeping with her too soon, but he didn't know she was going to be The One. He'd forgive her that. It was the wine.

Otherwise, she was a woman to make a man proud. Some men preferred statuesque, striking women, voluptuous women, blondes like Doris Jean from back home who turned other men's head's when you escorted them into a room. But in his more honest moments he'd have to admit that a woman like Doris Jean intimidated him. His own mother was much like Leah. She had always satisfied his old man. Fact is, there never was a finer little woman than Mom.

Jennings had been only an adequate student in medical school, but during his residency he hit his stride. He had a real feel for diagnostics. Each case was like putting together the pieces of a puzzle. It was a game, actually.

Once Leah asked him, "Is it always just a set of symptoms to you?" and he told her, "A doctor can't afford to get emotionally involved with personalities. It impairs his judgment." All said in a crisp, decisive tone that broached no argument. He felt good about that.

During his last year of residency, Jennings was chosen chief resident, which meant a modicum of minor administrative duties fell his way. He realized for the first time that he was no good at making decisions. Really faced the fact that there was never a solution that pleased everybody, and Jennings wanted more than anything else to please everybody.

He realized that Leah often worried about him during that year, for he frequently wore a harried, haunted look. He began to dread to hear the phone ring, and he often had her screen his calls. "If it's Bakerman, stall him," he'd say. "Tell him I'll call him later." Bakerman always had a problem that required a decision on Jennings' part.

Often, when minor disagreements arose over the duty roster, Jennings would find himself switching from one side of the argument to the other. It was so much easier to be agreeable. It was not an extremely productive year, but the residents voted him "Mr. Nice Guy" at the year-end picnic, anyway.

About the only place where he could be authoritative was at home, with Leah. Weslay Palmer had ruled his home; in fact, Jennings used to believe that he was a tyrant and something of an unreasonable scoundrel, but he found that he fell quite naturally into the same pattern with Leah. She seemed comfortable being the permissive one. But even with Leah, sometimes he found he had trouble.

"What do you want, spaghetti or meat loaf?" she'd ask.

Shrugging was his favorite gesture. "Whatever you say."

Or, "Do you want me to iron your blue shirt or your white one for tomorrow?"

He could never say. She always made the little decisions like that. Still, in big things, he was the man of the house.

It occurred to Jennings that everybody needs a goal, and that he had stumbled upon the ideal one for himself. He would be the best diagnostician Clarington ever had. No more slipshod back-country medicine like old Doc Grainger had been getting away with for fifty years. Jennings would bring bigcity medicine to the whole area. Word would get around in time, and people from as far away as Jacksonville would come to him. In time, he could bring in other specialists. Palmer Clinic would be Mayo Clinic for the whole South.

It wasn't a dream he shared with Leah, of course. It wasn't any of her concern, anyhow.

The thing had a lot of serendipities, this secret goal of his. There was the money, naturally. Even with all the deadbeats and coons, he'd still make a comfortable living. Then there was the prestige.

Also there was the satisfaction. It wasn't something he could admit to anybody, but he could thrive for a week on the look of adoration from the mother of an ailing child. It was probably how the Lord felt when he parted the Red Sea for the Children of Israel.

That was it: his patients made him feel like a Savior.

As to life in Clarington, for Leah, he never thought about it. She'd do just about what she'd always done, he supposed. Whatever that was. Except, of course, work. No wife of his could work anymore. Not in his hometown. Oh, she could help out in the office until he found someone permanent, but after that, she'd stay home. Of that he was certain.

Whatever else she might do, he'd never have considered she might spend her time plotting murder.

Jennings was an uncomplicated man, and he liked a stable, predictable life. He liked to pigeonhole things, to classify them good or bad, black or white, if he could.

61

This in part explained why he returned to Clarington in the first place. He had a house there. Mamie had given it to him.

"You're going to like the house," he told Leah. "Solid as a rock. Good thick oak doors. They don't build houses like that anymore."

She murmured her approval.

"The furniture's good, too!" he continued. "It may be thirty-five years old, but it's as sturdy as the day it was bought. And it's been sitting in just the same positions as long as I can remember."

She was glad, she mumbled.

"Dad's car, too. We're lucky to have it. You get a good Chrysler and take care of it and it'll run forever. Besides, it doesn't look good for a doctor to be running around in a new car. First thing you know, people would be jealous."

She'd never have thought of that, she admitted.

Jennings could easily become a morally righteous man. Oh, he'd climbed fool's hill often enough in high school, but he'd never done anything bad enough to get arrested for. Except the time he and Joe Billy caught the little Mexican girls down by the lake. You couldn't call that rape, although their momma had, when she called the sheriff. Of course, Malcolm Gunn hadn't really arrested them. But Weslay took a cane to Jennings and told him to respect all women, even dark ones, and to watch out for social diseases.

Weslay Palmer said grace at the table three times a day until he died, and Mamie heard Jennings' bedtime prayers every night until he was thirteen. Jennings went to Sunday school every week, and sometimes on Sunday nights Mamie let him go to Baptist Young People's Union over at the Baptist church with Coy. In short, his religious training was not neglected.

So if he were ever called upon to make a moral decision, such as the one he faced in the spring of 1960, anybody could predict that he would try to make what he felt other people would think was the righteous one. His old friend Joe Billy Tolliver should have known that. If only he'd thought it through ahead of time, Joe Billy might never have stirred up the whole mess.

7

LEAH WAS soon bringing in a little money from the sale of her watercolors at the frame shop. Hardly more than enough to cover the cost of her materials, but she gained a sweeping sense of gratification from this small effort. Painting, the use of her talent, remained the beholden duty which Sister Fain had always laid upon her, and thus much of its enjoyment and abandon were lost to her.

If she had ideas of setting up her easel on a hillside and painting the countryside, these were soon dispelled, for the clearings consisted of new-plowed fields or utility rights-of-way. All else was thicket and wood, a tangle of growth which almost choked itself in its closeness. The land was like the people, she decided. And so for the most part she contented herself with still life or painting an occasional country shanty which she sketched on country calls with Jennings. Rarely she would happen onto a decaying plantation which was, to some extent, still operating. She was to learn what even many Texans never realize: that East Texas is a pocket of the Deep South, the Old South, actually, unhampered by the contact with the outside world which has altered most of the rest.

She was always curious to know who bought her watercolors. She was pleased and flattered, one week, to learn that Jennings' Cousin Frank had bought a painting. Pleased, because she'd secretly wondered if the Ramseys' failure to appear at the Tollivers' dinner party was a desire to shun Jennings and his new wife. Flattered, because she'd been told by Aunt Ida that Cousin Frank was a sculptor of sorts, and she needed the approbation of another artist. But she was mystified by his choice: it was one of her poorer ones, she thought. Not a still life or a landscape, at which she was fairly adept, but the study of a woman, possibly modeled after Mama, made up from her own wishful fantasy. She hoped to run into Frank sometime, hoped he would mention the purchase so she could question him concerning his choice. But she was to learn that the Ramseys' failure to appear at the party was not a rarity. They neither socialized nor even came into town except to buy supplies. Gossip had it that they even refused to have either a television or telephone in their farmhouse.

In the golden vigor of a September noonday, Leah was drawn from her flower-bed puttering by the insistent ringing of the telephone. It was important, always, to answer the phone, now that Jennings was picking up a few patients. She was not expecting to hear the voice of Jennings' cousin, Frank Ramsey, whom she had never met.

"Frank! What a surprise! Are you in town?"

"I'm calling from Mom's place," he said. "Is Jennings in?"

"I'm expecting him soon. I hope Aunt Ida isn't sick?"

There was an awkward pause. "I'm not calling for Mom. She's always used Old Doc Grainger. But the colored folks who live on the place have a sick grandbaby. I understand

65

Jennings has been taking care of them. I think he'd better come out and have a look at the kid. . . . We'll pay, of course. Just have Jennings drop by the house after he's finished."

It was the chance she had been waiting for. "I—sometimes drive along with him to see the countryside, Frank. Mind if I come, too?"

He didn't hesitate, she was sure of that. "Be glad to have you. Do Harriett good to see a friendly face."

It was midafternoon when she and Jennings set out for the Ramsey place, Leah with a feeling of exultation she'd almost forgotten. She rode with the window open, breathing in the robustness of the bright day, smelling the freshness of the new-turned earth of the fields near the highway. Then the car plunged onto a back road which knifed into a thicket, and she could see the sun no more. It was midafternoon when they reached the old gray shack on the Ramsey place where the Johnsons lived, but the gloom of a false dusk had already crept inside the house, and a kerosene lamp was burning in the front room. Leah shivered as Jennings slammed the car door. She didn't want to wait alone.

"I'm coming in," she said.

He looked at her curiously and shrugged, turned and led the way up the two rickety steps and through the screen door. He picked up the kerosene lamp, offhandedly introduced her to Buck Johnson and his wife Pearlene, two grossly overweight hulks who hovered passively in the shadows of the room. Leah got the impression that the couple was in their fifties, but she scarcely gave them more notice than did Jennings. He ignored the several young children who skulked about and carried the lamp into the other room. Leah hesitated a moment then followed him, not knowing what else to do. The stench was unpleasant, and the dark interior of the cabin was both depressing and frightening.

In the bedroom, holding up the lamp to encompass them in

a circle of light, Jennings introduced her to two young women, Reeona and Dorothy. She didn't know which was which. A young man lay on one of the two beds. He made no motion to get up as they entered. A baby whimpered on the other bed.

The sight, especially, for some reason, of the young man who sullenly ignored them, transported her to another day, another time, and a strange, wistful loathing took possession of her. She did not wish to feel kinship to these people. She moved closer to Jennings' side.

"Leroy, can't you get up and the doctor be here?" one of the young women chided. The young man turned his head sullenly to the wall. "Leroy!"

And then from the other room came Buck Johnson's voice. "Leroy!" The young man got up, bowed slightly in Jennings' direction and left the room.

Jennings bent over the child. "How old is this baby, Reeona?"

"Pert near nine months this week, Doct. Palmer."

"You're still breast-feeding him, aren't you?" She nodded sheepishly. "I thought I told you to wean him. What else are you feeding him?"

She shrugged. "Wellum, he got but four teeth—"

"He's underweight, Reeona. You're starving him. I told you weeks ago that he has to have more food. And milk. Stop by my office sometime and I'll give you some vitamin samples. Do you have any baby bottles?"

"Wellum my sister do. But she got a baby just now."

He stood up and folded his stethoscope into his pocket. "I'll speak to Mr. Frank. Mrs. Ramsey probably has some bottles she can give you."

He shook his finger in her face in mock sternness. "You'll stay home and be a good mother to this boy. And you won't get pregnant anymore, hear me?"

She grinned and ducked her head. "Wellum all right."

Jennings took up the lamp and left the room, leaving them in almost-dark. Leah followed the light. Buck and Pearlene had risen respectfully to their feet. Leroy was nowhere in sight.

"Pearlene, you need to watch Reeona. She's not feeding that baby," he said. "And, Buck, you need to take that boy Leroy in hand. How old is he, anyway?"

"Wellum he be same as Mist. Frank. Same as you, he be," Buck answered.

"That boy needs to learn some respect. And he needs a steady job, instead of lying around this house," Jennings said, setting the lamp back on the table.

Buck straightened. "Leroy got a steady job. Me and Leroy in business now. Together!"

Jennings snorted and walked out onto the porch, out into the light. "We're going up to the big house and see Mr. Frank now. If they have any baby bottles or anything else you can use, we'll drop them by on our way home."

They were in the car when Pearlene banged the screen door and hailed them. "Doct. Palmer! Dorothy be around next week to work for Mrs. Palmer!"

Jennings hesitated a moment, then nodded and waved her off. Leah grabbed his arm as he reached for the ignition key.

"What's she talking about?" Leah cried. "Tell her no! I don't need a maid!"

But Jennings only patted her and started the motor. "Humor us all, then," he said. "Pearlene is looking out after Dorothy's future."

"How's that?"

"Somebody to look after Dorothy when she's gone. Pearlene's probably figured Reeona'll take her place with the Ramseys and Dorothy'll end up with us. I doubt if Pearlene will last much longer, and neither will Buck."

Leah shuddered in spite of herself. "What makes you say that?"

"Look at them! Overweight. . . . I suspect that Buck has already had a few little strokes. Sometimes he seems forgetful. And Pearlene needs all kinds of tests. I suspect she may have carcinoma. What are you going to do with these people?"

"You treat them like children," she said.

"You don't understand," he said. "You probably never will."

Aunt Ida's house sat high on a hill a half-mile south of the Johnson shanty. In what used to be called the East Pasture, Cousin Frank had built a small contemporary ranch house. This was what the Johnsons now called the "big house." At the entrance to the East Pasture were the mailboxes. Inside the fence, just over the cattle guard, a large hand-lettered sign announced: Mad Bull, Bad Dog, Naked Children, Mean Wife, No Visitors.

"Did Frank do that?" Leah asked incredulously.

Jennings was indifferent. "Frank is forever defending his freedom. Look at this spread—" His arm swept around all sides. "All of this his, and yet he turned his back on it. Only came back because Aunt Ida is widowed and can't manage without him." He pointed ahead. Two youngsters ran around the pasture, completely nude. "At least he can't say the sign didn't warn us."

The young woman who opened the door was tall, slender, serene. Her waist-length black hair was caught back with a piece of hemp rope. She wore faded jeans and a man's white shirt from which the sleeves had been torn. Around her neck dangled a long, single strand of watermelon seeds. Her feet were bare and not too clean. Her dark eyes lit with unmistakable pleasure when they introduced themselves.

"Jennings! Leah! We've been expecting you!" In one movement Harriett Ramsey half-embraced them and led them into

69

the house, into an enormous L-shaped room. Leah felt an immediate warmth for this woman, and with sudden longing knew that she needed a friend.

The house actually consisted of the two bedrooms and the enormous room they were in now. One end, dominated by a huge stone fireplace, served as the living room, while the other end became the kitchen. Frank's sculpture was everywhere. Each piece seemed to be accompanied by a message, carved below. The most prominent piece, an immense wooden phallus titled *Fallout Fertility*, reigned from its own pedestal near the door. There was clutter everywhere. Harriett kicked it aside and called for her husband. "They're here, Frank!"

Jennings stopped her. "Please! If he's working—"

Harriett waved him aside airily. "He's not creating; I only wish he were! It's paperwork, something about the feed bill. We're farmers now, remember? Far cry from Half Moon Bay huh?" There was no bitterness in her voice. She bounced out to get Frank, and Leah turned to find Jennings standing before a small watercolor.

"Do you like that?" she asked. It was a picture of a woman seated at a table.

"Mm? I don't know. I don't get it. The face—there are no features. Just a blob of brown."

"Maybe the face wasn't important," she said. "Maybe the artist was trying to create a mood without using anything as obvious as facial expression to convey it. Don't you get the feel of the somber shadows, the drooping shoulders? Look at the articles she's fondling on the table."

He took a step back and squinted. "Oh yeah. They must be—toys." He stepped back again, then his face lit up with a grin. "I get it! She must have lost a child, and she's grieving. That's it, isn't it?"

"Bravo!" The voice was Frank's and they turned to see him

70

poised in the doorway like the Angel Gabriel. A barnyard odor permeated his jeans, which hung an inch below the waistband of his shorts. He wore no shirt. Yet his looks were clean and aesthetic, almost delicate. His bright tumbled curls ended in ringlets almost at his shoulders. His deep-set gray eyes were sad and penetrating, and his voice was quiet, musical, tinged with culture. Leah couldn't make him out.

He walked over and took Leah's hand. "Your taste has improved, Jennings, both in art and in artists. Good to see you, Leah. I saw this at the frame shop and had to have it. What inspired that marvelous piece of work?"

Leah colored and looked sidewise at Jennings. "It was—just a television show I saw," she said. "Jennings, I—I hadn't mentioned it, I guess, but Mr. Hill down at the frame shop was good enough to take some of my watercolors on consignment. They—were just cluttering up the house. I didn't know what else to do with them."

Jennings, she could tell, did not like surprises. She had put him in an awkward position by not telling him before now, and she regretted it.

"Aha!" Harriett, who had gone into the kitchen area to open some beer, called through the passway. "So! Ratholing your pin money, eh, Leah?"

"Hardly!" Leah laughed. "It all goes for new supplies." She joined Harriett in the kitchen area while Frank and Jennings sat down on pillows near the stone hearth. The house was so open; she'd hardly have a chance to talk to Harriett alone, and of a sudden she felt an aching hunger to get to know her.

"Have you been here long?" Leah asked.

Harriett picked up the tray of beer and went into the other part of the big room, leaving Leah to follow. "Two god-awful years," she said over her shoulder.

It was clear that it would be a four-way conversation. Leah

sat quietly while the others talked, and she pondered her peculiar isolation, a solitude which she had longed to break on this day. Since the dinner party, she had felt that she might find a friend in Harriett. But Harriett was so very married, not like herself who had plenty of time alone. Yet she knew her instincts were sound; she felt no feeling of danger here as she had in Joe Billy's house. She felt comfortable here, and she was sorry when Jennings asked for the baby bottles and announced that it was time to go.

At the door, Harriett gave her hand a squeeze. "Thanks for coming out, Leah. Friendly faces are far between in these parts."

Leah's throat ached with the urgent desire to say—what? She wasn't sure. Instead, she said, "Come to see me whenever you're in town."

Frank handed Jennings a check for the Johnsons' house call. "Much obliged for coming out," he said. A grim, restrained smile played at his sensitive mouth. "I hope you make enough of this to keep you out of Joe Billy's back pocket."

Then he handed Leah a small metal amulet on a chain. It was carved in the shape of an eye. "I'd like you to have something of me, Leah."

She was touched. She turned the eye over and saw, carved on the reverse side, the words, "This above all . . ." She didn't know what it meant, but she had the feeling she'd read it in English class. She was afraid to ask, afraid it was something she ought to know.

Frank grinned. "It's just a little something I made. It's for gnawing on when this place starts driving you crazy."

At the Johnson place Dorothy and her younger sister Reeona stretched out on the floor near the screen door. Two younger sisters could be heard shrieking and splashing as

72

they washed dishes in the kitchen. Their older brother Leroy wrestled on the floor behind the couch with Dorothy's four-year-old son. Buck and Pearlene sat close to the television set in one corner of the room.

From the bedroom came a child's wail. Pearlene shifted in her chair and peered into the bedroom. "Dorothy, your baby's awoke."

Dorothy stretched her thin legs before her and leaned sluggishly against the wall. "Don't know why she don't sleep. I done moved the fan so it blows in there."

"Go shut her up before she wakes up mine," Reeona said peevishly. She ain't never going to quit by herself. You done got her so spoilt."

"Hmph! Like to know how I be spoiling her and I never see her!"

"Like crazy!" Reeona squealed. "Didn't you stay home all last week while I be up at the big house doing all that work!"

"All that work!" Dorothy scoffed. "Settin' up there under the cool of Mrs. Ramsey's air conditioner! And me and Momma taking care of all these kids and doing the cooking and washing—"

"Dorothy! Your baby awoke."

"Ain't no reason why either one of us got to stay home," Reeona reasoned. "You could go up to the big house, and I—"

"You could kite off to town!" Dorothy sniffed. "Why don't *I* kite off and make the money?"

"Because you never went to high school! Ain't nobody's fault but yours you so ignorant!"

"Shut your mouth!" Dorothy stormed, slapping the floor.

"All you ever done was run around with anything with pants on, getting yourself pregnant." Reeona ducked deftly to avoid the blow aimed at her head.

"Dorothy, did you hear your momma? Your baby's

awoke!" Buck's tone was impatient. You didn't mess with Buck.

"I'm going." Reluctantly, Dorothy pulled herself up and shuffled into the bedroom. She heard the sound of Dr. Palmer's car, heard Reeona greet him and take him into the kitchen. She didn't want to make conversation with the doctor again. She decided to take the baby outside.

As a precaution against insects she oiled the child before taking her out in the dusk. Then she carried her quickly, quietly through the front room. Carefully she backed through the warped screen door and pushed it to with her foot. On the porch was an old rocking chair, but Dorothy didn't care to socialize with the doctor on his way out. So laying the baby in the chair, she moved it off the porch and out into the side yard by the new clothesline. A galvanized-iron washtub was leaning against the tree. She turned it upside down and sat upon it so that she could face the chair, which she rocked gently. She hummed softly to soothe the fretting child. She paid no mind to Dr. Palmer's car, parked there in the yard, nor did she see the lone occupant sitting inside.

The child intermittently whined and screamed in angry protest of the heat as long as her mother consoled her. But after a time, as Dorothy's attention wandered and she spoke in hushed tones more to herself than to the baby, the child stopped fretting. Her black eyes became somber and attentive, as if she didn't want to miss a matter of importance.

Dorothy, hunched over, elbows on her knees, looked up at the clear indigo sky already flecked with starshine. She sighed as one of the glowing coals streaked downward and out of sight. She strained as if to hear, over noisily chirping crickets and frog songs from the bayou, some empyrean report.

"See that star, babe? One minute glowing bright and the next minute it's gone. Not a sound out of it, not a trace left. It don't do to be thinking you're too important, baby love.

74

"See the moon, baby love? See it up yonder? You want that moon, baby love? Stretch out them sweet-as-cream fat fingers and take it, then!"

She leaned forward and grasped a little foot in her two hands and pressed its sole to her lips. The child cackled gleefully. She patted the baby's middle and resumed her rocking, staring up once again into the gathering dark. Somewhere nearby a giant frog croaked grandly.

"Oh dear Jesus," she cried, "will I ever get outa here?"

Her words slashed through the quiet night sounds like a dagger and pierced the spirit of the lone occupant of the car, reopening a fulminating wound.

Eventually the baby slept peacefully, her legs dangling over the seat of the rocker. Dorothy picked her up gently and, swaying slowly from side to side, looked up at the now brightly glowing moon one last time. With a long sigh, she took the sleeping child quietly around to the back of the house as Dr. Palmer stepped out onto the porch.

From out of the east a restless breeze stirred, sending a wisp of cloud to obscure the moon and washing the night with a sudden unnatural black chill. Across the darkness a single firefly darted, then disappeared, inked out in the nothingness.

8

EARLY PAIN, enormous emptiness had molded her, left her both deft and cautious, prepared her to map out her moves so as to protect her position wherever she found herself. Leah soon glided into the mainstream of Clarington life, faltering only slightly once or twice.

The first was a near disaster, the lighthearted outing to Tolliver's Lake soon after that first dinner party. The guest list was identical: Joe Billy's sister Ernestine and her husband Coy Moseley, Blackie and Blanche Carnes and Jennings and Leah.

No apprehension warned Leah, and later she was to conclude that her own anticipation had blotted out everything else. She had wanted to be just right. She allowed herself a frivolity, marched down to Tolliver's Dry Goods and bought a smashing sun dress, too revealing, perhaps, but one which none would forget, she was sure. The halter top clung in soft purple folds upon the ivory curve of her breast, barely concealing its pink bud. The skirt fell in liquid undulations against her thighs. She excited herself, just looking in the mirror. It helped to look just right. But something was wrong. She reached up and removed the cross which hung from a chain around her neck. That was better. There was no break in the eye from her carved white throat to the plunging V of her dress. She let the necklace slip through her fingers into her lingerie drawer where it sank out of sight. Good. It reminded her of Sister Fain, who had given it to her. Sister Fain would not like her dress.

The dress had been her first mistake of the day, that miserable day. She knew it immediately when they reached the lake house and saw the others in shorts or swimsuits. The women eyed her suspiciously and the men merely ogled. She didn't want that, not enemies, not adversaries. She made some lame excuse about having dressed for an earlier occasion and not having time to change. They saw through it immediately. Morosely she suffered through the afternoon. When the others suggested a swim, she pleaded nothing to wear. She should have told the truth, that she didn't know how to swim. As it was, Doris Jean produced a perfectly horrid sunsuit left over from God-knows-when by God-knows-who and took great glee in making her put it on before they went out in the boat.

"O.K., girls," he said. "Time to get your hairdos wet. Last one in's a nigger baby!" And he skinned off his T-shirt and dove over the side, coming up a second later spewing lake water.

Blackie opened another beer and peered over the side. "Hell, Joe Billy, are you by God crazy? I ain't going to bust my head on no by God boulder out there!"

"Ain't no rocks here, Blackie, and you been knowing that since you was twelve! Now put down that beer and get your—"

"Come on, Leah." Ernestine was pulling at her arm.

Leah looked around frantically for Jennings. But he was down below. Ernestine and Blanche were easing over the side.

"It's not deep here, Leah," Ernestine called from the water. "Look: I'm standing on the bottom!"

She must not panic. Must not tell them how little she knew about being in the water. Gripping the rail, she let herself down over the side, sucking in her breath as the cold lake water ate its way up her legs. It was a sensuous sensation which took her breath away, made her forget about keeping up her guard.

Coy and Joe Billy were horsing around, squirting water at each other between their palms. Blanche squealed and ducked. Leah bounced away on tiptoes. She was exhilarated by the feel of the water against her skin. She rubbed her knees against each other and enjoyed a certain self-lust. She blocked out the voices of the others and bounced and worked her way to the other side of the boat. And suddenly she was in over her head. Literally.

Flailing, fighting, grasping for a hold on something, trying to call and sucking in a mouthful of green water, she realized, through her panic, that the others could not see her. And in that moment she said to herself, You see? Just like always.

But then she heard Doris Jean call, and saw Jennings peering down at her from the boat. But before he could dive in, she felt herself swept up forcibly by a powerful arm, which grabbed her head and pulled her up. Then she was being lifted out by the man, Perry—had he been watching her all along? She felt humiliated, misshapen clothes sticking to her slender body, her dark hair stringing down over her eyes. It was a wretched, mortifying experience. Especially since she was sure the other women were enjoying it so.

Moments later, as she crouched, soaked and gasping, on the shore and the others crowded around, she heard Joe Billy mutter, "Sonofagun! I never seen that sucker Perry move so fast in my life! What do you suppose got into him, I wonder?"

Her next error was a long time in coming. It was Christmas of that year, 1959, when the early spring bulbs were already greening. The season crept up on her, really, because of the weather. And because she didn't know the rules. On Christmas Eve the Tollivers swept by to leave a homemade fruitcake. Ernestine and Coy Moseley showed up with a bottle of wine. Blanche Carnes brought them a Della Robbia arrangement. And Jennings and Leah stood by awkward and empty-handed.

"Why didn't you warn me people were going to do this?" she demanded of Jennings.

He shrugged. "I left here a boy. Mama always took care of those things. You're supposed to be the one to know what to do, not me."

She'd never be caught again. She would learn.

During the first January snow, she was transported to another day long ago when she had waked to find her smutty ghetto had disappeared and in its place shimmered a fairyland. Rushing outside, she had marveled at the glistening new world. This is the real world, she had thought. She picked up a bit of the new world between her fingers and it, too, disappeared. Try as she might she could not grasp her new world for long. She felt that she was very close to discovering the true nature of things. But that truth eluded her now.

A gray drizzle hung about that heavy and threatening February day when her inborn will to survive again rattled its chains in warning. But Leah was misreading the signs these days, or believing them to be misleading or merely superstition. It was the day of the tea at Miss Agnes Crenshaw's big house on the hill. Doris Jean had wangled her an invitation and had taken her there, had linked arms with her and steered her through dozens of introductions. "Have you met our new doctor's wife? Such a talented thing! Sings in the choir, paints pictures, just reads every book you nearly ever heard of!"

She took it all, lapped it up, welcomed it, needed it. Resolved to get more of it.

By March trees were dabbling pale lacy-leaf fingers in the turbid streams, and she tasted the aromatic crispness of the south breeze. It drew her out of doors like a magnet. She spent hours strolling in the woods past the highway, savoring the sweet songs of a reverent robin against the proud sky, kicking aside the winter's layer of blackened leaves to discover the brave new shoots, breathing in the syrupy odors of honeysuckle and jasmine.

She was tardily planting caladium bulbs in the front bed one day when the postman surprised her with a small white envelope of expensive linen paper. She knew what it was immediately. It represented a minor triumph she'd been working toward for months. Without understanding exactly why, she decided not to mention it to Jennings just yet.

It didn't really matter about Jennings, anyhow. He was gone much of the time, was preoccupied when he was at home. On his afternoon off, he usually played golf with Joe Billy at the country club. Frequently he had to spend the day in court testifying for Joe Billy in a personal injury case.

The chief industry supporting Clarington was, of course, not the oil field, which the Railroad Commission was allowing only fourteen pumping days a month, but the chemical plant, which processed by-products from the oil field waste. Leah knew nothing of its operation other than it seemed that many of its five hundred employees must be doing dangerous work, judging by the frequency of injuries. Joe Billy seemed to get wind of these injuries early. Often he had sent clients to Jennings for treatment; in fact, Joe Billy's sponsorship was the main factor in their growing prosperity. It was on those occasions when these personal injury suits came to trial that Jennings was asked to testify.

Sometimes, Leah noticed, this made Jennings grumpy. He resented, he said, having to be out of the office for a whole day for a silly court trial. But it seemed to Leah a small price to pay for the business that had been thrown his way.

Occasionally Jennings would balk, unable to decide whether to testify at all. She would hear him tell Joe Billy on the phone, "You'll be sorry if you get me on the witness stand. I honestly can't decide if there's a damn thing wrong with him. I sometimes suspect he's nothing but a crock!" Then Joe Billy would drop the complaint, she supposed. Whatever Jennings said seemed to be the final word. No matter how he grumbled, how brusque he was, how unpleasant, Joe Billy seemed never to take offense. Leah was grateful for that. They needed his patronage.

Jennings found the linen envelope on her desk the next day and came bringing it into the breakfast room where she had set up her easel. "Why didn't you tell me about this, Leah?"

She knew what he meant without turning around. "I hadn't decided what to do about it yet," she said. Actually, she had already mailed her acceptance.

"Are you kidding? An invitation to join the Study Club? I thought you were dying to!"

She shrugged. "But the dues. . . . I know how hard you're struggling."

He waved that concern away. "We'll manage. You couldn't refuse, anyhow. What would they think?"

Leah turned back to her easel and smiled her secret smile and wondered if Tolliver's Dry Goods would have anything decent enough to wear to the initiation. Maybe she ought to drive over to Kingston. If she bought the new outfit here everybody would know it and know how much it cost. If only she knew what was right to wear. If only there was someone to ask. But it was O.K. She'd figure it out.

Mama was right. It was possible to break out.

Father Richard was right. There is justice in the world.

Sister Fain was right. I will get my share of the abundance. I am finally going to get mine. Make it a double helping. With a cherry on top.

Go away, knot. Leah Marie Evangeline Boudreaux Palmer can handle it. Got my man. Got my house. Got my ticket. Finally got my ticket, and it reads first class.

Tread water, kiddo. Used to be, anybody'd look at me, tears would come in my eyes. Not crying tears, just shame tears, shyness tears. Like excuse me for occupying space. Just hated those tears, such a giveaway! Had to wear dark glasses to protect myself from them.

No more. Got me a space and a deed to occupy it.

Leah went to the best dress shop in Kingston, picked out the most expensive suit on the rack and charged it to Dr. Jennings Palmer. A girl had to look exactly right for Study Club initiation. Especially if she was planning to use it as a stepping-stone to something bigger. For suddenly nothing seemed impossible, no goal too lofty.

Not even Miss Agnes Crenshaw's Fine Arts League, made up of the old-line moneyed families.

Standing before the mirror in the new suit, her ivory cheeks flushed with pleasure, her dark eyes sparkling with anticipation, Leah could imagine herself mingling with the wealthy old matrons, catching the admiring glances of the old codgers with diamond stickpins.

"It is coming true," she murmured to her reflection, "just like they promised. I wonder if there is any limit?"

9

THE ULTIMATE victory was less than a month in coming. It was as if Leah had some sort of psychic ability to alter events to make them come out the way she wanted. As if, once she could see herself as a member of the prestigious Fine Arts League, it was bound to happen. Still, when she opened the door to Miss Agnes Crenshaw herself, Leah was stunned speechless. She must have stared, mouth gaping, for several seconds at the elegantly turned out matron holding the coveted pink envelope in her gloved hand.

At length Miss Crenshaw smiled, showing a mouthful of gold. "I see I've taken you by surprise, my dear. I should have telephoned."

Leah recovered herself and invited Miss Crenshaw inside, but she couldn't persuade her to come into the living room. The old matron stood stiffly in the front hall and stated her business.

"My dear, I am here on behalf of the Fine Arts League. Perhaps you are aware of our work."

Leah was giddy with anticipation. "Of course! You bring cultural events to town, musicians and—things."

Miss Crenshaw patted her arm benignly, bestowing pardon for her ignorance. "Oh, we do much more than that, my dear, as you will learn—when you join us."

Leah feigned astonishment as Miss Agnes pressed the pink envelope on her. "This is your invitation to join us on the board of directors," said Miss Agnes. "When you have discussed it with the doctor, I hope we'll receive your acceptance."

Leah had known forever what she would say next: "Why of course, Miss Crenshaw, we would be honored to join!" She hadn't even opened the envelope.

Miss Crenshaw displayed the gold teeth. "Marvelous! Then I'll take this as your acceptance instead of the usual formal note."

Oops. Should have thought about a formal note. Well, no matter. She would learn, in time.

When the old woman took her leave, Leah fairly exploded with glee. Ripping open the envelope, she scanned the invitation hurriedly, sucked in her breath at the size of the initiation fee, then sought out her purse. She could hardly contain herself until the old woman's Cadillac was well down the street, so that she could pay Doris Jean a visit and crow.

She stopped at the opened back door, drew in the pungent spring breeze and called over her shoulder, "Dorothy, don't count on me for lunch. And be sure to put the chicken on early. It's Dr. Palmer's afternoon off, remember?"

"Wellum all right." Although going rate was two dollars a day, Leah found a pretext to pay Dorothy two seventy-five, and for this, Dorothy insisted on staying late to serve supper.

Leah sang along with the radio as she drove down the tree-lined street. Only pale brushings of clouds suggested themselves overhead. The sun splashed noisily on the April landscape, reflecting her own spirits. The redbud trees were in full bloom, and the dogwoods were budding. Gardenia buds peeked from luxuriant slick leaves, filling the air with their sweetness. The old street in St. Louis was a million miles away, maybe not even in this world.

She stopped in the drive of Doris Jean's rambling house and looked it over. Leah loved everything about the place. The two-acre lawn was landscaped meticulously, and the interior smacked of a decorator's touch. Someday she was going to blast Jennings out of that morgue and they were going to build something suitable.

The back door banged and a man rounded the house and came through the side gate. A big man he was, that dusky-skinned giant whose khaki shirt was unbuttoned almost to the waist. The sleeves were rolled almost to the shoulders, revealing his beautiful biceps. His black eyes bore into hers and she couldn't meet his gaze. She felt small prickles at the back of her neck as she realized that he was walking straight toward her. She knew him, of course. It was Perry Johnson.

"Excuse me. Would you let me move your car?" He motioned toward an old blue Buick parked in front of her in the driveway. "I'll be leaving soon. If you give me your keys—"

Mutely she held out her car keys and his hand closed unnecessarily on hers. His gaze on her, which she had to meet now, was frankly sensual. Leah recognized the stirrings within her, despised herself for observing that this one would be no complaisant lover. He tossed the keys lightly in his palm. Bastard! He knew exactly his profound effect on her.

"I'll see you get your keys back." His gaze swept down her one last time. She turned on her heel and pretended not to notice . . . that his look said, "I know. I know."

Good friends just didn't use front doors in Clarington, no matter how much trouble it was to get around back. Unlatching the side gate, she hurried up the walk to the back door and opened the screen without waiting for her knock to be answered. She could hear Perry revving the engine to her Chrysler. Unnecessarily. It isn't *that* hard to start, for God's sake. Just another thing to get her attention. He doesn't know for sure, she told herself. Let him make all the noise he wants.

Luretha, standing at the kitchen sink, didn't turn around to acknowledge Leah's greeting, but merely waggled her head. "Baby Love's in yonder messing up right behind me," she grumbled, motioning toward the breakfast room.

Leah found Doris Jean staring absently out the bay window into the backyard. The breakfast room was speckled with sun-and-shadow patterns which complemented the sunny design of her flowing jersey robe. Her usually carefully coiffed hair fell in random brassy ringlets against her tight-set jaws.

"Greetings!" Leah exclaimed. "Am I interrupting something?"

"What?" Doris Jean barely turned her head. "Oh. Leah. I didn't hear you come in." She walked over to the glass-topped breakfast table, picked up a cigarette and lit it. She indicated a chair. "Here. Sit down and I'll have Luretha bring us some coffee."

She disappeared and returned at length with a tray.

"That damn Luretha!" she grumbled. "Makes me do everything myself!"

Leah chuckled. "You might's well face it: she's bossed you too many years to begin taking orders now!" She stirred her coffee then let her spoon clatter. "Oh pooh! How can I be blasé?"

The idiot outside was still revving her motor. Vaguely Leah wondered what he was doing here, anyway.

"Blasé about what?"

Leah dug into her handbag and produced a large pink envelope. "As if you didn't know, you sneaky thing! You're probably responsible for this, but you didn't breathe a word! Why didn't you warn me so at least I could have had my house in order when Miss Agnes Crenshaw popped in?"

"What is this?" Doris Jean took the envelope almost fearfully.

She should have been warned, should have recognized the plaintive note among the astonished tones, but she was too full of herself to notice. Besides, she was playing a part, and there was the distraction outside.

"Don't you know? It's our invitation to serve on the Fine Arts League board! Just *think* what this'll mean for Jennings' practice!"

"What?" cried Doris Jean, ripping the invitation from its envelope. "How could they? I heard they had an opening, but—"

Leah was stunned. "You—didn't know about this?"

Silence filled the room. Sunlight sparkled through shadow patterns on the parquet floor. From the kitchen came the sound of water running and Luretha singing, "Precious Lord." Somewhere, somewhere storm clouds were gathering, and it was a more ominous storm than Clarington had ever known.

"You mean you're not a member, Doris Jean? I thought—I naturally thought that—well, when Miss Crenshaw said they'd decided the board was too stodgy and needed some new blood, I just *assumed*, of course, that you and Joe Billy were already *on* the board and that you had suggested us—" Leah stopped. She could still hear the echo of her own voice. And Luretha singing, "Take my hand."

Doris Jean dropped the letter on the breakfast table and snubbed out her cigarette. "Well," she said brightly, "I suppose this puts you out of our class! I've never known them to accept newcomers before—or anybody under fifty, for that matter. So you can consider yourself honored." She paused, fished out a new cigarette and lit it. "I hope you don't find yourselves in over your heads. That bunch has money. I hope you plan to think it over carefully."

Elation had spread over Leah like a warm flood. In the driver's seat, precious Lord. Lord, I've never been first in my life. Oh, let me savor it slowly, lick it carefully like a double-dip ice-cream cone, turning it round and round and just lapping off where the drips are running down. On top, precious Lord. So this is how it feels!

"Oh, I've already accepted—at least, verbally," Leah said. Plenty of time, plenty of time. No need to bite into it. Just turn and lick. "Miss Agnes came by *in person* right after breakfast. Can you *imagine? Miss* Crenshaw just *dropping in?*" Turn and lick, turn and lick.

Leah sipped her coffee and settled back cosily in her chair. As yet, since she first came in, Doris Jean hadn't looked her in the eye. It was delicious.

"In a very gracious way, Miss Crenshaw let me know that Jennings and I would be the only paupers on the board. But as vacancies occur, they mean to add other young people. I'm sure your name will come up next—in fact, I can guarantee it!" Oh, Blessed Virgin, Mother of God, let me ask no other blessedness!

But her composure was shaken moments later when Luretha came in, still humming, jangling a set of keys on her forefinger. "I almost forgot, Mrs. Palmer. Perry say to give you your keys." She turned to go, then came back. "Oh yeah, what else he say? Something about the way your car run. Oh yessum. He say tell you your spark plugs is *all black.*"

The changes had come over Leah gradually. Six months before she wouldn't have had the moxie to take on two pop callers in one day: Miss Agnes Crenshaw in the morning and Jennings' old girlfriend in the afternoon.

Ernestine Moseley had never before been in Leah's house. But she rushed past Dorothy and headed straight for the den as if she knew exactly where she was going. "I just heard the news!" she exclaimed, giving Leah a little hug. "Everybody's talking about the new league members—and you not in town six months yet! Oh, I'm so proud of you!"

Leah, who had been doing her nails when Ernestine came in, had a good excuse not to return the embrace. She waved her fingers stiffly, blew on them a couple of times and indicated a chair across the room. She had just come out of the bath, and her coarse brown hair was held off her neck by a clip. She wore no makeup, and she didn't like to be seen this way. She was a little too sallow, a little too tan without her liquid foundation. She wore a loose-fitting robe, and she used this for an excuse to leave the room.

"Just let me get into something decent, Ernestine. I won't be a minute. Dorothy, bring Mrs. Moseley some coffee." And she fled. Down the hall, into the bathroom, bang the door— oops!—not so loud. Get that foundation on. Peach bloom. Never should leave the bathroom without putting on the peach bloom first. Never can tell who's going to blow in.

She did a slap-dab job on the makeup and grabbed a skirt and shirt from the closet. When she returned to the den, she made straight for the drapery cord and closed the drapes.

"I hope it's not too dark in here for you," Leah said. "I find the afternoon sun is fading the upholstery on that chair."

It was O.K. Ernestine was too busy taking in every detail of the room to look at her, anyway. Leah perched on a footstool across the room and accepted the cup of coffee that Dorothy brought her.

"You know, Miss Agnes can't go anyplace without the whole world knowing," Ernestine was saying. "It's like the queen of England trying to go someplace. So I guess half the town knows by now that Miss Agnes paid you a visit this morning. . . . Man, don't you know Doris Jean's seething?"

Leah set her cup down on the floor and drew her knees up to herself protectively. "Ernestine, you're a Moseley, by marriage. I'm sure there are Moseleys on the board. Blanche Carnes is a Dawson. I'm sure there are Dawsons on the board."

Ernestine nodded. "I know what you're wondering. How come you were asked instead of one of us? Well, you see, having a parent on the board is almost the same as being on the board ourselves. I mean, we know we'll be there one day. What happened was, old Mr. Leonard Kerr resigned. He used to be a good friend of Jennings' daddy, and besides, he's a patient of Jennings' and thinks the world and all of him. *He* put your name up." She snickered. "Miss Agnes has been dotty about old man Kerr for a thousand years, so whatever *he* wants, *she* wants!"

The coffee was not warming Leah. She picked up the cup and tried to warm her hands on its outside. The day was growing cold. Cold and dark. She got up and turned on one small lamp beside Ernestine.

Ernestine smiled sweetly, showing her irresistible dimples. "My little sister-in-law, I know she's going to be heartbroken. I tried to call her, but she's incommunicado. . . . But here! Enough about that! I came to invite you to play tennis tomorrow."

My cup runneth over, she thought. She smiled sadly. "Oh, Ernestine, how nice. I—I don't know the game, but I'm learning. Can I take a rain check on it?"

"Anytime." The plump little woman jumped to her feet. After a few more pats and hugs she was gone and Leah was left alone to ponder this new victory.

She opened the drapes, but the afternoon sun didn't shine so brightly. For only a moment Leah's memory flashed back to that day in Tolliver's Lake when she had stepped off into a hole and had sunk in over her head. She remembered her panic, her flailing arms, the gasping, the choking.

She didn't hear the car drive up, didn't hear Jennings come in. He came up behind her and kissed her lightly on the neck. She turned and just let him enfold her against his chest.

"Why so glum, little chum?" he asked, pushing back a wisp of hair from her forehead. "Here the sun's shining and your husband's off early and is about to ask you out for another tennis lesson!"

"That'll be nice," she said absently. "Jennings, isn't it odd? I mean, you asked me 'Why so glum' and I can't remember—consciously. Have you ever had that sensation? I mean, it will have been a perfectly lovely day when nice things have happened and you have every right to be happy. But something keeps gnawing—something you can't even put your finger on." She surprised herself, talking like this.

He kissed her again. "It'll surface sooner or later. Now! Tell me about the nice things!"

She ran to the desk and brought him the invitation. Scanning it, he let out a low whistle.

"Wow! How did we rate this?" he asked.

"Leonard Kerr is retiring, I'm told," she said. "He recommended that we be asked to fill his vacancies."

"Leonard Kerr! Well now, that was nice of the old gentleman. I must remember to thank him. I just wonder whether or not we should accept."

"Not accept?" she cried. "What do you mean?" Don't take my double-dipper away, she thought.

"I mean that even if we want to devote the time to a project of this kind, there's bound to be expense involved. The parties, the elegant clothes . . . I don't know. . . ."

"But, Jennings, Miss Agnes, *the* Miss Crenshaw was here *in person* this morning! I couldn't say no to Miss Agnes!"

"You *what?*"

"What could I say?" she pleaded. "Oh, Jennings, I *want* to join! It's such a great honor. . . . Look: we can look on it as an investment! You admit yourself that these are the moneyed people, the old guard. If you could just capture the silk-stocking trade—"

Taking her by the arm, Jennings led her to a chair like a child. He sat down and pulled her down on his lap, then looked around to make sure that Dorothy was out of earshot. "Look, Leah. Remember how it was when we were in St. Louis? I was enough for you then, remember? Leah, do you realize that climbing is a disease? And this is such a big step up for someone as young as we! Some of our friends might resent us. I just don't know—"

"You're always so worried about what somebody else is going to think!" she said.

"Can you honestly say," he spoke deliberately, "that you care a hill of beans for the work of the Fine Arts League? That it's not for personal prestige that you want to join?"

Leah bristled. He would never, never understand. It was no use discussing it. She bit her lip angrily. I have to have this, she told herself. I need all the help I can get. It is mine. It is justice. Father Richard and Sister Fain would understand. Mama would understand.

"Jennings," she said evenly, rising and facing him levelly, "I'm sorry you feel this way. I have already accepted. It's too late to back out. It's just too late."

It was probably too late, too, to turn back the storm, the fulminating tangle of lives and events which would alter everything in a matter of months. No one person or no one change of events could alter the outcome. It was just too late.

10

LIFE HADN'T worked out half bad for somebody who had once been the fattest girl in the sixth grade. For somebody whose family had never amounted to much in a town where family was everything. For somebody whose mother was Wanda Peavy, the frumpy high school English teacher whom every kid in the whole school had to suffer through. For somebody whose daddy had hardly worked a day in his life, and everybody in town knew they weren't living on oil royalties.

But Doris Jean Peavy was ambitious, and maybe she was almost psychic. Nobody else ever figured Joe Billy Tolliver would be worth a damn, either. Time was, back in high school, when she would hardly date the skinny fool, herself. Always mouthing off. Talk, talk, talk. As much as a fairy. Who'd ever dream he'd amount to a hill of beans? But he had, made it through college and law school both. And by that time she had already latched onto him. And he figured *he* was the lucky one!

Actually, she always planned to marry a rich man. And she

sure as hell never figured on living in Clarington. Dallas, maybe, or Houston. New Orleans, even.

But in the end she'd just plain got the hots for Joe Billy. It happened when they both came home for Christmas. She'd been working up in Longview and had learned a lot. Like how to dress and how to talk and how to look like a cool million dollars. It was the year she'd first bleached her hair.

She had pranced into Tolliver's Dry Goods looking like a knockout and feeling like one, too. And there was Joe Billy, helping out behind the counter during the Christmas rush. She could see that, once he recognized her, he was stunned. More than that: smitten.

"Doris Jean? Good Lord in heaven, girl, is that you?" He came around the counter with arms outstretched.

But Doris had learned a thing or two up in Longview, and she avoided his embrace, catching his two outstretched hands in hers. He wasn't as bad as she remembered. Maybe he'd fleshed out some. At least he always had good-looking clothes. Got them wholesale.

"You look like Jayne Mansfield, did you know that?" He was always full of baloney, but she preferred to believe he meant it this time. Her estimation of him was rising.

She extricated her hands from his grasp and let him get a load of her new walk. She circled a counter of handbags, pretending to look them over. "Oh, Joe Billy, you haven't changed a bit! These purses real leather?"

He was not to be distracted. "My lordy, I just can't believe my eyes! Man, have you lost weight! Bet that ain't all you've lost!" He laughed in a way that told her he meant it as a compliment.

She shot him a reprimanding look. "You know me better than that, Joe Billy Tolliver! You know how I was brought up! Not like you and that wild little sister of yours!"

He looked offended, and for a moment she feared she had gone too far. She sidled up close and brushed against his chest. "I didn't mean that. Just teasing. . . . You're looking good, Joe Billy." She let her eyes travel down his length, and she meant it. "Real good." And she could see him suffering.

It had been so easy. She had flat laid him on his ear, Doris Jean did. A third-year law student who'd had to really hump it to make his grades all these years. Maybe he hadn't had three dates since high school—at least he sure didn't act like it. They were dynamite together from that moment on, and Doris Jean forgot all about marrying a rich man. Maybe she'd marry a *smart* one and make him rich!

And so she came home, soon as he passed his bar.

There was satisfaction in coming home, in making the whole town her conquest. In showing everybody that the fat little Peavy kid was all grown up.

When she was little she used to think Miss Agnes Crenshaw was God, sitting up there in her big white house with the turrets, giving teas that the Peavys talked about but were never invited to. Maybe now she secretly wanted to be Clarington's next Miss Agnes.

She'd made an impressive start: past president of the Study Club, social chairman at the country club, staging chairman for two years in a row of the garden club flower show, executive board member of the Women's Forum, circle leader, leader of the Wesleyan Service Guild . . .

Sometimes, these days, she found herself gritting her teeth. It was such a rat race. Parties, luncheons, dances, and Joe Billy never around when she needed him. It was such a strain. Especially for someone who operated at a perpetually high sensual pitch. Everybody needs some time to let down . . .

Maybe, she reasoned, that's why she allowed herself one small indiscretion—in the beginning.

That pompous caretaker! At times she almost hated him!

Lately she had felt that he was beginning to take her for granted, and several times in the past few months she had purposely stood him up for their usual Thursday morning together at the lake. But she always regretted it afterward. It was punishment to stay away.

Perry was so beautiful—an incredible man! Black eyes that stripped her to the soul, that captivating white smile that he flashed so seldom, that splendid tan body—she despised herself for being a slave to it. And she despised him for treating her like a nobody. Cheeky half-caste! From the first he'd been brazenly aloof. He never fawned over her. He never paid her a compliment, never called her by an endearing name—never addressed her directly at all. She couldn't remember a single time, since childhood, hearing him call her Doris Jean, Mrs. Tolliver or especially "darling." Fact is, he never said much of anything. It was exasperating that, although she'd known him nearly all her life, she knew practically nothing about him.

She knew his wife, of course. Mrs. Perry Johnson was a cousin of Blackie Carnes, one of his hillbilly cousins. Blackie wasn't the best, but he had money—or was it his wife Blanche who had money? Anyhow, the Carnes family was probably respectable enough. True, the hills were dotted with shacks whose mailboxes read "Carnes," but a few of them said "Peavy," too. But Johnson? It was such a common name.

She felt a stab of pain remembering the one time she had questioned Perry about his family. It was one winter afternoon a year ago. Lazily she had rolled over on her side and studied his handsome profile as he lay beside her. She nuzzled her head in his shoulder and ran a finger over his firm cleft chin.

"Who do you take after, your daddy or your mother? What do they look like?"

"I don't intrude in your private affairs," he said coldly, abruptly rising from the bed. "Leave mine alone."

96

"Oh, Perry, don't get huffy. I keep no secrets from you. If you want to know anything, just ask me! Ask me anything!"

He gave a snort and began pulling on his clothes. "Ask you anything? Is there anything I don't know? Haven't you been telling me since childhood about your blue-blood ancestors, waltzing till dawn in the 'Peavy plantation'?"

"Sweet! I didn't mean to sound haughty when I told you those things. That was a million years ago, when we were kids!" She was standing beside him, clutching his shoulder, forgetting the chill of the unheated room against her bare skin. "Forget whatever I said. You—you know as well as I that—my family is nothing special. It's us that matters. Don't be mad with me if I've hit a sore spot."

He thrust her gruffly from him. "You hit no sore spot. I'm proud, and I have every right to be proud of my family. I wish your mother was half the woman mine is. Then maybe you wouldn't have turned out so—so intolerable!"

When he was gone, she cried for most of the afternoon. She tried more than once to call his house, but each time his wife answered and she hung up. She had to go back to town without patching it up, and it was weeks before he would see her again.

Maybe he was right to be indignant, she reasoned now. Obviously he'd had humble beginnings, else he wouldn't have had to work as a child. For years he had been around. He had come on Saturdays, a tall, melancholy boy in immaculate denims and stiff-ironed cotton shirts, to do yard work for the Peavys. Doris Jean's mother had objected to John Peavy's hiring a boy to do work normally relegated to a colored man, for status reasons, quite naturally. But there was no arguing that Perry had been more dependable. He had never played sick, and he was meticulous in his work.

Mrs. Peavy had always been opposed to Doris Jean's friendship with Perry. As children, when he was working in the

97

yard, Doris Jean was called into the house. It was unseemly for her to play with the hired help. But when Luretha was in command, which was much of the time, Doris Jean was free to cultivate his friendship.

Perry never seemed to mind that Doris Jean was homely—and she felt, quite frankly, that she had been at that time. He never treated her as a "fat clown," which was what Blackie and George Bob Carnes had sometimes called her. She was his equal, and in those days he was the only boy with whom she felt natural.

Only once or twice had she ever felt shy with him. The first time had been the fall of her twelfth birthday. Perry must have been about fifteen—very old, she thought. She had worn a pullover sweater to the Saturday matinee the first cool afternoon in November. As she came out of the picture show, a group of boys huddled behind the billboard had yelled, "Lookit the boobies on the buffalo!" Puzzled, she had held her head high and walked past them, recognizing the voices of her male classmates, all of whom she topped by a head. They had followed her all the way home, keeping a good half block between herself and them and shouting, "Hey, buffalo boobies!" for all the world to hear.

Tears stung her eyes, and she knew she couldn't bear the questions of Luretha or her mother. Skirting the house, she ran through the side gate into the backyard and made for the haven of the grape arbor. Too late she saw Perry pruning the vines. He looked at her questioningly, but she ran past him into the arbor and flounced upon the ground. He stood at the entrance looking at her back. She fought down the tears and sat picking at a stem.

"Hi." Perry stepped inside.

"Go away." She didn't turn around.

He seemed genuinely surprised. "Why are you crying? I heard what they said. They're payin' you a compliment,

98

though I guess they don't know it yet." He knelt behind her and reached around to touch her breasts. "You're soft. Not like older girls who wear harnesses."

She batted his hand away and jumped up indignantly. "Don't you ever do that again, Perry Johnson!"

Grinning, he rose and backed out of the arbor. "Someday you won't mind so much." And he had been right. In time he had become a young bull of a man, magnificent of physique and with an irresistible wistfulness .about him which captivated her.

A lean-to had been built on the back of the garage to house Doris Jean's treasures: her dolls, her rock collection and, after her thirteenth Christmas, her chemistry set. If she felt particularly in need of companionship, she would condescendingly allow Perry to enter her sanctum and view her treasures. Usually he scoffed at them and made fun of her trinkets. But not the chemistry set. From the first he wanted to try it. He begged, but she refused, pushing him out of her lean-to and locking the padlock. He followed her to the back steps, pleading, cajoling.

"You'd only make a mess and use up all my chemicals, besides!" she said impatiently, sitting down on the back steps.

"I'll pay you for what I use," he argued.

"Humph! What do I need with your money? I've got more than you have already!"

He pondered. "Then I'll—I'll do something you like. I'll push you in the swing or play Monopoly with you."

"Oh, I'm too old for all that stuff, silly!" She looked wistfully at the gray winter sky and sighed with sudden longing. "Isn't spring ever coming? There's nothin' to do in the winter. Life is so dull. . . ."

He sat down beside her and blew at the flyaway wisps of hair covering her ear. "Did anybody ever kiss you?" he asked.

She caught her breath as little chills of delight trickled

down her neck. What should she say? "Not—very often," she said.

"That's not dull," he said. "You really ought to be learning how. Just let me use your chemistry set and I'll show you how."

"Yes," she said thoughtfully, "I guess you're right. I suppose I could use the experience. All right, you can try out my chemistry set—but only one experiment. But I think—you ought to—do the other first."

"O.K.," he agreed. "You want me to do it here, or—"

"No! We'll go out to the playroom." She stood up and, in a businesslike way, patted down her skirt and strode in front of him to the lean-to door. She bent closely over the combination lock so that he couldn't see the numbers. She went in ahead of him and pulled the light string in the middle of the room, then turned to ask, "Shall we sit down or stand up?"

He eyed the light dubiously and shifted his weight back and forth for a moment. "I never kissed anybody in the light before."

"Oh. All right." She pulled the string. "Should we sit or—"

She felt him groping for her shoulders and a surge of warmth rose in her as he found her and kissed her lightly on the corner of the mouth. He was drawing away when she wrapped her arms around his waist and found his mouth again. Her lips parted and she pushed her way between his two even rows of teeth. Gluing herself against him, she felt him responding, his palms moving, making circles on her back. Then she broke away and pulled on the light.

"Where did you learn to kiss like that?" he asked, astounded.

"Did you like it?" she asked timidly.

"Well, it was pretty good—for a fat girl."

She hoped the stab didn't show, even though it caused her to stagger a step backward. She got out quickly, flinging back

100

as nonchalantly as she could, "Stay as long as you like. I have other things to do now."

She had avoided him for six agonizing weeks, hoping he was pining for her and sure that she wanted nothing more to do with him. Then one day early in March she ventured out while he was raking pine needles off the lawn.

"It's getting to be spring." She stared up into the cool green shadows of the newly leafed oak. "Luretha's made lemonade. Want some?"

He looked up, then continued his raking. "I guess so."

"I made some new slides for my microscope of blood and fly's wing and stuff. If you want to see them, I could bring the lemonade out there."

He glanced up warily but said nothing.

"Oh, you don't have to worry," she laughed. "You don't have to kiss me, if that's what you're thinking."

"I wasn't thinking anything."

She sauntered into the house and made straight for the bathroom, where she took elaborate pains fixing her hair and applying Tangee Natural. After daubing great quantities of her mother's perfume behind her ears, she stopped off at the kitchen and picked up two glasses of lemonade. She barely arrived at the lean-to ahead of Perry.

He entered the dim little room and blinked, sniffing the pungent air in the close quarters. "Is that you?"

"You mean the perfume? Oh, I always wear perfume, silly!"

"Smells strong. You didn't used to."

"Well, I didn't when I was a kid, if that's what you mean. But then, I didn't wear lipstick—or a lot of other things." She giggled.

He looked at her breasts. "You mean a harness. I can tell you've got one on."

"I remember what you said one time—about me being soft. You said—"

His hands were under her sweater unfastening her bra, and then she was giggling and helping him, and then they were lying on the hard dirt floor of the lean-to amid the pervasive odor of leaf mold. It was awkward and painful, but they kept laughing and joking. She didn't like it much, but just the same she felt elation. Perry would be her boyfriend from now on.

When it was over, Perry got up and reached for his lemonade. "I'll never do *that* again!" he breathed.

She retrieved her clothes from the dirt floor and walked behind him to dress. "Why? Was it as bad as that?"

"Naw, it was just a dumb thing to do."

"Why?"

"You might get pregnant, stupid!"

She shivered with delight. "I never thought about that!"

Perry had kept his word for a decade. But ever since he became caretaker at Tolliver's Lake, their ultimate liaison was inevitable.

Lately something had been missing, and she had thought maybe it would be better to end it now, before he got tired.

But of course that was impossible. She could never break it off. Besides, he was such an absolute animal. No other word could describe the way he loved with every part of himself. No, she would never break it off, and neither would he, now. Now that she was *finally* going to bear him his first child.

Yes, things hadn't worked out half bad for Doris Jean. She had conquered Joe Billy, and she had conquered Clarington. Now she was finally going to conquer Perry.

11

HUMAN BITES are potentially more deadly than dog bites. Perry Johnson learned this the hard way. But actually he had to be told by a trespasser just how deadly.

Perry spotted the car from the house, a late model Dodge with Oklahoma plates. He picked his way quietly through the dense pines to a place directly behind the man, who had just chosen a lure from his tackle box. Only then did he make his presence known.

"Hey! Can't you read signs? This is posted!"

The short, thickset fisherman wheeled, blinking into the sun, sizing up the dusky-skinned giant. Then he extended his hand nervously. "I'm sorry, sir. You must be Mr. Tolliver. Clarkson's my name. I'm a drug detail man, just passing through. I'm glad to make your acquaintance, sir."

Chafing to see the stranger on his way, Johnson looked hesitantly at the fisherman, and the scowl faded from his face. He advanced a few steps and took the proffered hand.

"Pleased to meet you. But I'm not Tolliver. My name's Johnson. The—manager of this lake."

"Is that a fact!" Clarkson exclaimed. "Well, Mr. Tolliver is mighty lucky to have you looking out for his interests." He picked up his tackle box and made as if to go. "I won't trouble you. Just wanted to get in a little fishing this fine afternoon and thought maybe nobody'd mind if I fished off Mr. Tolliver's bank. Maybe I can find a place up the road somewhere where they wouldn't mind."

He ambled off a few steps toward the car.

Caretaking is a solitary life. Perry Johnson often hungered for male companionship. He made an instant decision.

"I was just thinking," he said, walking up to join the man, "you ain't going to catch much standing on the bank. I was just about to go out in the boat. You can come along if you want."

"Say! That'd be great!" Clarkson cocked a shrewd eye up at him. "You sure Mr. Tolliver wouldn't object?"

"Anything I do is all right with him."

They headed along the water's edge until they reached a clearing which sloped gently downward from the back of the large redwood ranch-style house to the pier. Two aluminum boats were tied up there. They took the smaller of the two, which was already loaded with Johnson's fishing gear and an ice chest.

The lake was L-shaped, and Johnson headed the craft swiftly around the bend and out of sight of the main house. They passed a smaller house, which Johnson pointed out as his place, and maneuvered quietly into a swampy-looking area where trees sprouted out of the water.

"You must know every inch of this lake," Clarkson said, looking over the side of the boat. "I can see huge logs and rocks just beneath the surface."

Johnson nodded. "There's just one little path through this

104

part of the lake. If you miss that path, you break a propeller. Here's the hole I want to try." He had cut the engine and glided to a cool dark hole.

They fished for almost a half hour in silence, letting the sun soak into their flesh. Then the caretaker opened the chest at his feet and drew out two beers. It was hot, and they finished them off in minutes. The darker man opened two more and pulled off his T-shirt, mopping his chest with it. On his right breast was a nasty red and purple wound. Clarkson couldn't ignore it.

"Looks like somebody bit you there," he said.

Johnson nodded.

"Human bites, they're the worst kind, they tell me," Clarkson said. "They don't heal good. Folks sometimes die of human bites, you know that?"

Johnson shook his head and looked down at his wound, worried.

"If I was you, I'd get that doctored. Good new doctor back in Clarington. Not very busy yet. Probably doesn't charge an arm and a leg, either."

"I might go," Johnson said.

"Name's Palmer," said the drug salesman. "Office right across from the hospital on West Main."

"I know him," Johnson said. He opened two more beers. Clarkson leaned back in the boat and looked at the pillowed clouds.

"Man, what a life! I envy you, getting to do this every day."

Johnson shrugged. "It's not bad. Gets tiresome after a while, fishing by yourself."

"Well, what's a sharp fellow like you doin' out here workin' for somebody else? Seems to me a fine specimen like yourself ought to be able to make enough in town to buy your *own* lake."

105

Johnson stared out across the water. The beer was making him expansive, loosening his tongue. "There was a time," he said slowly, "when I thought that'd be possible. Even went off to Kingston for a spell." He took a long swig from the can. "Fellow needs an education to get ahead these days, where-ever he goes."

"Don't be too sure. I bet if you went to Dallas—"

Perry glanced over his shoulder, in the direction they came from, a restive set to his sculptured jaw. "Maybe I can some-day leave this place," he said quietly, "but not now. No, not yet. Right now it suits me to stay."

It was much later, as the sun waned behind the west bank trees, that Perry Johnson bade his fishing companion good-bye, after promising again to visit his doctor. He had con-sumed too many beers, he knew, so he delayed going home until the buzz wore off. He didn't feel up to any more scenes with Ada Sue.

He took a turn around the main house, mechanically check-ing doors and windows. On the front porch in one of the chairs he found a yellow cardigan sweater. He picked it up and examined it. On the inside was a dry cleaning tag reading Tolliver.

He carried the sweater with him around to the back of the house. Draping it over one shoulder, he emptied the ice from the ice chest and threw the empty beer cans into the garbage can. Taking the sweater off his shoulder, he fingered its soft-ness for a moment. Then, with one swift, savage movement, he ripped off one sleeve and threw the whole thing in the garbage can.

Leah was filling in for Jennings' vacationing office nurse the day he walked in. His pain-racked face was so ashen that she hardly knew him, until he pulled off his shirt. The chest she knew. Here was the man who'd once pulled her out of the water at Tolliver's Lake. Like everyplace else, there was a back door at the alley for coloreds. He had come in the front. Who does he think he's kidding? she thought.

"Lucky you came in," Jennings told him, eying the festering laceration. "These human bites can be very stubborn. Leah, get some cotton and excoriate this wound. Your child bite you?"

Perry was sitting on the end of the examining table. He looked feverish. His eyes watered slightly. "Wife," he said dully.

"I'm going to give you a shot of antibiotic and something to bring your fever down first," Jennings said, disappearing into the adjoining room. "Let me see that wound after you've cleaned it, Leah, before we bandage it."

Timidly, gingerly, she went to work on his chest. She could feel his labored breath on her hair. Once or twice he winced, and she stopped for a moment to let the pain subside.

"Must have been quite a fight," she said.

He looked her up and down. "Who says we were fighting?" He watched her discomfort a minute, then said, "But you're right. It was a fight." He smelled of sweat. It was a compelling odor.

She commenced cleaning his wound again. He breathed on her some more, through his mouth. It made her uncomfortable. "You don't remember me, do you?" she said, to distract the breathing.

He played her game. "Should I? Seems I would remember you."

"You pulled me out of the water last summer, out at the lake."

He started the breathing again. "Your hair—you were wet that day," he said. He moistened his lips but said no more.

Jennings came in with the hypodermic needles and gave him tetanus, antibiotic and aspirin. He examined the clean wound. "Looks good," he told Leah. "Put a bandage on it." To Johnson he said, "When my—nurse has finished, why don't you just lie down here on the examining table until your fever subsides. Then come back and let me have another look on Tuesday."

Jennings had taught her long ago, just in case she ever had to help out, how to dress a wound. But he hadn't taught her how to make small talk with the patients. She busied herself cutting and folding gauze and applying tape. She could feel him watching her. She performed her tasks with studied non-chalance.

At length a trace of life came back into his feverish eyes. He said, "You from around here?"

She shook her head. "St. Louis."

There was an interminable silence. Then he spoke in a tone of gouging deliberation. "Then why are you here?"

She looked sharply. "This is my home now." Her voice had taken on a faint quiver in spite of her best efforts. He knows. He knows. It was not her imagination. She felt actually faint. She finished the bandage quickly and helped the patient lie down.

Then she fled into the hall. For her danger sensors had picked up a new warning. But she wasn't sure whether the danger came from Perry—or from herself.

12

THE SPRING rains came late that year and lingered into May, not showers by any means, but somber deluges which uprooted seedling crops, beat the wild flowers into the ground and choked old and ravaged streams, sending them overflowing their already indeterminate banks. But it didn't matter to Leah. She had, at long last, the whole pie. She was at her zenith, and she savored it, along with the tea cakes, at Miss Agnes Crenshaw's very exclusive evening "do" to introduce her to the other members of the Fine Arts League. Actually, it was meant to introduce both her and Jennings, but at the last minute he'd had a call.

"You'll have to go on alone," he'd told her as he hung up the phone. "I've got to go down and hassle with the admitting office over Buck and Pearlene."

She was completely exasperated. "Buck and Pearlene! Why is it always some charity patient? Half the time you miss your meals because of some problem out at Buck and Pearlene's! Now what?"

He shrugged. "I simply can't go on treating them when I haven't the foggiest idea what's wrong with them. I decided to put them in the hospital for diagnostic workup. But there are no facilities for the minority poor. I hadn't thought about that. I'll have to go make some arrangement."

Leah preferred not to think about it. She went to the party alone. She could handle it, handle just about anything these days. She was, according to Miss Agnes, "the darling of the town." At least, a few of the old codgers seemed to think so.

The streets were slick, and the streetlights caught the pelting rain and sent it shooting toward her windshield in blinding cascades. She crept along in the old Chrysler, and in spite of herself, she wondered if the weather were an omen. She reminded herself that every time in her life when things looked good, she had always known, "I'll soon have to pay." Had been afraid to enjoy herself with complete abandon, had always held back something of her joy, knowing that she must not spend too freely, for some calamity lurked just beyond her vision, just past her power to control. The threatening rumblings of the heavens just might be a reminder that it was almost time to pay for all her comfort.

But her premonitions were dispelled when she swept into the chandeliered vestibule of Miss Agnes' magnificent home. A doddering old mustachioed gentleman bowed grandly as she stepped inside. "Agnes, honey, let the party begin! The goddess Diana has just walked in!" He offered her his arm, and escorted her over to the hostess, who was just descending the majestic staircase.

"Leah, my dear! The doctor held up? Well, no matter; the charming half of the team is here!" The grand old dame held up her jeweled hands for attention. "Attention, people: may I present the newest member of the Fine Arts League, Dr.

110

Palmer's lovely little wife—now isn't she just precious? Come, dear, let me introduce you around."

And thus it was that Leah was lulled into a false sense of well-being and safety. In truth, the corner had already been turned, but she held her new station so close to her gaze that it obscured the larger view. She smiled and accepted the attentions of Clarington's old guard, and she became sloppy about currying her protective mechanisms. And for two solid days afterward she floated on a cloud.

Her calendar was crowded with club meetings, parties, choir rehearsals. She was deluged with phone calls and finger sandwiches; she waded through rules of order, etiquette books and spiced punch. It was dizzying, but she was coping. She could handle it. Because it was part and parcel of what she'd always dreamed of: acceptance.

It was Tuesday before the rains stopped, and as the sodden earth drank up the sunlight, Leah longed to take a break from the endless round of meetings, to get out into the country and paint. She had always been a private person, and she felt the need to escape.

Her watercolors were already packed into the car when Ernestine Moseley drove up. Now what? Leah thought. But she waved gaily, one foot already in the car.

"Can you spare a glass of iced tea?" Ernestine called.

Leah sighed and beckoned her in. What is this all about? she wondered. She looked longingly at her paints and closed the car door.

They sat facing each other over the Palmer kitchen table, tall glasses of tea between them. Leah waited impatiently for the preliminaries to end. She was beginning to wonder if this visit had any purpose, after all, or if it was, as Ernestine would have her believe, just a pop-in social call. And then the whole thing began to take shape.

Ernestine rested her pretty round face on a plump little fist and gave her a cozy, intimate smile. "You know, seems like you and I have become such good friends all of a sudden!"

That is an entire vat of it, and you know it, Leah thought.

"Some people stay newcomers here till they die, almost, but not Leah Palmer! No ma'am! You've made such an *effort*, seems like, to fit in."

Leah smiled and squirmed in her chair. She felt it coming, but she just didn't know what it was going to be.

"And you're so reticent! How can one person be so outgoing and friendly on one hand and be so shy and retiring when it comes to talking about yourself? Oh, you are a rare bird, Leah!"

Here it is. Now we know. Leah took a deep breath. She had rehearsed for years. Now it should come easy.

"Well," she said, "there's so little to tell. My parents were killed in an automobile accident when I was small—"

"How awful for you!"

"They—were very well off financially. I was put in an exclusive sort of boarding school."

"Really! Where 'bouts?"

"Outside St. Louis. Saint Agnes Academy."

"A *Catholic* school?"

Blunder. Watch it, Leah.

"An old maid aunt's decision. Actually, my parents had intended to send me to Stephens in Columbia." Leah picked that out of the air.

Ernestine reached over and patted Leah's hand. "You poor little thing. Such a sad childhood—out there with all those nuns and monks and stuff!"

Leah shrugged and smiled in spite of herself, and she backed off—way off. "Oh, it wasn't like that at all. It was a —very—happy childhood. Actually, it's a very exclusive school. Some very fine old families are Catholic, you know."

112

Ernestine tossed her curls deprecatingly. "I thought all Catholics were Mexicans with pierced ears." They both laughed.

There had been too many sessions like this lately. Too many questions, too much probing. Sometimes at night Leah lay awake and planned her answers to hypothetical questions. Belatedly she always remembered that the best defense is a good offense. She remembered it now.

"Enough about me . . . what about you? Do you realize I hardly know anything about you and Coy?" A lie, of course.

Ernestine's chair creaked as she squirmed and shifted her girth and laughed. "What is there to tell? Got married right out of high school. Never been anyplace. That's what love'll do. I do come from a fine old family, though. We're even related to the Crenshaws."

Leah's interest was genuine now. "I never knew that! What relation are you to Miss Agnes?"

"Just distant, just distant," Ernestine hurried. "I—doubt if Miss Agnes would even claim kin. But then," she began recovering herself, "Miss Agnes actually comes from one of the more *questionable* branches of the family."

"Ernestine! What *ever* do you mean?" Back her into the corner. Game time. Cat and mouse. Leah was enjoying herself.

The big blue eyes widened in the little round face. "Oh Lord, *nothing* against Miss Agnes! She's just the finest lady I ever knew! It's just—"

Leah leaned across the table. "Yes?"

Ernestine threw up her fat little hands. "Well, who knows whether it's even so or not!"

"You can't stop now, Ernestine."

Ernestine didn't look as if she wanted to stop, anyway. "Well, folks have always said that Miss Agnes' daddy got to

113

messing around with one of the colored girls and had another daughter almost exactly the same age as Miss Agnes. There's been a lot of speculation over the years about who it is—or was. Could be dead by now. Anyhow, this town's full of mulattoes, in case you haven't noticed."

That right-angle turn in the conversation had almost stripped her naked. She could hardly wait for the Moseley woman to leave. She went immediately to bed as soon as Ernestine left, turned her face to the wall and tried to calm her pounding heart.

Too close. Going to give yourself away. Going to blow your whole world wide open. Going to panic and blurt out, *scream* out—

"Mrs. Palmer?" It was Dorothy at her bedroom door. She'd forgotten about Dorothy. "Otis be about through with the yard. Would it be all right if I go along when he leave?"

Leah struggled to a sitting position in the bed. She had also forgotten about the yardman she'd hired, Dorothy's beau. "Oh sure. Otis going to take you to the hospital?"

"Wellum yessum." Dorothy just stood there, waiting for Leah to ask. Waiting to talk about Buck and Pearlene. Wanting the doctor's wife to tell her they were going to be O.K.

Leah couldn't make the effort this time. Just didn't want to hear anybody's problems. Didn't want to hear about Buck's stroke or Pearlene's various ailments. She had no sympathy left to share this day. She dismissed the girl quickly and set about composing herself before Jennings got home. Her world had got out of focus during the past hour or so, and, as yet, she couldn't put her finger on what was wrong. How could she fix what she couldn't understand?

It was seven o'clock when Jennings drove in. Leah met him at the door, her mouth drawn in a thin line the way Mama used to do.

114

"Can't you telephone when you're going to be late?" she asked.

"Sorry, honey." He pecked her on the mouth. "You didn't wait supper, I hope?"

She shook her head. "Dorothy left early. I'd planned to eat out. Where've you been?"

He dropped onto the den sofa. "Aw hell, old man Molesworth Carnes died."

Old man Carnes had been Jennings' concern for weeks. He was the father of his old school chums, Blackie and George Bob Carnes. Always called himself a farmer, but he did very little of that. Did very little of anything except hunt in the woods around his place out at Pine Hill. Took sick about a year ago, but nobody could get him to come into town to see a doctor. Finally Blackie persuaded him to let Jennings come out. The young doctor suspected cancer of the prostate, but there was no way to know for sure. Old man Carnes wasn't going to come into town, and that was that.

"Blackie called me this morning," Jennings said. "Said he was suffering something awful, so I loaded up on drugs and went out. The old man doesn't have a phone, of course, so I couldn't call you. I got there about noon and couldn't do a damn thing, of course, but sit around until he died."

Leah sighed. They really should do something. "I guess we ought to go see Blackie and Blanche, take a dish, maybe."

Jennings nodded numbly. "Let's go eat first. Then we'll drop in. You can get Dorothy to fix something for them tomorrow."

They were almost out the door when the telephone began ringing. Leah pulled at Jennings.

"Let it ring. Just this once," she said.

He shook his head. "Think how many weeks I waited for the damn thing to ring just once."

Considering all that came after, it would have been much

better if he had let it ring. Or maybe it wouldn't have made any difference. Leah waited impatiently by the back door as she heard him pick up the den phone. Thank God it wasn't a patient. It wasn't long before she could guess that he was talking to Joe Billy Tolliver. There was a definite edge in Jennings' voice that surprised her.

"I thought I made myself perfectly clear, Joe Billy. I have definitely changed my mind for good. I'm not your man."

She moved closer to the den door, and she could see Jennings' angry face in the mirror on the opposite wall.

"Benefit of the doubt?" He laughed derisively. "What doubt? The man is a crock, and you know it. He no more has a back injury than I do, and you sure as hell better not ask me to testify unless you want me to say just that!"

He slammed the receiver down abruptly and strode past her and jerked open the back door. "Let's get out of here."

"What was that about?" She followed him to the car almost at a trot. He flicked on the ignition and roared out of the driveway. "Jennings?"

He didn't say anything, just gunned down the street like a wild man. The traffic light caught him. He sat there at the red light and cooled down.

"I should have figured this out," he said finally.

"Figured what?"

"The big play-up Joe Billy's been giving me. He and Doris Jean. I've been part of his meal ticket. The sonofabitch has cultivated himself his very own personal expert witness to put in his back pocket!"

"I don't believe it," she said. But of course she did.

"No wonder that bastard can afford to live in that house and blow money like there was a diamond mine out back! I should have suspected. No lawyer that fresh out of school can make that kind of money."

She was quiet for a while, trying to piece the thing to-

116

gether, to understand that somehow it was possible to make a living—by what?

"Didn't he send you one of your first patients?" she asked finally.

"That's right. He suckered me right away. That was a 'neck injury.' Only I was so eager for the business that I gave the old bird the royal treatment. Guess he soaked the insurance company for plenty."

She pondered this. "You're saying some of his 'personal injury' cases are fake."

"I'd say most of them are at least exaggerated."

She was having to reassess Joe Billy completely. "What about tonight? What was that about?"

"He's got another pigeon. John Tom Bacon. I've examined him—strong as an ox. Stepped off the loading dock backwards and Joe Billy knew about it almost before he hit the ground. Joe Billy thinks this one's worth a million dollars. Wants him declared totally disabled. Says there's a good fee in it for me. I think John Tom's faking, and I think Joe Billy knows it!"

They drove on in silence until they reached the restaurant. She wished they didn't have to go in. She wished she had time to be alone, to think. He reached across her and opened her door.

"Jennings? What will you do?"

He ignored the question, got out, locked both doors and took her arm. They walked into the smoky café. The noise was deafening.

"Jennings?"

"What can I do, Leah? I can't get tied into this kind of thing. I can't play ball with that sonofabitch anymore."

For a moment—just for a moment—she wondered why not. He could at least give John Tom the benefit of the doubt.

"But won't he be furious? What will he do?"

Somebody dropped a tray in the back, and the tenor of the

noise rose to cover the disturbance. Jennings led her to an empty booth in back and settled down across from her.

"Maybe nothing," he said at length. "I hope to hell he cools off about it. Joe Billy could be a bad enemy to have."

And now Leah knew it was the truth.

13

WITH THE exception of his widow, only three people cried when Molesworth Carnes was laid away. Leah was one of them.

Services were conducted to an overflow crowd within the wooden walls of Pine Hill Community Four-Square Gospel Church, off Farm Road 69, and graveside services followed at Pine Hill Community Cemetery a half-mile this side of the bog.

Leah had resisted going, for she had never in her life attended a funeral. But Jennings was going, and he seemed to need her by his side.

"He was only a backwoods bum, but he was Blackie's dad," he said. "I remember how I felt when my dad died." Jennings did not admit that he might be going out of guilt, because he had not been able to save Molesworth's life, but Leah speculated that Jennings needed her there as a show of support.

Still, she was not unsympathetic, for she knew something of

119

grief. Although Mama hadn't actually died, Leah had been deprived as if she had, just the same.

But that was not the main reason she cried.

Blackie, she noted, wasn't particularly bereaved on this occasion. She couldn't guess the resentment which smoldered in Blackie's breast against the old man who had beat him savagely and knocked him around at a whim.

Still, Blackie felt a responsibility to preserve the life of the old tyrant, which is why he'd called in Jennings. He noted with satisfaction that Jennings had come to the funeral, and he wondered if it was only because he had signed the death certificate. He also noted that Leah Palmer was obviously shaken by the proceedings and that she had put on her sunglasses, even though the interior of the church was dark. Nice touch. He wished he'd not left his in the car.

Blanche Carnes, as might be expected, was one of the three who cried. Trust Blanche to do the proper thing. She cried not for Molesworth's immortal soul, which she knew was this day in paradise with our Lord. No. She cried for Molesworth's widow and for Blackie and for George Bob, who would be deprived of Molesworth's company for a spell.

Blanche, too, noted that Leah was crying, but it did not seem peculiar to her. "There goes a good Christian woman," she would tell Blackie later.

The third mourner was Molesworth's ugly niece. Ada Sue cried more from excitement, perhaps, than from grief. She was on an emotional high, on the brink, really. From a lifetime of ostracism, of harassment for no better reason than her ugliness, she had now come to acceptance by reason of her marriage. Perry's incredible handsomeness overshadowed to some extent the questionability of his blood. And his diligence to work, his provision of a regular salary, thus affording her luxuries unknown to her peers, placed her in a class by herself —in fact, separated her even from her father. But on this day, for once, they were all here together under one roof, and she and Perry were a part of the whole. She had been stunned by his decision to come, and grateful. She cried in gratitude.

Perhaps Ada Sue, of all those present, could have understood why it was that Leah cried.

Jennings could not, certainly. He was, in fact, inwardly distressed to hear her snuffling beside him, and he hoped it would go unnoticed. If he'd told her once, he'd told her a dozen times, "A doctor has to maintain a certain dignity, and so does his wife." In many ways Leah had not yet proved equal to the task of being a doctor's wife. Take that business of not wanting children, or the ridiculous notion about wanting to work, or the rather cheap practice of displaying her pictures down at the frame shop like a common peddler. But she would learn in time. He'd see to that. After all, what would people think?

Joe Billy, taking in the whole proceedings, filed away many bits of information for future reference. Some were puzzling. Like why Leah was crying. And why Perry showed up and why he didn't seem to notice Doris Jean at all, but had cast a furtive, hooded glance at Leah. Nothing peculiar about a man looking at a beautiful woman. But it was Leah's reaction which interested Joe Billy. Her face registered what, from the oblique angle at which Joe Billy viewed it, appeared to be fear. . . . Leah and Perry. What was their common denominator? A possibility crossed his mind.

Doris Jean did not cry, although she felt like it. Felt like screaming, in fact. She alone knew why Perry Johnson had come to the funeral. Ordinarily he'd never be seen in public with that scarecrow wife of his. But he had come just to thwart Doris, to hurt her by his nearness and his remoteness. And all because she'd questioned him about the wound on his chest.

"Leave it alone! The doctor's wife put that bandage on." He

121

pushed her away roughly when she'd tried to peek under the bandage.

"What is it, a knife wound?"

"Of course not!" He got off the bed and pulled on his shorts. She was mystified, incensed.

"*Now* what did I say? Honest to God, Perry, you're so touchy!"

He hadn't slowed down but dressed quickly and pulled on his boots.

"How can you leave me like this?" she cried.

"I'm out of the mood," he said. "You're always prying, always picking—"

She was exasperated. "My gosh, I'm only concerned . . . Wouldn't you be curious or just a little surprised if I turned up with a bandage?"

He stopped in the doorway and looked down at her. "Surprised? Yes. Because it'll be a cold day in Havana when Joe Billy Tolliver bites you."

She was up and chasing after him, dragging a sheet for cover. She stopped at the back screen door as he hopped off the back porch. "Are you telling me your wife *bit* you, Perry Johnson?"

He turned one last time to look back, an amused glint in his black eyes. "It would surprise you what my wife does to me," he said. And she felt like throwing something at him. She knew he was only goading her. He got tremendous pleasure from teasing her.

It also chafed her to think that Leah had dressed his wound. Come to think of it, Leah had cast several glances across the aisle toward Perry. And once he had looked at her and their glances had locked. From her place behind Perry and Ada Sue, Doris Jean could see it all, and it set her wondering. But no, it was impossible. Who knew that better than she?

122

Leah cried, she herself decided, because of self-pity. For her feeling of deprivation. Because, looking around this assemblage of mourners, she could see Carneses of every ilk—recognizable by their noses—and she envied their sense of belonging to each other. It must be such a comfort to have someone to stand up with you when you marry and someone to mourn when you die. It would be nice to have a family tree, even if some of the branches were rotten. Like George Bob Carnes. Rotten relatives are better than no relatives at all. And that's what Leah had: no relatives at all.

It's too bad that Leah was so wrapped up in her grief. Otherwise she might have been on the lookout for danger. Because she was surrounded by it.

It was out at the cemetery after the first spadeful of dirt had been thrown in and a musical group from Sacogee Bayou were fixing to play that Joe Billy Tolliver pulled George Bob aside.

"I want to offer my respects, George Bob," he said.

George Bob didn't know what he was supposed to say. He just shrugged and looked up into the trees. He almost felt like crying.

"Too bad he had to go so young," Joe Billy said. "Too bad you couldn't get someone out here to save him."

"What do you mean?"

Joe Billy didn't answer. Presently he said, "Were you here at the time?" When George Bob shook his head, Joe Billy looked disappointed. But he clapped George Bob on the back. "He was a fine man, George Bob. Maybe someday you and I can do something nice for your mother in his honor."

"Like what?"

"Like sue for malpractice."

14

JOE BILLY was a different kind of a fellow. Jennings probably would have told anyone who'd listen that Joe Billy was motivated by money rather than prestige. Jennings would have been wrong.

Not that Joe Billy had anything against money. No, he always planned to have lots of it. And he didn't have anything against prestige, either, and someday down the road he meant to try for a judgeship. But Joe Billy Tolliver had larger aspirations than either wealth or prestige. Joe Billy wanted to be God.

Joe Billy was a manipulator. He'd rather sit in the background and finagle people and events to achieve whatever end he happened to fancy. He didn't even mind that nobody else ever knew who was *really* responsible for the outcome. He liked the power, the feeling that he was too smart for any of them, Moseleys, Crenshaws, Carneses, the lot.

Nothing that he did was accidental, no matter how incidental it seemed. From his slick, social-climbing wife to his own casual, country-boy demeanor, it was all carefully arranged for. And even Doris Jean didn't know that.

Just now Joe Billy had his sights on a big haul. He made it his business to know what went on out at the plant, to be the first to know of any injuries or accidents. In his several years' practice, he had found that back injuries were almost impossible to disprove. Occasionally, he ran across a worker who was also ambitious, who was willing to become disabled, at least until a settlement was made. John Tom Bacon was such a man. John Tom had "fallen" off a platform, and John Tom had brains and a certain talent for acting. Joe Billy was suing for a million dollars.

It wasn't the money, although Joe Billy would get the biggest portion of whatever settlement was made. It was the game. Manipulating as many of those people as possible.

Someday, when he'd run the personal injury thing dry, or when he tired of it, he'd approach it from another angle. Malpractice suits. He could use some of the same cast of characters. He was already laying the groundwork for that, and dropping a seed of suspicion here and there.

He needed Jennings, of course. Needed *some* expert witness. Jennings was the obvious choice. Hell, didn't he need the money, piss-poor bastard? They were old friends. Jennings'd come through, eventually. Just in case he needed special persuading, though, Joe Billy had been looking for his chink.

It was the first thing Joe Billy did when he met anybody. He looked for the weakness. It was hard to find Jennings' chink. Unless it was Leah. But he wasn't so sure but what Jennings'd throw Leah to the wolves if the chips were down.

On the other hand, Leah was just full of chinks. She was self-conscious, ill at ease and full of baloney. That girl had

125

things to hide. A shady past, maybe: an abortion or a few tricks on the street. Or if not that, questionable lineage, at least. He would ferret it out, whatever it was.

It was no use expecting Doris Jean to help him; he didn't trust her anyway. The day he had to let Doris Jean in on any of his plans would be the day she lost her value to him. Blanche was accurate, but Blanche had entirely too many scruples. His sister Ernestine was the perfect choice, and it was easy to drop a suggestion in her ear one evening while they were dancing at the country club. "What do you know about Leah?" he asked. "Isn't it peculiar that nobody knows much about her? Reckon it would take a mighty clever person to find out anything about somebody as closemouthed as Leah." He knew Ernestine. He could tell by the set of her round little jaw that she took the bait, and that she would take great personal pride in reporting back to him. For whatever that was worth.

And when all was said and done, either Jennings would cooperate, or he'd have to get a new boy. The town wouldn't support any more doctors, so he'd have to herd one out to make room. Either Jennings played ball, or he'd move out, be starved out, maybe be ridden out on a rail. Joe Billy'd work out the details if it came down to that.

As for this current case, Joe Billy would win it, no question there. And if Jennings wouldn't cooperate, he'd have to discredit him, somehow. Make him look bad, make his testimony unacceptable to a jury. He'd work it out, if he had to. Lay the groundwork, just in case it came to that. He hoped it wouldn't, though. Jennings was his friend.

The clubhouse of the Clarington Country Club was a wretched rambling redwood affair which belied the splendor to which its members aspired. Its saving grace was its golf course, whose lush fairways, if unchallenging to the expert, at least offered a restful view. Joe Billy spent a lot of time on the course, and a little more in the clubhouse. It beat sitting in the office all day.

Sometimes he even amazed himself with his own improvisation, his ability to utilize the raw material at hand. In this case, it was Blanche Carnes, hunched over on a redwood bench outside the clubhouse. He ambled over and took her angular hand and squeezed it respectfully. You didn't kiss Blanche Carnes on the cheek. Or chuck her under that servile chin.

"What in the world are you doing out here in the heat, Blanche Beth?" he said, slipping down easily beside her. She inched away from him a little.

"Waiting. Just waiting. Picking up Blackie when he gets through playing." She held up the car keys to prove it, then looked off down the green as if he weren't even there any longer. Blanche wasn't much for chitchat.

Joe Billy got out his handkerchief and mopped his neck. "Well, I don't know why in heck you ain't burning up out here! I sure am, and I just got here! Hey, how about coming inside and drinking a Co-Cola with me?" Before she could refuse, he hurried on: "Besides, I need me some good Christian advice, and you might be just the one to give it to me!"

He knew her chink, you see. She followed him mutely, her beige polished-cotton culottes making a swish-swish noise as she walked. Joe Billy chose a table in the far 'corner of the dining room and, with extreme courtliness, held her chair for her. Sensing her eagerness, he deliberately held off, asking after Blackie and the kids, inquiring about the health of her mother, stringing it out until she had to ask.

"Joe Billy," Blanche finally interrupted, "didn't you say you wanted to ask me something?"

He snapped his fingers, as if he'd forgotten. Looking around to be sure they were alone (and they were the only ones in the dining room, as he well knew), he leaned over, affecting an anxious mien. "That's right, Blanche. I need a good Christian opinion about what to do. Now, you know how much I think of Jennings. Almost as much as I think of Blackie."

She looked a little dubious at that last statement. He'd better not spread it on too thick.

"I'm afraid he's in for trouble. Jennings, that is."

"What kind of trouble?" she asked.

He was improvising. He really didn't know yet what he was going to come up with. "You know his practice depends on keeping people's goodwill. And if the silly rumor I heard today gets around, it could ruin that boy!"

She stiffened, sat up straight. "I don't listen to rumors," she said flatly. "They're the tool of the Devil."

Joe Billy nodded with his whole body. "Exactly! That's my whole point! It would be so easy for a pack of lies to ruin Jennings, and yet there's no good way he can protect himself if he don't even know the dangers . . . but how're you going to warn the man without being a part of the rumor spreading yourself?" He leaned way back in his chair and tucked his thumbs in his belt. "And it's *got* to be lies—can't no way be true!"

Blanche flicked a small piece of lint from her lap. Blanche was a tidy, impeccable person. She had no illusions about her long horse face or her lanky, rawboned figure. But she could at least be neat, and she always was.

"I don't want to hear them, whatever they are," she said. She had finished her drink, but she didn't get up. Joe Billy took that as a good sign.

Joe Billy felt of his midsection. A while back he had had an ulcer, and he called it into being again whenever it was needed. "Dad-dang if I don't believe that Co-Cola has set my ulcer churning again!" He shook his head. "I ought to be more

128

careful, especially when I'm all wrought up about something, like today. Blanche, do you mind sitting here with me while I drink me a glass of milk to sort of settle things down?"

Blanche didn't say anything.

"Would you like anything else, yourself?"

Blanche shook her head. Joe Billy had the idea that she wasn't convinced of his sympathy for Jennings. Blanche was a hard cookie. Maybe he'd said too much already.

She watched him get his milk and sip it slowly. Neither of them spoke for a long time. Joe Billy was about to give up. Then she let out a long sigh.

"You asked me in here for some Christian advice, didn't you? Well, here's what I think: I think if a person's your friend, you ought to let him know what's going on. I don't think that's spreading any rumors." Her duty done, she was about to get up when Joe Billy reached out across the table and caught her.

"Bless your heart, I wish it was that simple! But right now I just can't approach Jennings about a dad-dang thing!"

"Why not?" she asked.

He drained his milk glass and set it down slowly so that he could think. "It's a legal matter, Blanche, that I'm not at liberty to divulge, even to someone as trustworthy as you. But at the moment our professional relations are a little strained, and I just feel like Jennings might take any warning from me in the wrong way. Now, of course, somebody else, like Blackie—"

"Leave Blackie out of this," she said sharply.

He shrugged, then caught himself. Wrong tack.

"You're absolutely right," he said. "The fewer people who know about this, the better."

She pressed her paper napkin firmly to her mouth, then got up deliberately. "And that includes me."

He got up quickly and followed her out. "Did I ask you to

do anything? All I asked for was advice, and you gave me that. Good advice. What was it you just said? 'If a person's your friend, you ought to let him know.'"

She was intractable. She returned to the redwood bench outside the clubhouse. He was right behind her, plopped down beside her and leaned close to her ear.

"O.K., O.K. You're forcing me, Blanche. I'm just going to have to give you a hint about how serious this really is."

"I don't want to know," she said, trying not to want to.

"And I'm not going to tell you," he said. After all, how could he? He hadn't thought of anything yet. "I said I am going to give you a *hint*. That's all. A hint. I'm just going to say that if this were true, it could affect every decent, law-abiding man, woman and child in this county." It was the best he could do on the spur of the moment.

Her head snapped up. "Child? Are you saying that Jennings Palmer's an integrationist?"

He couldn't believe his good fortune, and he congratulated himself on his flash of genius which had led her to put the needed words into his mouth. He could have thought all week and not come up with anything better.

"I didn't say that," he said. "Just don't go jumpin' to any conclusions, Blanche. Just because he went up north and lived up there all those years in St. Louis. Just because he married a girl from up there who probably has a different attitude about it than we do down here—"

Blanche narrowed her eyes. "I do know she raised Dorothy to two seventy-five a day and now every maid in town knows about it," she said.

"I hear he's got two of 'em in the hospital right now," he said.

Blanche pondered this. "It's the Christian thing to do."

He nodded. "My point exactly. He's just doin' his Christian duty."

130

Blanche shook her head. "Jennings grew up here. He knows how it is."

"You're forgettin' Leah's influence," he reminded her. And then he remembered himself. Never argue; it only solidifies the other's view. "I mean, after all, they don't have any children, so why should they be interested one way or another? You're right, of course, Blanche." He patted her shoulder as he rose to leave. "Ain't no truth in it. We all know Jennings. Still, a false rumor is just as damaging as the truth. Pity, ain't it?"

He sauntered off the lawn onto the gravel parking lot, not sure he had stirred up anything at all, and not sure, if he had, that it would reach Jennings, prod him into taking another look at Joe Billy's proposition. Well, maybe he'd better not count on Blanche. She might decide to hold out on Blackie. He'd puzzled a minute on why she was so anxious not to involve Blackie in this, but he thought he had that figured out. Blackie's brother George Bob was still such a hothead. Blanche was always afraid of knowing what George Bob was up to.

Oh well, it was just a shot. After all, he hadn't been doing anything else this afternoon, anyway. It was an interesting little diversion, and Blanche had certainly come up with a winner for him.

Blanche Beth Dawson Carnes sat primly on the redwood bench in the sweltering shade of the eave of the country clubhouse, and she thought about Satan. Sometimes it was so hard to see his hand in things until it was too late. Often she had been the Devil's unwitting tool, played right into his hands, believing all the while that she was thwarting him. It was a daily struggle, she supposed, with Christians around the world. He threw temptations in her path daily, tried to make them seem like her Christian duty, and if she succumbed, then he plagued her with guilt about it. She knew wily Satan.

In the matter at hand, the lines were fuzzy again. She knew the Lord did not mean for the races to mingle. They had been scattered at the time of the building of the tower of Babel, as punishment for trying to reach God. Segregation was Biblical. But this matter of Jennings: maybe he was just being like Albert Schweitzer. You couldn't fault that.

Perhaps she would talk to Brother Willoughby about it. Most certainly she would pray about it. And she would search the Scriptures. They would tell her what to do. Yes, she would move very, very cautiously. Because on Judgment Day she didn't want it said of her that she had been maneuvered by the Devil.

15

It was a day like any other.

Leah and Jennings were jerked into consciousness at five thirty by the strident ringing of the bedside telephone. Old man Leonard Kerr wanted to know if it was all right to eat a slice of bacon for breakfast just this once.

Jennings, who was due in surgery at seven to scrub to assist old Doc Grainger, had an early breakfast and was ready to leave by six forty-five. As he was going out the door, Leah remembered that she must lead the program for the circle meeting at ten.

"Jennings, do you suppose your mother left a Bible around here?"

He shrugged. "I wouldn't be surprised. How is it that you went all the way through a Catholic school and don't own a Bible?"

"Catholics only use them to record births and deaths," she said.

"I don't know," he said. "Look in the bureau in the front bedroom."

She took an early shower then set about to find the Bible. It was tucked away in the bureau, just as Jennings said. Reluctantly she sat down to study her Scripture lesson. She was clammy with fear at the thought of having to speak before a handful of women.

At eight thirty Grace Puckett called to ask Leah to speak to Jennings about writing a letter of recommendation to help her son Melvin, Jr., get into med school. Leah made a note to speak to Jennings. As she was writing, she noticed on her calendar that this meeting of her circle was the covered-dish luncheon meeting, and she hadn't a thing prepared. With telephone wedged to her ear by her shoulder, she sidled to the refrigerator and peered inside. It was a completely uninspired conglomeration of leftovers. With difficulty she extricated herself from the telephone conversation with Grace Puckett, who wanted to impress upon Leah what a splendid record Melvin, Jr., had at Lon Morris College.

She had nothing, absolutely nothing to fix. Her stomach was churning. How could she have forgotten? All the girls brought such fancy things to the luncheons; she always felt intimidated by them. She wasn't a fancy cook, and maybe she wasn't even a good cook. Cooking was just one of those things she never had a chance to learn. Why didn't Dorothy hurry up and show?

She dressed haphazardly, although she had meant to take great pains on this day. Intermittently she returned to scowl into the cabinets and the refrigerator, hoping for an inspiration. At nine fifty-five Dorothy still hadn't come, and she would be late to her circle meeting as it was. She pinned a note above the kitchen sink:

Dorothy—Please make a pie by 11:30. I'll be home then to pick it up. Don't fix lunch for me. Dr. P. will be home at noon. Show him note from Grace Puckett.

The circle meeting, held in the home of the local undertaker's wife, was a ghastly fiasco. In her rush to get out of the house, Leah forgot her notes and the Bible. She had to borrow a Bible from the hostess and speak extemporaneously. She found herself quaking and stammering, found the women inattentive and rude, whispering audibly during her talk.

She returned at eleven thirty to find that Dorothy still hadn't come. Jennings was due home for lunch in half an hour. She scurried around opening a can of soup and mixing a salad, still wondering what she could throw together for the luncheon, already in progress.

Jennings arrived shortly after, and the phone began to ring even before he took his first mouthful.

"He just sat down to eat," Leah told the caller. "Could I have him call you back?"

"No, just tell him Mrs. Simpson called. Just thought he'd like to know my period started."

"I'm sure he will," Leah said lamely.

Elbow on the table, Jennings leaned glumly over his soup, a dour expression on his face.

"I'm sorry there's nothing better," she said. "I've been gone all morning and Dorothy didn't show."

He looked up distractedly. "It's not the soup. It just seems things are piling up on me. I've got a lot to think about."

"You wanted to be busy," she said. She refused to discuss with him again the events of the evening before, when he was asked to appear before the hospital board to explain why he admitted two colored charity patients to a previously all-white hospital. Jennings had felt he acquitted himself well before the board by explaining that his desire to bring diagnostic excellence to the community must extend to all his patients. The board had countered that, for all of his charity patients, he would have to take full financial responsibility. She had listened to his account of the evening's events with all the calm she could muster. But she didn't intend to go through it again.

Maybe she would just open up a can of mixed fruit and pour some brandy over it for the luncheon. No, brandy was taboo. Besides, there didn't seem to be any fruit.

Jennings was talking about something else. "This morning I was ordered by Doc Grainger, in his capacity as county coroner, to turn my 'complete file' on Molesworth Carnes over to his office. Now what do you suppose that means?"

"I thought old man Carnes refused ever to come into town to see you?" she said.

"That's right. Seems peculiar to me Doc Grainger would wait until after the funeral to begin an investigation."

"It's probably nothing," she said.

The doorbell rang. It was the next-door neighbor, who'd seen the doctor's car and thought maybe he'd just pop over and let Doc take a look at the fester on his leg. It would save a trip to the office.

At the same time, the back door opened and Harriett Ramsey appeared with a hangdog Dorothy in tow.

"Buck's truck broke down," Harriett told her. "Dorothy had no way to get to work. I just happened along a while ago and saw her sitting out in the yard, so I brought her along."

Dorothy smiled sheepishly at Leah.

Leah was awash in relief. "Dorothy, I'm due at a covered-dish luncheon right now. Is there any dessert you could throw together in a hurry for me to take?"

"Wellum yes ma'am." Dorothy headed for the kitchen, where Jennings sat at the table with his spoon poised while the next-door neighbor propped his foot in a chair and rolled up his pants leg to display a large pustule.

"Leah, I've come to talk to you," Harriett said. "You might say Ida sent me."

Ironic that Leah had longed for a chance to visit with Harriett, but not, dear God, today. "I'm really sorry, Harriett. You've caught me at a bad time. I'm late for a luncheon—"

"Screw the luncheon," Harriett said. And she led Leah away with a firm hand, past Dorothy and Jennings and the man with the disgusting sore, out the door and into her pickup. Leah was content to let someone else take charge. Somehow she'd made a mess of the day.

They chose a booth at the motel restaurant so that they could talk without interruption. They ordered sandwiches, and Leah sat back in the booth and began to enjoy herself. It beat the covered-dish luncheon all the way to kingdom come.

Harriett lacked her usual openness, and Leah could never carry the ball alone. They ate in silence until Leah could stand it no more. Eventually she pushed back her plate in exasperation.

"O.K., Harriett, I'm no good at fencing. What did Aunt Ida send you here to say?"

The gristle of a sardonic smile played at the corner of Harriett's mouth. "You don't mess around, do you? O.K., out with it: Aunt Ida thinks the rumormongers are out to cremate you. Or rather, Jennings."

"Jennings! You mean the hospital thing with Buck and Pearlene?"

Harriett shook her head. "That's not it exactly, although I guess that started it. It's a much more insidious rumor, more damaging. They're saying that Jennings is an integrationist."

There was no safety anywhere, not even here, tucked away in a corner booth, not even with Harriett. Leah was not going

137

to discuss such a thing as this with Harriett or anyone else. She had known for years that she could not possibly *ever* discuss it with anyone, not anyone. That having made her decision to pass, these other things were not her concern.

And that what Harriett suggested could be possible? It was much more ludicrous than she had guessed when she married him. It was a breathless moment before she could say, truthfully, "That's the silliest thing I ever heard!" And she got up and paid the check. If Harriett wanted to follow, that was fine. The discussion was over. She got in the pickup, and she felt her throat ache, constricted as it was that day she first met Harriett. She was almost choking with the need to talk and knew now that she never could.

Harriett got into the cab and turned to her, her self-cut bangs, ruffled by the breeze, looking for all the world like a jackdaw's nest. Looks were the least of Harriett's concern. "Don't hold it against me for telling you. Ida thought you ought to know."

Leah blinked and turned her head, stared out the side window. Harriett started the pickup.

"This is the damnedest town," Harriett said.

They drove home in silence. Harriett pulled in the drive just as Jennings was driving away. They waved.

"God, I wish we were back in Half Moon Bay!" Harriett said. "Free to be ourselves, you know?"

Leah didn't know.

She stopped at the front door to pick up the mail. There was a schedule of events from the Fine Arts League for the fall season. Dr. and Mrs. Jennings Palmer were listed as hosts and local arrangements couple for the October 16 guest pianist. Leah wondered what that meant.

She had missed the luncheon, but there was plenty of time to get ready for the Study Club staging committee meeting to plan the Fourth of July activities. She cursed Harriett for having come to town at all. Now she would drag through the hours, trudge through her days, wondering what they were saying. She didn't need that burden.

It was midafternoon when the committee meeting broke up and Leah made her escape. Returning home, she recognized the Cadillac parked in front of her house, and she could see Joe Billy sitting behind the wheel. She stopped in the driveway and got out, forcing a smile, motioning him to get out, too. But he shook his head and rolled down the window on the passenger side.

"Wouldn't look right," he called, "Jennings not being home. Only take a minute."

Reluctantly she walked over and leaned on his window.

"There she is, pretty as a picture, just like always," he said, grinning disarmingly.

She looked long at his hard, steely-blue eyes. The grin was allaying, but the eyes didn't smile. "What is it, Joe Billy?"

He kept smiling, but he managed to look a trifle wounded at the same time. "Leah doll, Jennings is just not treating his old friends right."

She straightened and stepped back. "Listen, Joe Billy, I don't meddle in Jennings' affairs, especially his medical affairs."

The grin broadened. "Well, honey, maybe that's the trouble! Maybe this is one you ought to meddle in. Jennings is passing up a good deal! Hell, it ain't as if anybody is asking him to do anything illegal!"

She snorted. It was a mistake. Joe Billy slammed his palm down on the leather seat, and the smile vanished. The rims of his glinting eyes showed red. "Almost forgot! I'm thinking of running up to St. Louis one of these days. Anybody you want me to look up at *Saint Agnes Academy?*"

Ice had formed instantly around her heart and chilled the blood in her veins. She felt sweat pop out on her upper lip,

139

and she heard buzzing all about her. But it hadn't drowned out his voice. She climbed above it all and forced a level tone.

"That's nice of you to think of me, Joe Billy, but not necessary."

As if it just occurred to him, he said, "Hey! My sister was mentioning that you're an orphan. I bet there's a lot about your family that you don't know that it'd be easy for me, being a lawyer, to find out for you!"

She swallowed hard. "What do you really want from me, Joe Billy?"

He shrugged apologetically. "Hell, Leah, I don't want your gratitude, that's for sure. But if you *do* feel like doing something, you could persuade Jennings to testify for the plaintiff in this back injury case. I mean, hellfire, we'd make a great team, me finding the injury cases and sending them to him for workup, and him being my expert witness, testifying as to the extent of injury." He leaned over in the seat onto his elbow and said in a loud whisper, "I'd make it worth his time, Leah. Percentage of the damages. Do you know what kind of money I'm talking about, Leah?"

He motioned at the house behind her. "Do you want to live in this place for the rest of your life?"

She could think of no words, because she was not sure she knew the answer. Finally she said wearily, "Joe Billy, even if I wanted to help you—which I haven't said I do—I couldn't influence Jennings if I tried."

He thought about that a minute, his thin, boyish face growing dark with resentment at being thwarted. "You may be right, Leah, but if I was you, I'd sure as hell try!" And he ground on the starter and roared away.

Her rage and fear had melted to weariness even before she reached the front door. Why does everything have to be so complicated? she thought. What the hell did I ever do to deserve all this garbage? Why me, Lord?

She spent the late-afternoon hours calling hospital volunteers with new assignments. It could have been her imagination that some of the women sounded cold, distant.

While at her kitchen desk, she glanced again at her calendar. It was choir practice night. She was emotionally spent, but she would go. It was easier to go than to come up with an alibi later.

It was almost suppertime when she heard a crash in the front room. That damn Dorothy, she thought. What has she broken now—probably on purpose? Her paranoia was mounting, translating itself into rage again.

Rage that smoldered, bubbled always just beneath the surface. Rage, with which she had beat her small breast at the sight of Mama, bone-tired and wilted, cajoling, groveling, promising the landlord much too much. Tormenting rage which gave off an odor all its own, moribund rage.

Swallow it stifle it bury it. Grasp control. Cope.

She couldn't immediately come to grips with what she saw as she rushed into the living room: Dorothy whimpering there, the dust rag fallen forgotten at her feet, the shards of glass which spewed all over the room—glinting from the top of the old spinet piano, from the coffee table, from the open leaves of the forgotten Bible, from the couch—the jagged hole in the front window and finally, the thing on the floor.

She didn't pick it up right away. She had to assess the threat, as if it were a thing alive. As if she could hear Mama's voice: "You going to like it." And knowing that it was not so.

After several seconds Dorothy's whimpering escalated, became a wail and then a yowl, and Leah's brain began to function again. She could connect the object with its name. It

141

appeared to be a brick. Yes, it was a brick, wrapped with a piece of brown paper secured by several rubber bands. It was all too stylized.

"Lord Jesus, just like on TV!" Dorothy's eyes grew as big as half-dollars.

Something this histrionic can't really be happening, she thought. She picked it up and removed the paper, knowing that something would be written there:

Jigaboo.

She wadded the paper in her palm and felt calm, absolute control. Except that her nails had cut arcs in her palm from which the blood oozed. She never considered that the paper might be a denunciation of Jennings for hospitalizing Buck and Pearlene. She only believed that somebody knew the truth about her. Her thoughts flashed to Perry.

Leah was still trying to calm Dorothy, making light of the incident so that Dorothy wouldn't call her boyfriend Otis to come after her, wouldn't leave her all alone in this house, when Jennings phoned a half hour later. His manner was brusque, and he began speaking before she had a chance to tell him.

"I'll be later than usual. Something's wrong with the car. It's stalled on the hospital parking lot. I've called an all-night garage to come out. Meantime, they've brought in a woman who's about half dead. Husband beat her up something awful. Probably be midnight before I get away, so don't wait supper. If they don't get my car fixed, you'll have to come get me."

Leah bit her lip until she tasted blood. It is always this way, she thought.

She hung up and called the sheriff. Funny, she hadn't thought of it sooner. But once she had made the call, she regretted it. Dear God, why did I do that? she thought. I can't show him the note. What will I say? Maybe he won't come.

But they did. In about twenty minutes the old Ford squad

car swung into the drive and a pudgy, balding man who reminded her of Tweedledum stepped out. His partner was a tall, thin red-neck with several teeth missing. She went out front to meet them, carrying the brick. She had stuffed the note in her pocket.

"This is what they used." She handed the brick over to Tweedledum. Now that she was close she recognized him as a patient she'd once seen in Jennings' waiting room. "You're Malcolm Gunn, aren't you?"

"That's right, Mrs. Palmer; I'm proud you remember. And this here's Fen Ledbetter." He indicated his partner, who tipped his greasy straw Stetson. "Can you think of anybody's got it in for you or Doc, little lady?"

She thought of Joe Billy. Not his style, of course. "No one."

"Appears like the work of a teenage prankster," Gunn said. "Not much we can do except patrol the area, keep your place under surveillance, you might say, 'case they come back."

Fen Ledbetter was studying her hard. "You positive you can't think of any reason somebody would do this, ma'am?"

She felt intimidated. What was there about this man, what was he getting at? She didn't like him. It was dark now; he couldn't see her. What did her voice betray?

Got to get away; losing my control. God help me, what is happening? . . .

She got rid of them, fled into the house. Told Dorothy to phone Otis to pick her up. Told her to go home. No, she needn't come tomorrow. No, there was nothing on that paper, no, no.

Got to be alone. Got to pull myself together.

She paced through the house, wringing her hands and talking aloud, shoring up her defenses, fighting panic. She had always thought she was special. Didn't they all say so? Even when she was very young they had said it.

143

"She could pass," they had said. And Leah had taken it for the truth.

Maybe they all know. Have always known. Maybe Jennings knows and doesn't care. My God, maybe it doesn't matter. Dear God, why does it have to matter? What is wrong with me, why isn't it all right to be Leah?

She paced into the front room, where sparkles of glass still glistened on the Bible page. She picked it up and brushed them off and read:

> How long, O Lord? Wilt thou forget me forever?
>   How long wilt thou hide thy face from me?
> How long must I bear pain in my soul,
>   and have sorrow in my heart all the day?
> How long shall my enemy be exalted over me?

The tears rose, spilled out and flooded over. She paced and shook with great shuddering heaves, grappling with hysteria. Like when Father handed her over to the Sisters. Like when she poured out her desolation into the pillow on her cruel little iron bed. Like always. Even to Mama it wasn't all right to be Leah. Just like forever, her grief remained on her spirit like an enormous contusion, perpetually sore to the touch.

Set apart. That was what she had finally decided. Singled out to take the hard knocks.

Or, by God, give them.

It is eight hundred miles from the ghetto in St. Louis to the house on Redbud Street. Father Richard had promised her justice. He did not promise mercy.

She wrestled with her madness for almost two hours before Jennings called again. He wanted her to bring the car. His car couldn't be repaired and had been hauled away. He would

144

have to use hers indefinitely until they could order a new motor from Dallas.

"Some sonofabitch put sugar in my gas tank," he said. He sounded tired, defeated. There was no need to add to his burdens. She took him the car. At least now she had an excuse for missing choir practice.

He was waiting for her on the hospital parking lot. He had a house call to make; he'd drop her off. She put off telling him about the window.

He had bowed to hospital administrative pressure in dismissing Buck and Pearlene. But he was worried about them both. He would visit them every evening for a while. He told her not to wait up. She didn't, and she pretended to be asleep when he came home sometime past midnight.

Sister Fain had promised her abundance, but she hadn't promised freedom.

16

JOE BILLY sped away from Leah Palmer's that afternoon sensing that he had struck the mother lode. The granddaddy of all chinks. And he'd just blundered onto it. He couldn't contain the broad grin which crept over his thin face. Driving down the street grinnin' like an old blind sow found an acorn!

Joe Billy had learned to crawl before he could run, and he still found it best to keep his nose to the ground, sniffing and inching his way along. Operating moment to moment. It was the secret of his success in the courtroom: a jury was captivated by spontaneity. Often he progressed literally sentence by sentence, weighing the expressions on the faces of the jurors before forming his next statement. When he detected a flicker of interest, of sympathy, he bore down hard, hammered it in, said the same thing twenty different ways until he had the jurors in his palm, actually nodding with him.

Not that he ever went into court unprepared, no sir. Joe Billy always came in loaded for bear. But he never felt

146

cheated if he didn't have to uncover his big guns. He wasn't after prestige, remember. He only wanted results, creative results. Like God.

Joe Billy began preparing for his success early. He was actually still in prelaw when he uncovered the state law about acquiring property by paying its delinquent taxes. Came home that summer and spent two weeks going over the county tax rolls before he found the Graff place: two sections of marsh and thicket out off Farm Road 69 once belonging to Henry Graff and later to his widow Ivanell, now buried at Pine Hill Cemetery. Joe Billy drove out and looked the place over. His excitement mounted when he saw that it was familiar territory to him: the land north of Pine Hill Cemetery, called "The Bog," marked the westernmost boundary. To the east the land encompassed the very hole of water, a spring-fed lake, which he and his friends had frog-gigged as boys: Bullfrog Pond, they called it, after the huge frogs they caught there. He went straight to his father and asked for a loan, explaining that all he had to do was pay the back taxes, then continue paying the taxes, which were extremely low for undeveloped marshland, for five years and the property would be his! Grady Tolliver was no fool. He lent Joe Billy the money. Why, there might even be oil on the place.

Not that it mattered, but just because he was curious, Joe Billy went back to the courthouse to search out possible heirs of Ivanell Graff. Not surprisingly, he found that she had once been Ivanell Carnes, and that she had been the aunt to old Molesworth and Otho Carnes. Joe Billy was gratified to learn the property didn't belong to someone who could afford to pay the taxes, if they happened to find out it belonged to them. But all the same, he kept his project quiet. Never told anybody what he'd found out. And as soon as the property was legally his, he posted a large sign announcing: "Tolliver's Lake. Posted. Trespassers Will Be Prosecuted."

The acquisition of the Bullfrog Pond property was one of the circumstances that influenced Joe Billy to come back to Clarington to practice law, but not, by any means, the prime one. For one thing, he found Clarington completely vulnerable, totally susceptible to manipulation, like a little kingdom. The possibilities were endless.

For another thing, there was George Bob.

Joe Billy was no fool. He'd never let himself get messed up that way. Oh, there was once, during high school, when the others had gone to the sock hop. He and George Bob hadn't cared to go, instead had gone out and tied one on, had ended up in the old house out on Bullfrog Pond—the one he later learned had been Ivanell Graff's home—and had given vent to their lusts. But Joe Billy had claimed an alcoholic blackout the next day, and so had George Bob. To this day he never knew if George Bob really remembered or not.

He had little contact with George Bob these days, and usually only in the presence of his brother Blackie. Being around George Bob provoked a certain gnawing hunger still. But it pleased him to manipulate George Bob, and he did it often, without George Bob's ever knowing. It gave him a sense of ownership, of possessing George Bob, which is what he wanted most. It was probably what held him to Clarington most firmly.

His marriage to Doris Jean had been calculated, a business move which had turned out to be a predictably brilliant one. Except for her insatiable sexual appetite. He had seen early on that that could present a problem.

Until he found Perry.

He was driving up toward Kingston one day when he saw Perry working on a road crew: a glistening, strapping giant stripped to the waist. As usual Joe Billy's instincts served him well. He remembered Perry from years past, seemed to recall Doris Jean mooning over him in junior high. Suspected at the

148

time she might be showering him with her favors. Was even jealous of her, perhaps

At that moment an idea was born, a solution to his dilemma with Doris Jean. He pulled over to the shoulder and beckoned the powerful man over. Up close he was incredibly handsome.

"Don't I know you?" he asked.

"Perry Johnson." He spat casually over his shoulder.

"Used to work for the Peavys, didn't you?"

Johnson's gaze hardened. "So?"

A chink. File that away for possible future reference.

"I'm lookin' for an overseer for my property. Tolliver's Lake. I'm Joe Billy Tolliver."

Johnson studied him. "I know you. Where 'bouts is this lake?"

"Out east of Clarington. 'Bout fifteen miles out Farm Road 69. East of Otho Carnes's place."

"I know it," Johnson said.

"House already on the place. I'll fix it up real nice for you," Joe Billy promised.

The deal was made, but Joe Billy was distressed when Perry had moved in with a newly acquired wife: Blackie and George Bob's ugly red-haired cousin, Ada Sue. He couldn't figure that one out, unless Johnson just didn't like to keep house. But he wasn't stymied for long. He sent a construction crew out to build a cozy little redwood love nest around the bend from the original house. This would be the trysting place; he was sure Doris Jean would see to that. And in between he could use it for entertaining. Write it off as a business expense, maybe. Have some of the boys out for fishing. Even George Bob someday, maybe. If it still pleased him to do so.

Now, as he sped away from Leah Palmer's, remembering her stricken look, he congratulated himself anew for his perspicacity. He had felt his way along with her until he hit a

149

nerve. He'd seen the alarm in her face when he mentioned Saint Agnes Academy. An embryo of suspicion was forming in his mind, the gem of a notion which was too delicious to be true. He hurried to his office and dictated a letter, instructing his secretary to locate the address of Saint Agnes Academy and send his letter, a masterpiece of a letter, if he did say so.

Joe Billy flipped through his calendar. It was fast approaching time for a hearing on the John Tom Bacon case. He could probably get a postponement if necessary, but he would rather not. He was having a helluva time keeping John Tom in line. He was supposed to be lying at home in traction. Every time Joe Billy saw George Bob's car, he could see John Tom crouched down in the back seat. Who in the hell did he think he was kiddin'? He hoped to God Jennings never saw him.

The hearing was looming up. Time to put the squeeze on old Jennings. Joe Billy hadn't found anything Jennings was susceptible to, except maybe peer pressure. Joe Billy envisioned a showdown, maybe a dinner party with all his old friends, when Jennings would have to commit himself publicly either to stand with him or against him.

He flipped on his intercom and told his secretary, "Honey, get my wife on the phone— No, never mind. I don't much think she's home."

He'd just remembered that it was Thursday and that Doris Jean was probably still humping out at Tolliver's Lake.

It can wait, he told himself. I sure don't want to disturb them. Let him wear her out good and proper!

17

SOMETIMES, AT odd moments as she rushed through her days, Leah would be brought up short—by the terrible aching beauty of the countryside, by some plaintive sequence of chords in the offertory, by the haunting look of eternal destitution in Dorothy's sloe eyes. And grief would come pouring down upon her like a bath of black tar, paralyzing her, beseeching her to give in to it. Sometimes she could feel her heart shudder, longing to yield to the weeping of her spirit. But she shook it off angrily, this weakness. She could handle it. Yet always with her, lurking just out of sight like a bandit who would rob her of her new life, was the memory of too many years of impoverishment, indifference, neglect. Too many hard times to blot out completely.

Blanche Carnes, on the other hand, wasn't old enough to remember hard times. The oil field was discovered the year she was born, and she had no memories of poverty on the farm.

Yet wherein Leah's marriage to Jennings represented a sort of rescue, so it resembled Blanche's marriage to Blackie. No one could call Blackie a good catch: he was wiry and short, a good three inches shorter than she, and he bore the prominent hook nose which branded him as a Carnes. But considering Blanche's plainness, and more than that, her inability to exude an ounce of sexuality, Blackie was as good as she could have expected. He gave her a "Mrs." before her name, and, of course, he gave her the children. What matter, then, if he did not choose to be provider? Their arrangement suited them both.

But it was not without its difficulties, and the chief intruder on her tranquillity showed up the next Thursday afternoon, just before supper. Blanche watched from the kitchen window as George Bob Carnes and two of his friends cut across the back lawn toward the bricked patio where Blackie sat reading the paper.

"Hey, big brother, you reading about us in the paper? We finally made the front page!" George Bob, a taller version of his brother, his ignoble mouth curled in a smirk, sauntered over and took the highball out of Blackie's hand. His two companions followed him and draped themselves over the lawn furniture. "Ain't you got a little booze for my friends here?"

Blackie eyed his disappearing drink. "Yeah, sure. Hey, Blanche! Trundle out here with some setups and a bottle! . . . What do you mean, you made the front page? You murder somebody?"

The other young men laughed raucously. Blackie shifted uncomfortably in his seat. Somehow, in the presence of his brother's casual crowd, he always felt so stodgy. He scanned the front page again.

"I don't see— Hey! You didn't have anything to do with sugaring Jennings' gas tank?"

George Bob strutted up and down before his older brother. He loved to show off for Blackie. "You damn right we did, and we also left his wife a by God calling card—right through the front window! . . . Hey, Blanche! Let's get on the by God stick with the booze!"

Blanche's face reappeared at the window. "I wouldn't even waste rotgut on gutter scum for anybody's brother!"

Blackie's face grew crimson. "Now, Blanche, dammit, get your ass off that damn by God high horse and bring us some bourbon or I'll come in there and give your tail something to droop about!"

This witticism caused much amusement among the young men. But apparently it didn't strike the same chord with Blanche, for she banged the window down and let the blind down with a crash.

Blackie, glowing with self-assurance at a job well done by the Head of the House, lay back in his chair. "She'll bring it," he said with a confidence he didn't feel.

Blackie and George Bob had been such a successful team until Blackie got married. Then George Bob got a new bunch of friends. Blackie couldn't help but feel a little jealous of them. He found it hard not to find fault with them.

"If it was me," he said finally, "I'd never ruin a perfectly good motor, no matter what the man did." George Bob looked guilty. Blackie had him. He went on.

"Thing is, I just hope you ain't got the wrong guy. That bull about Palmer, that was just something Joe Billy told Blanche. Probably baloney."

John Tom Bacon, one of the other boys, suddenly spoke up. "Did you ever wonder if the nigger he loves might be the one he's married to? Ever look at her real close?"

Blackie spat again. "Come off it, Bacon. You know Jennings Palmer. He wouldn't marry one, for crissakes!"

They all agreed that this was so.

Blackie felt compelled to play devil's advocate, just because these young toughs intimidated him so. "Look, he said, "I can't condemn the man until I'm sure. Far as I know, all he's done is put two niggers in the hospital. Maybe he's just a by God humanitarian. Didn't he come out to Daddy's and sit with him until he died?"

George Bob nodded sullenly. "Didn't save his life, though."

"Hell, he wasn't no damn magician!" Blackie said. "O.K. Here's what I'll do: I'll find out *for sure* about him. Next time I see him, I'll point-blank *ask* him. Until then, you blockheads just lay off him!"

George Bob kicked the chair stubbornly. "Communists is infiltrating everywhere. Going to have a field day pretty soon. And us just sitting by letting it happen."

Blackie was beginning to feel intimidated by his brother's insolence. It was time to draw some lines. "I said lay off until I find out for sure, you hear? Or else—"

The younger man drew himself up over his brother and leered menacingly. "Yeah, little man? Or else what?"

"Or else I'll by God quit handing out the dough, tough guy! Got a smart-ass comeback for that?"

George Bob shrugged and sat down. "So what's a few days? . . . Hey! How by God long we going to have to wait for a drink?"

Blackie leaped to his feet and stalked toward the house. He tried the back door. "Well I'll be damned! She done locked me out!"

Leah Palmer was not destined ever to meet Blackie's Uncle Otho, or to know about the two games he played to make life bearable. But she was to be profoundly affected by the events that occurred when he quit playing them.

The first had to do with his intentions. This particular afternoon Otho Carnes sat in his rocker on the leaning front porch and studied the rotting boards of the porch floor.

"One of these days I'm going to have to fix this porch," he said, "else the whole damn thing is going to fall down."

His red-haired wife Juanita was standing a few feet away on the hard-packed ground, hanging the wash on the broken and burned fence boards by a field of ancient stubble. She flapped some overalls a couple of times before draping them on the fence scraps. It was an angry gesture. "Where have I heard that before? One of these days you was going to get some money, too! Going to take that stray pup in town and see what you could get for him. Only now look at him! He's well-nigh grown!"

"Yeah," Otho mused. "I bet Blackie could use a good coon dog. One of these days—"

"The queen of England's going to drive up and give you a hundred dollars just for sitting up there looking so fine!" She shot a zinger through her teeth which landed dangerously close to him.

Juanita could be so grinding on the nerves. He ought to get up and pop her one. One of these days he would.

She was studying the dog in question, one of several that sprawled on the ground in the shade of a huge old tree, the lower limb of which threatened to dislodge the porch roof.

"He'd make a nice pet for Blackie's high-toned wife," she said hopefully.

"High-toned, hell! Ain't she a Dawson? I remember when Casper Dawson's whole spread weren't no bigger'n my front pasture! Back then us Carneses'd think twice before we'd even wipe our feet on Dawsons."

Juanita sighed, and Otho understood. It didn't seem fair. The Dawsons had more money than good sense, and the company that leased Otho's land had never even core tested. Still, it was forty dollars an acre every single year, just for oil lease. You couldn't fault that, specially since it was the only income they had. But then, Otho could hardly be expected to farm with his bad back.

Juanita must have read his mind. "I have to do everything around here. Even had to dig the potatoes. If it hadn't been for Ada Sue's help—"

This almost, but not quite, brought Otho out of his chair. "Now listen, you old slut! Don't you go throwing her up to me! The day she married that darky she stopped being my daughter," he growled.

"He ain't no more colored nor you or me," Juanita said stoutly.

"You just can't face it, can you?" he sneered. "Any gotch-eyed idiot can tell, just by looking at him! He's got colored blood, and they damn sure ain't going to be no colored blood in my family. It's just by the grace of God they ain't had no kids. Probably be black as a coal post stove!"

It was an old argument; they both knew their lines. It was the other game they played: Otho insisting, Juanita denying, and thus reassuring him. He didn't have to listen to know what she would say next.

"Perry Johnson don't have an ounce of colored blood in his body! He's got manners better'n any Carnes and he's got looks and brains, too. Look at how far he's gone already!"

He was pacified, but the rules of the game required that he finish his part. "What's so damn special about bein' caretaker of somebody else's property! There's no honor in that."

She was deviating from her part. "Honor ain't everything, you old toad! If you'd ever come over with me to see them, you'd know. Propane stove in the kitchen and an indoor bathroom and rugs on the floor. And a cooler in the window. I'd say that's better'n your precious honor!"

Otho was stung by that. Women set such store by things

around the house. His rancor at his son-in-law flamed anew. "Well, if he ain't a nigger, why'nt he prove it? Where'd he come from? What does Ada Sue know about him? They's a lot of things more important than a goddam bathroom, I ganny!"

Juanita was through talking. She whipped Otho's wet clothes with renewed vigor, jabbing them sharply against the pointed boards of the fence. The conversation had taken such a hopeful turn when they had talked of selling the dog to Blackie. But somehow he always got the better of her, diverted her onto something else so that he had an excuse for not getting up out of that chair.

Otho viewed his domain with satisfaction. Only one thing was missing. "Go in yonder and fetch me my Red Man," he commanded.

Juanita grinned triumphantly and sent a mouthful of tobacco juice spinning his way. "Reckon you'll have to go into town sooner'd you thought," she said. "I done chewed the last bit!"

Too bad about Otho and his Red Man. For his first part in the tragedy was in being gone when he was needed most.

18

THREE-QUARTERS of a century before Pavlov gained international acclaim for his delineation of conditioned reflexes, the stimulus of the mere mention of the name Moseley was already producing a response of awe and deference among inhabitants of East Texas. Zebedee Moseley was possibly the most illustrious citizen ever to settle in that land. A war hero and statesman, he accumulated extensive land holdings during his long and eminent life. The fact that subsequent generations squandered his fortune and did, in several instances, step over the line onto the wrong side of the law, could not dispel the mental genuflection of Clarington folk toward a Moseley.

The father of Ernestine Tolliver, of Tolliver Bros. Dry Goods, was overjoyed by her choice of a mate. And if her mother was less than enthusiastic about the prospect of her daughter's assuming a monastic living standard, Grady Tolliver quickly squelched her. ("He's a Moseley, don't forget.

She'll never do better than a Moseley. One day she'll inherit half of what's ours, and your grandchildren will be named Moseley!") So, on the tenth of April during her senior year in high school, Ernestine Tolliver became the bride of Colton (Coy) Zebedee Moseley with her brother Joe Billy as best man. The happy couple moved into two rooms which Grady Tolliver converted into a temporary apartment on the back side of his house. For fourteen years now it had been their home.

Ernestine was still on the telephone on the tenth of June when Coy unloaded the last case of booze from the back of the station wagon. It was always a tough job, having to be executed in total darkness with the greatest stealth.

"Lot of help you've been," Coy growled, kicking the door to. "You could of at least held the door open."

His wife frowned and held a forefinger to her lips. "Oh, that's just Coy, back from a trip to Kingston," she said into the telephone. "Thanks for the invitation, Doris Jean. We wouldn't miss this show for anything!"

"Miss what?" Coy asked as she hung up the receiver. "And listen! What do you mean, telling Doris Jean where I've been?"

Coy and Ernestine both lived all these years under the delusion that no one knew about his "sideline." Otherwise, neither of them could have held up a head in public. She followed him now into the bedroom and watched him secret the last case in the closet under an old rug.

"I didn't tell her why you were there," she said. She plopped down on the bed, grumbling: "The stuff is pushing us out of the house. One of these days my mama's going to wander in here and go poking around—"

"Wish that was the only thing I had to worry about!" He stood back and eyed his handiwork, then placed the suitcase which he used for deliveries in front of the rug-draped booze.

Running his hand over his bullet head, he sat down heavily beside her. "Notice what a light load I brought back this time? Pretty soon they ain't going to *be* any bootlegging business!"

He lit a cigarette and stretched out full length on the bed. She watched for a while as his cigarette ash grew precariously long, but she said nothing. Coy could be so touchy about things. Explosive, sometimes.

"Times is changing, Ernestine. Nowadays, half the niggers in niggertown has got a car, and a lot of jigs are getting into the act." He got up and stepped to the doorway of the closet-of-a-bathroom and sent the half-smoked cigarette spewing into the toilet. Ernestine sighed in relief.

He walked over to the one pair of double windows in the small room and stared out into the backyard morosely, shoving his hands deep into the pockets of his tailor-made trousers. It would be nice to look out a window into a *front* yard, for a change. "I've lost some of my best customers," he said. "Chocks I been hauling for ever since I started! And the pity is, if I try to lower my prices and undersell my competition, those damn niggers just keep on sticking together. Gradually they're squeezing me out."

She picked at a tuft of chenille and offered cautiously, "You could always quit—and get a full-time job somewhere."

Coy frowned, pondered the possibility. "I think the best thing," he said slowly, "would be to take to the woods. There's still a big market up in the hills, if a fellow wanted to go to the trouble to fish out the ones who're not making their own. Say! You being sarcastic with me?" He wheeled on her viciously, but she presented a placid smile as she busied herself smoothing the bedspread.

Reaching atop the old chiffonier, he tossed a sheaf of envelopes on the bed. "Because if you are, here's about twenty good reasons why they ain't no salaried job in this town—

including the one your old man offered me—that'd cover these bills! Times is getting harder all the time. I just heard they're thinking of raising the green fee at the club."

She'd heard it all before. It wasn't the time to mention the fur stole. Daddy would get it at market for cost, anyhow. She gathered the bills in a neat pile and stacked them again on the chiffonier, the same placid smile on her round little face. It was time to change the subject.

"I know who put sugar in Jennings' gas tank: George Bob and John Tom and them. And that's not just hearsay. Blanche heard George Bob admit it to Blackie," she said.

Coy shook his head and whistled slowly. "Well, I'll be— Man, that's bad! I bet Blackie feels like hell about it. Where does he get off telling a damn hothead like George Bob everything that Blanche tells him? Damn! To ruin a man's car like that and not even know for *sure* he's guilty!"

"Oh, he's guilty, all right," she said. "If Blanche tells it, you *know* it's so."

She turned to arrange her bangs in the mirror, a puzzled frown creasing her brow. "Joe Billy's up to something. Wonder what it is?"

"How's that?"

"Doris Jean just called up and invited us to a dinner party Friday night. She said Joe Billy *insisted*, even though she's dog-tired and hasn't been feeling too well lately." She looked at her reflection thoughtfully. "Do you suppose she's pregnant?"

He thought about this. "Not unless Joe Billy's found a customer for a black market baby."

She shot him a killing glare. "Watch it, big shot! That's my brother you're talking about!"

"Hell, you're the one that said he was up to something, not me!"

She was pensive. She was no fool: Joe Billy *was* up to some-

161

thing. Thought he was so clever, getting her to find out what she could about Leah. Not that she minded, because she was curious herself. And there definitely was something to find out. Her instincts told her so. He wasn't the only Tolliver with brains.

"He may be planning some sort of confrontation," she mused. "Joe Billy loves to be dramatic!"

Coy snorted. "Well, if Jennings *ain't* an integrationist—and knowing him all my life, I find that hard to swallow—I just hope he never finds out how all his friends were so anxious to believe the worst about him. Ernestine, I don't ever want to catch you talking about this to anybody—until we get the straight of it."

With raised eyebrows and closed eyes, her mouth set in a prim, expressionless smile which deepened the dimples in her full cheeks, she said haughtily, "People who do things they oughtn't to can expect to get talked about!"

"Oh yeah?" he gibed. "You've kind of moved over to the other side of the fence since high school, haven't you? Have you forgotten who was three months' pregnant when she got married?"

She clamped a pudgy hand over his mouth. "Shut up! Do you want everybody in town to know?" She slammed the closet door shut and stalked out of the bedroom. He followed her into the kitchen, his face mirroring derision as he watched her rattling pans.

"Yeah, you're mighty anxious to condemn *somebody* in that Palmer household of being a nigger-lover. But you didn't think niggers were so bad, did you, when you went to that nigger abortionist?"

She turned on him, a mountain of grief welling up in her blue saucer-eyes. "I panicked, I told you! And you see what he did to me, don't you? He ruined me! Ruined!" She ran from

162

the room sobbing loudly, and he heard her bang and lock the bathroom door.

Brokenly, he dropped into a kitchen chair, mist clouding his own vision as he picked at a piece of peeling white paint on the table. "Well, you didn't have to go," he whispered. "The baby would of had a name. And talk would of died down. And now there'd be somebody to carry on the family name . . . maybe a son . . . Now there'll never be another Moseley."

The monstrousness of such a tragedy, the death of the Moseley name, must finally be faced. He brought his fist down so hard on the table that the saltcellar bounced off onto the floor. They had avoided the subject all these years. He wondered how he could have kept, all this time, from finding that so-called "doctor" abortionist and castrating him—then slitting his ugly black throat.

And if not his, then some other black bastard's!

"I'm going to get me a coon someday, if it's the last thing I ever do," he muttered. "One less jig in the world would never be noticed, anyhow."

Coy was prophetic about the first part: it would be the last thing he ever did. But he was wrong about the world. The eyes of the world were on Clarington almost as soon as it happened.

Part 2

Leah's Vengeance

19

SUMMER CAME on hard in 1960. By the twelfth of June, the day the murder was conceived, the spring rains had long since seeped through the East Texas clay, leaving the earth in cracked tiles which children loved to pry loose and chuck at one another. The sluggish streams were even more constipated, choked with layers of moss which collected around the trunks of trees growing on marshy bank. The sun pressed down hard, and you could feel the pressure. Only the giant pine seemed impervious to the heat, thrusting up past the closeness to reach a free breath.

Clarington seemed smaller in summer because the foliage grew up and covered the town. The redbud trees met over the brick paving, making dark tunnels of the streets. Main Street took on a wan, deserted look, and even down by the courthouse most of the sitters moved indoors. The late-leafing big oaks in front of the Methodist church dwarfed the only dome in town, making it seem somehow insignificant.

It was a tolerable-sized congregation for the second Sunday

after school let out. Around the corner at the Baptist church, they drew a good crowd year round. But the Methodists generally lived up to their name "backsliders" once school let out.

The air was soft early, for a light sprinkle had fallen just before church time, giving Brother Willoughby inspiration for an opening remark about how the whole town "has been baptized this glorious Sunday morning." Then the sun came out and the landscape steeped in its own juices.

That was the day the murder was conceived.

"Conceived by the Holy Spirit . . ."

Leah stood in the choir loft, her narrow, taut face impassive as she chanted the Apostles' Creed by heart. After the anthem she could settle back to sort things over. And study her victim, sitting about midway back on the left-hand side.

Possibly she wasn't completely serious in the beginning. Probably it was only an idle game. Like as not she figured there was another way out at first. Certainly it had seemed the only way during the night, when she had lain there seething, staring wide-eyed into the dark, gripping the damp mattress to keep from flopping around and waking Jennings. But she had known it was only the night; things would be better by day.

"suffered under Pontius Pilate . . ."

How much suffering, do you suppose, makes murder justifiable? She reckoned it a cumulative thing and not all inflicted by one person. Actually very little by any one person, really. It was just such a crushing weight, even when she was little— especially when she was little. Her sigh was heaving, broken, hidden by the chant of voices.

"Was crucified . . ."

My God, yes. Forever crucified. All my life.

She was a small woman by anyone's standards. She had long legs, but she was still tag end on the front row of the

168

choir. And not just short. She was slender. Small bones. Beautiful bones, Jennings used to say.

"Christ, what a model you'd make if you'd been born a foot taller!" he told her once.

Smaller than almost everybody. No physical match for an adversary.

She pictured a shotgun blast going off in the face, just exploding away flesh and bones and spattering blood in every direction. She supposed Jennings had a gun. Of course, she would have to learn to load and fire it. Besides, there might be a struggle. She might be overpowered.

And then she would be caught and tried. And everyone would know and her life would go up in smoke, and even Jennings' practice would be ruined.

No. No one would blame him. "He should never have married a girl from up north," they'd say. And he would be excused. They would feel sorry for Jennings.

Father Richard had said, "God is just, Leah Marie." And then he had given her the royal screw.

She used to wonder what Jennings would do if he ever found out. At first she believed that later, sometime after they had made love and felt very spiritually attuned, she would tell him and he would chuckle and hold her close and tease her for supposing it would make a difference.

But he had been different in St. Louis. Since he'd come home, he'd settled in, gradually. Back in the old familiar rut. He'd slipped back down into the primordial ooze.

"We can leave this place and go far away," he might say. "We can start all over someplace where it doesn't matter."

No. That wouldn't be the way it would be.

Besides, when were they ever spiritually attuned after making love?

Anyway, whoever named it "making love"?

A car accident, maybe. A hit-and-run accident.

Absurd! What was she supposed to do? Sit out on Pecan Street with the motor running, just waiting? That might take forever, and she had so little time. Besides, some people survive car accidents.

The organist had begun the anthem intro. The choir director raised her hands.

"Oh love, that wilt not let me go . . ."

What kind of love would make you turn your back on family, on roots, on church? When she was small, she used to dream the dream, used to sit on the wooden steps of the slate-blue frame row house and look up past the tacky roofs and the coal-smoke-covered buildings and watch the clouds and the blue, always the blue. Bright promise somewhere in the blue, away from the particles of coal soot. Just love. No faces, no handsome prince, no people at all. Just romance. She was in love with love, faceless love. Bliss, forever bliss.

"I have a boyfriend, Mama," she had said on her last visit. Not, "I'm married." But Mama had known. Beautiful Mama, now grown shabby and shoddy. Those piercing black eyes had burrowed into her soul and had seen.

"Is he good to you, babe?"

Leah had nodded and lowered her eyes, so Mama would not look into her heart anymore. "He is better than good," she had said, and Mama had let her go. Mama had drawn her new baby to herself and Leah had looked upon his yellowness and had felt revulsion, and she had gone.

"I'll be in Chicago," she had lied. "I'll call you from time to time." And she had meant that. But Mama knew. Maybe Mama loved her, after all. She didn't say, "You're going to pass," but she let on like she didn't know. She let her go. It was like a funeral. Mama let them take the body away.

Stabbing with a butcher knife. It used to be a common method back in the ghetto.

Battering with a cast-iron skillet.

170

The shotgun blast. Back to the shotgun, pieces of skin flying ...

Slitting the throat, blood gushing.

A hypodermic needle! A syringe full of something lethal that she could steal from Jennings' office ...

Oh, sure. Just walk up and say, "Stick out your arm so I can give you a shot."

How do you get *close* enough to somebody to commit murder?

She was weak and trembly when the anthem was over. The bottom had dropped out of her blood sugar level. It takes tremendous reserves of strength to hate so much.

A wire twisted around the neck.

Suffocation with a pillow. No, there would be a struggle. Always a struggle.

Poison. Arsenic. Used to, you could buy it at the drugstore. "I've got a red ant bed," she could say. Or rat poison. She had seen it at the grocery store. Wouldn't have to say anything. Just put it in the basket and march out through the checkout stand ... But then what? A dinner party? But then everybody would know. A drink at a public place? She could slip it into the coffee. But how much? It might taste funny. They only do that in the movies.

It is not easy to murder. She never knew that before.

Drowning. Ridiculous! The whole world could swim better than she. But then, there weren't many pools in the tenements' backyards where she grew up. And there was no pool at Saint Agnes. What chance had she ever had to learn?

She remembered last summer, her first summer in Clarington. A party at Tolliver's lake house. Drinks out on the redwood deck. And skimming along the water in the magnificent boat. Stopping in the cove for a swim. How could she admit to them, "I can't swim"? Then there would have been questions, lots of questions. So she had almost drowned.

She had hated the man who saved her life that day—for somehow knowing about her.

Still, it had been her idea to stop at his cabin on the way home. "I never got a chance to thank the man," she had told Jennings.

A spindly-legged red-haired woman had opened the screen a crack and heard them out before she summoned the man. "I wondered how come he come in soppin' wet," she had said.

Leah had stammered her thanks but he never looked her way, only addressing Jennings in monosyllables. But she was more certain than ever. *He knew.* And by then, of course, she knew why he knew.

Now her pulse throbbed in her throat just as it had that night coming home from the lake. Drowning was out.

Pastor Willoughby was reading the scripture.

> "In the path where I walk
>   they have hidden a trap for me.
> I look to the right and watch,
>   but there is none who takes notice of me;
> No refuge remains to me,
>   no man cares for me . . ."

She looked over the congregation, saw the upturned faces of Joe Billy and Doris Jean, of Coy Moseley and of Blanche Carnes. They are all his friends, she thought.

What am I doing here, anyway? In this place, in this town, in this life? So naive. To believe that finding Jennings was the beginning of finding my good, the act of a benevolent, intervening God. I've got to get out of here.

"Will you come forward during the singing of our closing hymn?" Brother Willoughby said finally. "Will you come?"

Leah Palmer rose and opened her hymnal to number 52,

"Just As I Am." As she raised her eyes to the congregation, she allowed herself the delicious luxury of one last look at her victim.

Their eyes met, and she smiled.

Dorothy Johnson fanned herself languidly with a limp cardboard fan which read "Compliments of Jackson Funeral Home. Sympathetic Attention in Your Hour of Need." Jackson Funeral Home was the only colored funeral home in Clarington, and the Mount Ebenezer Baptist Church was proud to count Attaway Jackson, the richest man in the county, as its member. From her place in the choir loft, Dorothy could tell that Brother Jackson was growing more and more restless. He had announced earlier that he had an important matter to discuss with the congregation at the end of the sermon, and at twelve thirty it looked as if the sermon would never end.

Dorothy loosened her collar and wiped her sticky neck with a tan palm. She was sure it was hotter in the choir loft than anywhere else in the steaming little church. The acrid smell of warm flesh filled her nostrils. If Brother Griggs didn't quit soon, she was sure that she would wet her pants.

The preacher had long since removed his coat, and now his white shirt was plastered to his stout back. Now he paused to pour himself another glass of water from the big pitcher on the table beside the lectern, and to mop his glistening head. But Dorothy knew, as did they all, that he was far from finished. For the topic of the sermon this morning was money, and Brother Griggs had already promised that he would preach until "every man, woman and child in this room lays a offering of cash on this here altar!" For emphasis, he banged the lectern with a broad fist.

That had been over an hour ago, and so far, only a sprinkling had come forward with an offering. Dorothy sighed. She

173

recalled that following the last money-raising sermon, the benediction had been pronounced at a quarter to three o'clock.

"Now you may be sayin'," he went on, " 'What for do we need money?' " He strutted the platform, imitating his flock. He was very good, Dorothy would have to admit.

"That's right!" from the congregation

". . . when the Lord has blessed us with the finest church on the hill!"

"Amen!"

"Given to the glo-ory of God by our distinguished Brother Jackson—" His baritone had taken on a rich vibrato.

"Amen, brother!" The congregation loved it.

"—who single-handed—" He was almost singing now.

"Yeah, brother!" And the crowd was providing the beat.

"—put this magnificent roof over our head!"

"Hallelujah!" It was a symphony, and they were swept away.

The portly gentleman in an expensive black silk suit nodded in acknowledgment from his front row pew.

"Yes, brethren," Reverend Briggs challenged, pointing a menacing finger at his flock, "I hear you out there 'amening' but I don't see you coming up this aisle with no offering!"

"Amen," came the voices of those few who had already come forward.

"I'm talking to you, Brother Morris, for the sin of omission is just as great as the sin of commission."

"Amen!"

"Oh, my brethren, don't be the Devil's willing tool no more!"

"Amen! No more!"

Brother Morris, his eyes blazing in indignation, jumped to his feet, his slender, long-boned hands clutching the pew back in front of him. "Brother Griggs, I resent you calling me the Devil's tool!"

"Amen!" said the crowd, out of habit.

"Respect the cloth, brother!" said Griggs.

"The day I get white folks' wages is the day I'll walk up this aisle!" Luther Morris had fallen into the singsong naturally.

"Amen! Hallelujah! Yes Lord! That's right!"

All over the room men had jumped to their feet, and Dorothy felt swept forward, the way she always did during a revival. She felt a surge of pride, of unity, a sort of patriotism.

Encouraged by their response, Luther Morris drew his slim, lofty frame up taller and turned around to face the people.

"Give me white folks' pay to spend on white folks' goods!"

The rhythm was broken as the men went wild, cheering, jeering. But the women looked on, wondering, doubting, fearing. Near the back sat the five generations of Winona Strong, her daughter, her granddaughter, her great-granddaughter, who was only fourteen, with her own newborn baby cradled in her child arms—and Winona not yet sixty herself. Dorothy knew what apprehension lurked in Winona's heart. Times could get hard, and talk was not cheap. Talk was dangerous.

There was a general shushing as Attaway Jackson rose slowly, deliberately, and stepped upon the dais. His pretty little wife beamed proudly in the choir's direction and she caught Dorothy's eye as if to say, "Everything will be all right now." Dorothy sighed, relieved.

"Preacher," he began in his rich commanding bass, "I think the good Brother Morris is missing the point of your fine sermon. He is overlooking the fact that he don't have no education for no big paying job. He done forgot that in the Lord's eyes, his tithe is just as important as mine, or as Mist. Tolliver's or Miss Agnes Crenshaw's or any other white man's."

The crowd had reluctantly seated and now murmured its approval. But Luther Morris still had his honor to defend.

"I ain't overlooking the fact that what I make mowing lawns don't hardly feed my family, Brother Jackson," he retorted, "much less leave any left over for building no fine church building."

"Amen to that, brother!" boomed a voice from the back. The crowd turned to see poor, sick Buck Johnson lifting his girth heavily from a back pew. Dorothy caught her breath. It was bad on Buck's heart to get so worked up. She looked at Pearlene and it seemed to her that her mother's lips were moving, as if in prayer, as she jiggled Dorothy's baby on her fat knees.

"It be easy for you to preach at us, Brother Jackson," Buck challenged, "being's how you done got more money than all the rest of us put together. But I'd like to see you tithing on what most of us has got!"

"You makes enough to afford a bottle every Saturday night, brother!" roared the almost-forgotten preacher. The crowd stirred uneasily. Dorothy couldn't meet Mrs. Jackson's eye.

The crowd seemed cowed and looked expectantly to Buck. The sweat was running in rivulets down each side of his face. Pearlene reached up to take his hand, to pull him down beside her, but he waved her off. "I don't rightly know how you got your education, Brother Jackson, but you know and I know that they ain't none of the rest of us but had to work hard all our lives—since we was kids, even—"

"Yeah!" bellowed Luther. "Let the white folks pay us a living wage and we wouldn't *have* to take our boys out of school!"

There was scattered applause. Dorothy squirmed uneasily.

"Amen to that, brother!" boomed Buck. "And give us some decent schools—"

The tension was mounting. Even Winona Strong was fidgeting.

"Amen!" came a shrill woman's voice. "Let our children go to the same schools as the whites!"

The crowd roared and the pianist struck up with "Jesus Loves the Little Children." The congregation sprang to its feet, singing, clapping hands, stomping. Dorothy couldn't stop herself. She was both laughing and crying, for some reason.

". . . all the children of the world, red and yellow, black and white, they are precious in His sight, Jesus loves the little children . . ."

Attaway Jackson leaped to the pulpit and raised his hands. "Please! Listen! Sit down! Everybody! Sit down!"

The crowd obeyed, reluctantly, as Attaway Jackson pulled a long envelope from his inside coat pocket. A hush fell over the room, and people forgot the heat and leaned forward expectantly.

"As you all know, next Sunday is Juneteenth," he said.

"Amen!" burst out all over the room.

"Naturally, we've all been making our usual plans for celebrating Emancipation Day. But as president of the Negro Chamber of Commerce of Clarington, I have a letter here from Mr. Gaylord P. Jones, president of the National Institute for Racial Equality—"

The crowd gasped in awe.

"—and he suggests that we ought not celebrate Juneteenth this year."

This time the crowd gasped in dismay. There was general grumbling, and Dorothy knew that Buck was thinking about the truckload of liquor he and her brother Leroy planned to sell. She herself had a date with Otis to the picnic.

Attaway Jackson raised his hands again. "First off, June nineteenth ain't the date of anything. Not the day of the Emancipation Proclamation, and not the day the war ended.

177

It's only the day when the slaves found out they were free, is all."

Buck Johnson's voice boomed from the back. "You ain't free until you know you is!"

"That's right! Amen!" said the crowd.

"Besides," Attaway went on, "if we aim to be equal someday, we have to quit calling attention to the fact that our people were once slaves. So I hereby suggest we cancel our usual picnic at Booker T. Washington Park."

"No way! Not our only holiday!" The crowd was angry, many of them on their feet, shaking their fists.

Attaway raised his voice, bellowing above the din. "All right! I guess it's too late now to change this year's plans. But this National Institute for Racial Equality is trying to help us all. They done made a study of the thing, and this is what they say. So how many votes with me not to have no more Juneteenths after this?"

Reluctantly, one by one, hands rose throughout the room, but there were mutterings from every side. One woman cried out, "Ought to be a national holiday, anyway!" Several murmured in agreement, but gradually the crowd settled down.

Jackson nodded in satisfaction. "Good! Then, since this is goin' to be the last Juneteenth, let's make it the best!"

They yelled and cheered for a long time, and Attaway Jackson let them spend themselves. Then he raised his hands again, his large diamond rings glittering in the false light.

"And now, brethren, I think it'd be a good idea if we wouldn't take no more of our good pastor's time. He done preached a fine sermon, but he done run out of anything to say a good while ago, so I think it'd be a good idea if all you good people who ain't yet come forward to lay an offering on the altar would do so right now. And if you ain't prepared to offer no cash this mornin', I think I and the other deacons could be waitin' down front here to take your written pledge

178

that you'll pay somethin' out of next month's earnings. Can we have a little music, please, while the congregation steps forward?"

The pianist struck a chord, and Dorothy rose with the rest of the choir to sing "We Shall Overcome." Dorothy was aware of a new coursing of proud blood against her temples. And she was relieved when Buck stepped reluctantly out into the aisle and followed Luther Morris to the altar.

20

Sometimes I feel like I want to go home,
Sometimes I feel like I want to go home,
Sometimes I feel like a motherless child,
A long ways from home, Lord,
    a long ways from home.

Had he seen him in time, Perry Johnson would have avoided
meeting Frank Ramsey. But the thick underbrush along the
winding back road made it impossible to see another car coming around the bend until he'd already crossed the cattle
guard. As was the custom, Perry pulled his old blue Buick to
one side to let the landowner pass. But when Frank drew even
with him, he braked his pickup and leaned out the window to
shake hands.

   Perry didn't like to admit to himself that he was ashamed to
be seen coming here. It wasn't that he didn't like Frank,
whom he'd known all his life—played with as a kid. But with
Frank, as with any of the other people with whom he'd grown

up, he felt himself slipping back into the old niche and assuming once again the old ways.

But he was compelled to come. Ever since that day in the doctor's office, when he had seen the receptionist slip his card into the file behind one marked Johnson, Pearlene. He had stood there a long moment, wanting to ask the receptionist, but of course he could not.

"How're you doin', Perry? Haven't seen you in years."

"Wellum doin' all right, Mist. Frank." Perry fell easily into the old vernacular. "Heard you was back runnin' the place now."

"Yeah, after a fashion. You forget a lot about farmin' when you're away for a while. Sure could use a good hand. What're you doin' these days?"

Perry was no good at lying. He would have to trust Frank. "I'm workin' about forty mile from here over east of town out at Tolliver's Lake. Caretaker."

"Gettin' paid good?"

Perry nodded. "Wellum pretty good."

"Enough so I couldn't entice you away?"

Perry paused. "I got a wife now, Mist. Frank." And he could see that Frank understood the situation.

"Oh. Sure. Reckon I couldn't pay you enough to support a wife. But if you ever change your mind . . ." He never would, they both knew. Frank put the pickup in gear. "Give my regards to your family. Oh. Say!" He cut off the engine, maybe to emphasize the importance of what he was about to say. "See if you can't do something about that situation up there."

Perry felt his heart skip a beat as apprehension swept over him. He waited, but he couldn't ask. He didn't want to know.

"The place is a pigsty."

Perry felt his face grow hot, his heart pound. He swallowed and gripped the wheel. "Wellum yessir."

"See if you can get them to clean it up a little."

"Wellum all right."

"Well, be seein' you, Perry." Ramsey started the motor and rode off in a cloud of dust, leaving Perry trembling with long-forgotten rage.

At length he shifted the Buick in gear and jogged the remaining half-mile through the ragged scrub to the house. Frank was right, unfortunately: the place stunk. Memories flooded in as the smell filled his nostrils. Memories of days before they had any indoor plumbing, before Mist. Rade Ramsey ambled by that day with young Frank beside him.

"We're goin' to have to get these niggers some piped-in water and some indoor plumbin' else they're liable to run off all the quail and possum," he had joked.

The very large, very black man lolled on the porch in a leaning wicker rocker. Buck had put on even more weight since Perry'd seen him last. He couldn't be much help to Frank Ramsey anymore. More than likely he never worked at all, anymore.

Buck squinted, then, recognizing him, hailed him amiably. Buck never made any distinction between any of the children, but then it was doubtful that he even remembered anymore which ones were really his own.

The sound of Perry's car seemed to bring people out from every direction. Two dusty, barefoot children appeared from the thicket, and three older ones darted from the side of the house. They ranged in shade from black to tan, but Perry noted with satisfaction that none of them was as bright as he. He parked very near the front porch and got out.

"Hey, Buck, is Momma about?"

"She workin', boy. Up at the big house."

Perry turned to Reeona, who by this time must be about twenty years old. He looked her over. "Why you let Momma do housework?" he demanded. "Why you not up there, instead?"

Reeona let out her usual high-pitched shriek. "I worked all blessed mornin'! Done the housework and the ironin'! Then I come home and Momma went up there to help Mrs. Ramsey do some cannin', is all!"

Buck chuckled. "Don't worry none. These girls ain't goin' to let your momma do housework. She done work her last job. She don't never go up to the big house no more, else it's for the cannin'. Can't nobody do cannin' like your momma."

Dorothy came out on the porch carrying a baby which she handed over to Reeona. Perry looked over his sister in disgust. "That your baby?"

Buck spat off the porch. "That's Reeona's. She got three now and never be married yet."

"What I want with a husband?" Reeona whined. "Woman's got to have children, but she ain't got to put up with no man."

"Well, put him down and go up to the big house and take over your momma's cannin' and tell her I'm here," Perry commanded.

Reeona handed the child back to Dorothy, who protested mildly and then disappeared into the house through the sagging screen door. Perry settled himself on the porch step and called to the children who were crawling all over his car.

"You kids get off of there! And come here. I got somethin' to say."

They scampered over obediently to their uncle. Perry wrinkled his nose.

"Don't nobody ever make you all take a bath?"

They tittered and Buck guffawed. Perry glared at Buck.

"I mean, man, the whole place stinks. Smell like white trash."

Buck spat again and pulled himself up in his chair. "Who you callin' white trash, boy?"

"Ain't callin' nobody white trash. Except that's how it smell."

Buck bristled. "Well, you don't smell like no gardenia bush. Talk about smellin' like white trash, you the one!"

Perry colored and dismissed the subject. He got up and walked around the dirt-packed yard. Then he returned to the porch and touched a wringer washing machine which stood near the end of the porch. "I see you got a washin' machine."

"Yeah," Buck replied, once more amiable. "It come from the big house. Mrs. Ramsey be gettin' a new one. We goin' to connect it up one of these first days."

"And a clothesline!" said Perry, noticing for the first time the shiny new poles strung with wire which stood at the side of the house.

"Mist. Frank done put that up, him and Leroy," Buck said proudly. "He come up here and say, 'You wash them clothes and get them nice and clean and then hang them across a rusty bobwire fence.' Your momma, she so tickled, she want to put it right in front, but Mist. Frank say put it around back. So she put it right in between." Buck leaned back, puffing. It was a long speech, for him. It worried Perry to see him so winded.

Perry peered in through the screen door. "Where 'bouts is Leroy?" Referring to his younger half brother.

"Leroy done got him a good payin' business. Me and him we in it together." Buck squared his shoulders and shot a zinger through his teeth.

Perry narrowed his eyes suspiciously. "How's that?"

"He use the pickup to haul beer and pay me rent on the pickup."

"You mean bootleggin'?"

Buck nodded, his round face breaking into a wide grin which showed his new false teeth. "Got him a passel of good customers, too. Make maybe twenty, thirty dollar every weekend."

Perry thought this over. "Where 'bouts is he at today?"

"He done took the pickup and light out for Kingston. Fillin' orders. Used to, he had to collect in advance, but business be so good now, he use his own money." Buck chuckled. "Appears like he be runnin' Mist. Moseley clean out of business!"

Perry kept clear of town, but he went in often enough to know that Coy Moseley, the last of a long line of hotheads, had the bootlegging business all sewed up. And nobody messed with a Moseley, especially nobody colored. He was about to tell Buck that, when he said, "Here be your momma now."

Perry turned to see Pearlene laboriously making her way up the tangled path which cut across the field to the big house. Despite her extra weight, she was still pretty at fifty, he thought. Her dusky skin was still unwrinkled, and the soft freckles which peppered her nose gave her an impish look like a child. Her black hair was barely streaked with gray. But he was pained to see how crippled she'd become. He should have gone after her in the Buick. He ran up the path to meet her and hugged her long and hard, feeling a dangerous catch in his throat. It left her gasping and panting, her pale skin growing flushed from the exertion and excitement.

"Lord a'mighty, look at my boy! Just look!" she exclaimed, holding him at her plump arms' length. "Handsome as a movie star, nice-lookin' clothes, big fancy car, whoo-ee!"

He felt embarrassed and scolded her to hide it. "What you be doin', goin' up to the big house for, Momma? Whyn't you let one of the girls do that?"

"Ain't nobody can do cannin' like Momma," Buck repeated. "Come up here on the porch and rest."

Pearlene shook her head, her soft brown eyes gleaming with pride. "I want to talk to my boy alone," she said, opening the screen door and ushering Perry before her. "And besides, I want him to see what I got."

"What you got?" Perry looked around the front room at the familiar old studio couch, an army cot, the same sagging dou-

185

ble bed, several old easy chairs and a television set. On the floor beside the couch stood a large round floor fan. Pearlene pointed to it, beaming.

Perry was impressed. "Where'd you get that?"

"Green stamps. Young Mrs. Ramsey give me a whole stack of books. Two-three hundred, maybe!"

Perry eyed her warily. "More like ten-twelve, more'n likely."

"No, more'n that! Because I had one left over, and look what else I got with it!"

She hobbled over to the wall shelf and took down a bundle wrapped in newspaper. Carefully she unwrapped the paper and drew out a bright red corduroy pillow which she caressed against her large bosom.

"What that be?" he asked.

"It's a sofa pillow," she said, her large dark eyes glistening with pleasure.

Perry snorted and threw up his hands in a gesture which he'd seen Doris Jean use but which he'd never intended to imitate. "What you need with a sofa pillow? When you need dishes and clothes and sheets and everything in the world but a sofa pillow!"

She clutched it to herself harder. "I never had a sofa pillow, leave alone a red one. Can't I have one nice thing before I die?" She looked at it fondly before she rewrapped it in the newspaper and returned it to the shelf.

Perry did not like to hear her talk about death. "Why you not keep it on the sofa? Ain't that the place for sofa pillows?"

Pearlene snorted. "How long you think my sofa pillow be pretty in this house and I keep it out here with this mob of children?" She let herself down heavily on the couch. "Now come over here and sit down by me. You don't never come to see your momma no more. Why you never come home?"

Perry dropped beside her on the sofa and took one of her

gnarled tan hands in his. He pressed a five-dollar bill into her palm. As was her way, Pearlene took no notice of the money. Perry did not come out here to answer questions; he came to ask Momma why she'd been to the doctor. Now he was afraid to ask.

"Since I took this job, I can't get away much. It be about as far on the other side of town as this here place is. Maybe forty mile from here."

"You never bring your wife. You still be stayin' along?"

He nodded and shifted away uncomfortably. Momma had never asked him much about Ada Sue. Maybe she suspected the truth. He almost wanted to tell them sometimes, tell them all. Tell Frank Ramsey. My wife's white as yours, smelly bastard.

"How come you work like that, out in the country? Make more money in town, a handsome boy like my boy!"

"I got my reasons," he said darkly.

Pearlene was as perceptive as any mother about her children, even if her children were grown. She was silent for a while, and Perry could tell she didn't like what she was thinking.

"Son, is that why you taken that job? Are you thinkin' to get even?"

"For all your years of hardship? I never could," he muttered.

Pearlene closed her eyes and shook her head slowly. "Lord, Lord. Will you hold a grudge forever?"

"Maybe not, Momma. Maybe not. Maybe someday I'll settle up," he said.

21

It was ten thirty the following morning when Dorothy answered the telephone at the Palmer residence and summoned Leah. The caller was Joe Billy Tolliver.

"I'm just leaving the house, Joe Billy," she lied. "I have a very important meeting."

A chuckle. "Not as important as this one, I ganny."

Something about his cocksure manner made her throat constrict. She motioned Dorothy out of the room, made certain that she was out of earshot and said quietly, "Look: if you want to talk to me about Jennings, I told you I can't help you influence—"

"Leah," he interrupted, "I don't have time to play games with you. I've got to be in court this afternoon, and I'm soon going to need Jennings' testimony on that Bacon case. Now, better cancel whatever you've got and get on down to my office. I've just received some very interesting mail from St. Louis."

Leah held the receiver from her ear and looked at it dumbly.

Briefly she imagined her world cracking, falling apart and disintegrating into dust. She didn't answer Joe Billy, just hung up the phone. And she went, of course.

He kept her waiting for thirty-seven minutes. She sat in his outer office under the sour scrutiny of Mrs. Blodgett, Joe Billy's secretary. Leah leafed absently through a magazine and simmered.

He's sitting in there with his feet on his desk just wearing me down, she thought.

It was an effective technique. By the time Mrs. Blodgett ushered her into his office, she was a quaking, gelatinous wreck. He observed this and smiled, satisfied. He handed her the letter without ceremony and stood by grinning broadly as she took it. "Have a seat," he said.

She hadn't planned on sitting down until she glanced down at the signature on the letter. Then she put her hand back and almost felt her way to the chair. It was from Sister Fain at Saint Agnes:

Dear Mr. Tolliver:

In answer to your inquiry on behalf of your client, Leah Palmer, I can only tell you that she came to Saint Agnes in late September of 1944 as a fifth-grade student. She graduated in May of 1952. During all that time she had no visitors, I remember well. She was enrolled here by Father Richard O'Mally, who was priest of her mother's parish in St. Louis. She was enrolled as a permanent boarder, a ward of the church. Her full name was given as Leah Marie Evangeline Boudreaux. Much as I would like to help, I am not at liberty to give you the name of her mother or her address, which would do you no good at any rate, because that section of the city has been razed to make way for a freeway. Our only copy of her birth certificate is sealed in a vault and would require a court order to obtain.

It is with great pleasure that I learn that you are representing her interests. I am assuming that it is an inheritance case. Leah was always a favorite of mine, such a quiet little mite with those great sad brown eyes. At that time I was serving as a counselor for our boarding students. Please give her my kindest regards. I hope she remembers me.

Sincerely,
Sister Fain, Headmistress

With trembling hand, she tossed the letter over onto his desk, assuming a bravado which she didn't feel. "What is this garbage about 'representing' me?"

Joe Billy shrugged and walked around behind his desk. Light from the window behind him made it hard to see his features, made her squint to make them out. "In a way, I am representing you, you know. Because if you play my game, you stand to come into a passel of money!"

His cheek! She couldn't believe it! "What is this, Joe Billy? Some cheap attempt at blackmail? What do you think you've got on me, anyhow?"

He leaned over the desk and leered at her, not saying anything, just leering. She dropped her gaze and fidgeted. Still he said nothing. He was a master at suspense.

Finally he said, very softly, very kindly, "Do I have to spell it out, Leah? Have I got to say the words? You're no orphan. You told Ernestine you were an orphan. Is that what you told Jennings, too? Do I have to tell you what you are?"

"You don't know what you're talking about!" she blustered angrily. "Of course I'm an orphan! Doesn't that letter say I—never had—any visitors? Not one." The tears were dangerously close.

He measured her closely for a while and then smiled. "What pretty big, black eyes you have. Sister Fain was wrong about the color, though. They are great, they are sad, but when you are scared, they are black, and the pupils are huge —and frightened, like a cat's. O.K. I reckon I can get a postponement until after the weekend. It so happens that I have an old classmate in St. Louis who's already working on that court order for me. Think I'll run up to St. Louis next weekend and pick it up from him. Then I'll rent a car and drive out in the country toward, say, Saint Agnes. If I find myself nearby, I might drop in. See what Sister Fain could tell me then."

She gasped. "You mean you'd actually go to those lengths— for what? You must be sick!"

Joe Billy shrugged. "O.K., I'll play your game. But to answer your question, 'for what?' We are talking about a million-dollar settlement in a personal injury suit. You know that! Honey, you ain't *seen* the lengths I'd go to for a case this size!"

He came around the desk and grasped both her arms, pulling her to her feet. She tried to pull away, and he tightened his grip. She felt a curious thrill, realizing that she was captive.

"Leah hon, Jennings and I have been friends all our lives. I don't want to spoil that by bringing pressure on him. Fact is, I know him well enough to know he might bow his neck just out of orneriness if I was to pressure him in the usual way. But dad-dang it, I need his testimony! Now, we are going to be living right alongside of each other for a long, long time. Wouldn't it be better if you *persuaded* him to throw in with me without my having to cause hard feelings?"

She struggled against him. "You are crazy, Joe Billy! Turn me loose!"

He released her with upstretched palms in a gesture of surrender. "Have it your way. You'll have time to think it over while I'm gone. We'll see how you feel about it when I get back—and Leah: Doris Jean's a wonderful little woman but sometimes she talks too much. This'll be just between you and me . . . if you cooperate, that is."

She had stormed out the door and slammed it behind her before he finished.

I will kill him stab him stomp him hammer his head to a pulp. I will carve him up in little pieces. I will mutilate him. I will gouge out his eyes with my fingernails.

She drove aimlessly, carelessly, recklessly around the town, thinking, heaving, plotting, berating. Passing the Tolliver house again and again. Eventually she parked across the street and down the block from the house. Doris Jean's car was not there.

". . . During all that time she had no visitors, I remember well. . . ."

I will burn the house down. Oh Holy Mother, why am I so helpless? Give me a weapon give me justice give me peace, peace, dear Blessed Mother.

Luretha stepped out on the front porch with her broom. A sign, thought Leah. God is giving me a sign.

Leah started the car and eased across the street and into the Tolliver driveway. She bounded out of the car and hailed the maid cheerily.

The old woman squinted into the sun, shielded her eyes, then grinned widely in recognition. "Baby Love's not here just now, Mrs. Palmer."

Leah feigned disappointment. Her mind was whirling. "Oh, too bad! I guess I'll call her later. But would you mind if I just come in and use your—telephone, Luretha?" Oops . . . should have said bathroom . . . but no matter.

She was inside before the maid could answer, down the hall and into the master bathroom. She flushed the commode and turned on the water in the lavatory to mask the noise of opening the medicine cabinet. She had no idea what she was look-

192

ing for, but she knew she didn't have long to find it before Luretha finished sweeping the porch.

Her stomach was in knots. Her hand trembled on the handle of the cabinet. What is this doing to me? she thought. I'm a quivering bowl of jelly. I've always been so in control.

Dozens of bottles. Most of them Joe Billy's. Of course! She'd heard him talk about his fabled ulcer. But the dates on most of these bottles were not current. She scanned the labels frantically—was that a car she heard? She held her breath for a full twenty seconds.

She tiptoed to the window, breathing heavily, and cautiously drew the curtain aside. A dry cleaner's truck was pulled up the driveway and its driver had engaged Luretha in a lively conversation. She could hear Luretha laughing. He had bought Leah a few more minutes of time.

Back to the medicine cabinet to search for a bottle with a current date. Her heart was pounding audibly.

Maybe I will die of a heart attack right here on Joe Billy's bathroom floor. That would spoil all his plans, she thought.

For the briefest of moments the prospect of her own death loomed enticingly. It would be so simple. Simpler, by far, than planning someone else's death. Then she glanced at herself in the mirror and saw the face of a person who had fought too long, too hard to survive to give up now.

Then her eyes fell upon what she had been looking for: a prescription dated June 6, 1960. "Joe Billy Tolliver. One capsule three times a day thirty minutes before meals to prevent nausea," it read. It was signed, "Jennings Palmer, M.D."

What now? Send him off to St. Louis with poison. The reflection in the mirror nodded, acquiescing. The "great sad brown eyes" which Sister Fain remembered now glinted at the expectation of sweet retribution. She hardly recognized herself. She almost scared herself.

Let's see . . . (striding up and down before the dressing table mirror) . . . Quiet! Almost forgot where I am. . . . It must not look like murder. Jennings' name is on that label. Must be careful. Death by natural causes. A perforated ulcer. Lye. Yes, lye will do it. Lye in a capsule that dissolves in the stomach, preferably when he's somewhere out on the Flat River Road, miles from help.

Leah clasped and unclasped her hands as her excitement mounted. Maybe there was lye in this very room—but no! It must be done cleverly, carefully, thoughtfully, no mess, no evidence. Home. Go home.

She opened the bottle and took out three capsules, slipping them into her handbag. She was out of the house and into her car in seconds, waving good-bye to Luretha, who was still sweeping the walk. Maybe Luretha would forget to tell Doris Jean she stopped by.

She fairly sang all the way to town. He would be gone . . . Dear God, it was meant to be! Surely he would be taking along a bottle of pills which he'd had only a few days. Yes, it was meant to be. But she must be calculating. Clever. The lye capsule mustn't be the first one on top, or Joe Billy would take it too soon. She must arrange it so that it was, say, third down from the top. Put it in just before he left town. That would be easy to do. At Doris Jean's insistence, Leah and Jennings would be at the Tollivers' on Friday night for dinner. Joe Billy had said he was leaving for St. Louis on the weekend. That would have to be Saturday morning. She could place the capsules back in the bottle easily, arranging them so that Joe Billy wouldn't take the lye capsule until he was miles from Clarington, hopefully on the back road to Saint Agnes. It wasn't as satisfying as strangling him, but it would have to do.

She felt tremendously alive, creative, exhilarated. She viewed the world, experienced it, really, through heightened senses. Downtown was spectacular to her today. It was like stepping into an instant snapshot superimposed on an old tintype.

A string of old Christmas lights circled the clock tower of the century-old courthouse on the square. Beside the Confederate statue stood a once-white signboard listing the fading names of those who lost their lives in World War II. Between the iron hitching posts at the curb, parking meters vied for space. Leah parked near the corner, where she scraped her bumper on the handmade concrete watering trough. This corner of the square was occupied by a smaller building, a two-story box of unpainted stucco with barred windows. A lone figure could be seen looking out an upper cell window.

Maybe he is looking at me and maybe even knowing, she mused. It takes one to know one.

Before she reached the grocery aisle she'd thought of a flaw in her plan. Someone might remember later, if there was an autopsy and the lye showed up, that Mrs. Palmer came in a few days earlier and bought *only* a can of lye. So, although she could hardly bear to take the time, she filled her grocery basket with half a dozen cleaning products and a few groceries. The wait in the checkout line was interminable. But eventually she stepped out into the sun with the precious lye tucked somewhere in her sack of groceries.

The prisoner in the two-story stucco box was still watching. Maybe he knows what I have in this sack, she thought. Maybe he wishes me well.

Once home, she locked herself in the bathroom with the can of lye and a stainless spoon. Taking the capsules from her purse, she opened them carefully and poured their contents down the drain. Then, with sudden calm and deftness, she spooned out the lye and filled each capsule, hardly spilling a grain. Everything must be perfect. She wiped each capsule

195

clean with a tissue before wrapping them all in a tissue and returning them to her purse.

Must remember to take this purse Friday night. Must remember. How silly! She must be getting giddy.

After methodically cleaning the counter of all traces of lye, she took the spoon and the can of lye to the kitchen, where she put both in the trash can.

It is so easy, she thought. I wonder why it isn't done more often? Maybe it is. I wonder why I didn't ever do it before? Never had reason to—or, more precisely, never could narrow it down to one target before. Would have needed a machine gun to mow 'em all down.

Suddenly Leah felt very powerful, like an eighteen-wheeler in the fast lane.

22

Friday, June 17, 1960

I<small>T WAS</small> a terrible, endless evening. Leah was ready and waiting, the fateful purse in hand, long before Jennings had finished shaving. She fidgeted all the way over to the Tollivers' while Jennings told her about his day, something he never did. Fact is, he never talked to her about anything these days. He'd become more preoccupied than ever, although, of course, he had never been one to confide in her, not even in their early days. But tonight it was different. It was talk and more talk. She wondered what it meant.

Joe Billy met them at the door and gave her a questioning look behind Jennings' back. She risked a smile, but it was more in the nature of a grimace.

"Hold everything," she managed to say. He nodded and a triumphant twinkle came into his eyes. She felt reasonably sure she had stalled him at least for the evening.

They were the last to arrive. The Moseleys and the Carneses were probably anxious to get started with the roast, she supposed. Blackie and Blanche were extremely subdued, not unusual for Blanche, but a departure for Blackie. It was almost as if he were embarrassed to be here. Coy had been drinking and was more churlish than ever. Only Ernestine seemed to be in a jubilant mood.

"Leah! Sweet! I heard about your terrible accident! Do you have your house put back together yet?" Ernestine sidled up between them and looped an arm cosily through both hers and Jennings'.

Leah was ready, because she had rehearsed. She gave an airy laugh. "Why, Ernestine, you sound as if you thrive on misfortune! But I know that isn't so. Besides, it was only a little window, and we've forgotten all about it."

Joe Billy came to her aid. "Gosh, yes, Ernestine, can't you think of something cheerful to talk about? We here to have fun! What y'all want to drink this evening? Co-Cola?"

Jennings leaned back expansively and clapped his hands on his middle. "Think I'll have a light Scotch and water, Joe Billy. It looks like it's going to be a quiet night at the hospital."

Leah felt a momentary alarm, some warning, but it was too nebulous to grasp. She let it pass.

Doris Jean was especially subdued. Lost in her own little world, Leah thought. Wonder who she's planning to kill? Still, there was no hostility bristling from Doris Jean; she emanated a sort of serenity which Leah only vaguely detected, it being a quality which she had not, and she envied her.

Joe Billy brought Jennings a Scotch and steered him to a big deep chair. Jennings dropped down and settled in; he was completely at ease. He was with his people. It was obvious to

198

Leah that he didn't connect the hostile acts of the week before with his friends. He was talkative, animated, jovial. Watching from her old spot on the sofa, Leah felt alienated from this Jennings.

Coy had gone to the kitchen to freshen his own drink. When he returned, he stood in the doorway surveying the group with a loutish leer. "Hey, Doc," he said loudly, "been treating any more niggers lately?"

Joe Billy was across the room in less than a second, grabbing the glass from Coy's hand. "Let me freshen your drink, Coy." He bustled out of the room.

"I just did!" Coy protested, following him.

"Glass is dirty," Leah could hear Joe Billy say from the kitchen.

Blanche stirred uneasily and Blackie picked up a magazine from the coffee table and pretended to be very interested. Doris Jean belatedly remembered her hostessing duties and got to her feet.

"I should see if Luretha's about ready," she said, and she left.

Ernestine was crimson, and Leah felt shame for her. She looked to Blanche expectantly, and Blanche came through, bless her.

"How's your tennis game coming, Leah?" she asked.

"Not so good," Leah admitted. "I don't seem to get enough time to practice."

"It takes a lot of practice," said Blanche.

"My, yes," Ernestine put in lamely. They lapsed into silence.

Across the room, Jennings enjoyed his Scotch and had even managed to draw Blackie out of his shell, suggesting a fishing trip soon. What is with this man? Leah thought, so effusive.

Dinner was announced, to everyone's relief except Coy's,

who grumbled that he hadn't finished his drink yet. But Joe Billy told him, "You can bring it with you to the table," with a side wink at Leah. She hoped he had watered it lavishly.

Much of the dinner conversation centered around women's club activities, a proposed fishing trip for the men and Joe Billy's upcoming trip to St. Louis. Everyone was curious as to why he was going.

"Just doing my duty: protecting truth, justice and the American way," Joe Billy joked, not looking at Leah at all.

"Ooo!" Ernestine, doing her Betty Boop imitation, drew her round bow mouth up to match her round blue eyes. "What a great chance for you, Leah! Have you given Doris Jean a list of friends to call?"

"Oh, I'm not going with him," Doris Jean put in quickly. She squirmed in her chair for a moment and then the serene facade returned.

Ernestine looked puzzled. "But I thought you told me you'd be gone this weekend. I *know* you did!"

There was an uncomfortable pause while Doris Jean seemed almost to glare at her sister-in-law. Finally she stammered, "I—am going up to the lake house to—do some cleaning. I need to get out there and air out the place to get it ready for the boys' fishing trip. That's all."

"Aren't you afraid to spend the night alone out there in the woods with all those poachers running loose?" asked Ernestine. "I know *I* would be!"

"Doris Jean's perfectly safe," Joe Billy said. "I've got that good couple up there living on the place who watch out after her every need. Ain't that right, sugar?"

Doris Jean nodded feebly.

The purse was burning a hole in Leah's lap. She was losing her nerve. It wasn't going to happen at all if it didn't happen soon.

Joe Billy's plane was to leave Love Field in Dallas at ten

the next morning, which meant that he would have to drive out of his driveway about six to make it on time. With this in mind, Luretha had kept the meal moving at a steady pace. Time was slipping by dangerously fast.

Conversation lagged from time to time, despite all Joe Billy and Jennings and Ernestine could do to keep it moving. Blanche, of course, was never much help, but Blackie could usually be counted on. Tonight he continued to act cowed all during the meal, bending his head low over his plate and shoveling in the food in a dispirited fashion. Coy was completely irascible, having lapsed into his own small world where he was doubtless plotting black deeds. Or so it seemed to Leah. And Leah: Leah was too keyed up to talk. It was her high moment, and she didn't know whether she'd be able to pull it off. She had stage fright, she supposed.

Ernestine pulled her out of it. "Leah, what in the world is wrong with you? You haven't said two words all night!"

Leah was grateful for the reminder that she must keep up a front. Someone later, after it was accomplished, might hark back to this evening and comment that Leah Palmer had acted peculiar. This would never do. She shook off her apprehension and grinned.

"You're right!" she said brightly. "And I might as well tell you what I've been so preoccupied about: what would you think if I knocked out the wall between my living room and my dining room? Think it would look too open? I mean, ever since I saw Frank and Harriett Ramsey's house, I've wished for one like it!"

Jennings looked aghast, the green peas spilling from his open mouth. She enjoyed, inwardly, his discomfort.

"Gosh, nobody else has seen their house!" Ernestine said. "But let me tell you that a house of *any* kind sounds mighty fine to me." She shot Coy one of her killers.

The conversation took off in the direction of dream homes

201

and decorating, and Leah was off the hook once more. She allowed herself the delicious agony of putting off the moment she'd been waiting for until well into the evening. Finally, when the dessert plates were taken away and they were moving into the living room for a last cup of coffee, she knew the time had come if ever it was to come. She excused herself and made her way down the hallway to the bath adjoining the master bedroom. Through the bedroom doorway, she could see a suitcase opened on the bed. She shut both bathroom doors and sat on the edge of the tub. Now that her moment had arrived, she felt giddy.

This is it: like being in a voting booth. Time to pull the lever, now or never. Time to decide. Death or life. No write-ins. But she knew, really, how she was going to vote all along.

She opened the medicine cabinet slowly so that it wouldn't creak—but the bottle was gone! She felt overcome with a wave of sick dismay until reason returned. Of course, if he was leaving at 6:00 A.M., he would already have packed the pills. They must be in the bedroom. Dare she wander in there? What excuse could she make if she were caught? She squared her shoulders and decided to risk it.

Cautiously she opened the connecting door and tiptoed into the bedroom. It seemed to her that the voices from the living room grew louder—it had to be an illusion. In the light from the open bathroom door she could make out an overnight bag on the dresser. Not daring to turn on the light, she felt around in the case tray until she found the bottle. She took it back into the bathroom and closed the door.

Yes, no doubt about this being the same bottle. It took less than a minute to put the three doctored capsules into the bottle and return it, stealthily, to the case in the bedroom. Then, as an afterthought, she took the bottle out again and wiped it clean with her skirt. It was that extra few seconds that trapped her.

She was just returning the bottle to the case again when the door from the hall creaked slightly. She whirled and gasped to see a man silhouetted in the open doorway.

Oh dear God, let it be anybody but Joe Billy. I could explain being here to anybody else, somehow. She held her breath as he moved inside the room and closed the door behind him. But just before he did, she could see him tuck his elbows close to his waist and give his trousers a hitch. There was no mistaking that gesture. She was trapped by Joe Billy.

Leah's pulse was beating in her eardrums, and yet she didn't fear him any longer. From the light of the open bathroom door, she could see him look around the room and back at her. He had her now. She felt almost relief that she could yield, could surrender, could submit.

"I thought I heard you in here," he hissed. He grabbed her roughly by the arm and pushed her back into the lighted bathroom, closing the door behind them. "What're you up to?"

With his hand upon her, she was completely calm. "Why are you so jumpy?" she whispered. "I thought you saw me signal to you. I motioned for you to follow me." She was astounded at how easy it was to lie when she had nothing to lose in the attempt.

He let go of her arm. "I didn't see you," he said testily.

"I—wanted to—tell you I've—decided to—cooperate. I'll convince Jennings to testify, somehow." In a delayed reaction, she began to tremble, and her insides were quaking. Pray God he doesn't notice, she thought, clasping her shaking hands behind her, willing the tremor to subside.

He relaxed and a victorious smirk lit his boyish face. His eyes traveled down her body, her chest upthrust insolently as she gripped her hands fiercely in back of her. He ran his tongue slowly over his bottom lip. "I knew you would; you're too smart a girl not to. Too bad you decided so late; I'll have

203

to go through with my trip now. Still, it won't hurt to have a little insurance policy. You're quite a gal, Leah." He reached over and tweaked her on the breast. Enraged, she drew back and threw herself at him, her whole self, forgetting all her composure, trying to strike him. But he caught both wrists and held her there, rigidly.

"Don't you ever do that again, Joe Billy Tolliver!" She was gasping now, raging against him, breathing fire. I will strangle this dirty white bastard.

He tightened his hold on her wrists and drew her gradually to him. He was speaking softly now, still talking about his trip being an insurance policy, in case she had a change of heart, but Leah wasn't listening. She was only trying to master herself, to bring herself into control. Don't ruin it now, Leah. In another twenty-four hours he will be a corpse and in another week the maggots will begin to eat out his eyes.

She allowed herself to go limp against him, and it wasn't all bad. He relaxed his grasp and his hands moved along her sides. He was small-boned and spare. It was like letting a girl fondle her. She heard his mirthless chuckle.

"This is more like it. No need to fight me, Leah. What was it Sister called you? Leah Marie Evangeline? I like Evangeline. It has a genitalian ring to it. We're a team now, a winning team." And he tilted her face upward and kissed her roughly, his hands roving her freely. She forced herself to respond, and then found that in spite of herself he had aroused her, had awakened a certain ardor simply by accepting her for what he knew her to be. Then the insanity of their brazenness gripped her and she broke away abruptly.

"We must be crazy!" she whispered. "Somebody will wonder about us." She pushed him through the bedroom door and let herself out the hallway door, straightening her clothing and her hair as she went.

It is over. It is finished. Let this night now end so you can hurry off and die, bleed to death from the inside out, white trash bastard. Tomorrow all will be accomplished and I will bathe, bathe and scrub away the vermin of your touch upon me. And I will hate myself for my weakness, detest myself unto eternity for prostituting my mouth, my mind to you for thirty seconds.

She returned to the living room to find thankfully that the evening had ended, for the Moseleys and the Carneses had already left, and Jennings was waiting in the hallway for her.

"What happened to the others?" she asked Doris Jean.

"I think Blackie must have been sick or something," she said. "He couldn't wait to get out of here, and he hardly said three words all night—did you notice? As for Coy," she wrinkled her nose, "he's got his nose out of joint. Coy gets that way sometimes when he's had a little too much to drink, but it'll wear out by morning."

"Don't drive so fast, for God's sake! Didn't that meal sober you up at all?" Ernestine Moseley laid a hand firmly on her husband's knee. He glanced at the speedometer and let up on the accelerator.

"Hell, I've never been so cold sober in my life! I think Joe Billy must have been watering those drinks; I must've had six or seven, and I never even got a buzz on!"

Ernestine sucked in her breath as he wove dangerously over the yellow line toward the oncoming car. "Watch it! What's the rush, anyway? You broke up the whole party, leaving early like that!"

His head bent low over the wheel, he peered at the road with intense concentration, as if trying to get it in focus. "I've got some business that can't wait until morning," he said, his voice an ominous growl.

205

Ernestine snorted. "Now what? Something to do with your illustrious profession, no doubt! What kind of delivery do you have to make at this time of night?"

"I wish to hell that's all it was," he said. "What happened, see, one of my old regular customers—that jig that owns the colored funeral home—he's having a brawl for Juneteenth, and he so much as told me that if I'd get a case of some kind of domestic champagne that wasn't too high, he'd buy it. Otherwise, I'd never stock the stuff, you know that. You can't move champagne amongst a bunch of coons. Anyhow, I carried three cases out to the funeral parlor this afternoon, and some bird out there said *Mister*—get that: *Mister* Jackson wasn't in, and that he wouldn't be needing my services anymore because he had switched to another goddam dealer!"

He veered sharply around the corner, slamming Ernestine against the door. "Slow down, for Christ's sake! You can't do anything about it now!"

"The hell you say! I'm going to find my jaybird competition and scare the living hell out of him! Teach him to steal my accounts!"

She knew how Coy was. She knew all about his temper, inherited from his grandfather, they said, who'd wound up in prison for shooting a man. He was too much a Moseley, Coy was. He believed all the legends. Thought he was royalty, almost, like folks always felt about the Moseleys. Thought he was indestructible, too. Now she was genuinely concerned. Times were changing. Sometimes the coloreds struck back, these days. Maybe even against a Moseley.

"Oh now, Coy, isn't that just asking for trouble?"

"Naw," he said confidently. "This nigger is nothing but a dumb kid from out in the boonies. He's one of the Ramseys' niggers."

"You're going all the way out *there?*"

"Aw hell no. He hangs out at the Red Roof on Friday and

Saturday nights. Takes his pickup full of hooch and sets up stand right there."

She wished him well, this colored boy. She hoped he cornered the market so that Coy Moseley would stop this crazy traipsing back and forth across the county line and staying out half the night. Still, there was all that money, tied up in champagne . . .

"Well, just the same, I'd feel better if you were taking somebody with you. Blackie, or Joe Billy, or even Jennings."

"Yeah," Coy said wryly, "*especially* Jennings! Ever since he put them two jigs in the hospital, he's got every one of them in town licking his boots!"

He pulled into the driveway, leaned across her and opened her door. "Don't wait up. I ain't coming home until I get me a piece of coon hide."

23

"PERRY? WHAT you doing?" Ada Sue's voice rose above the din and clatter of dishwashing. When she was in the kitchen, it sounded like a herd of buffalo had got loose.

"It's Friday night, ain't it? Fixing to watch the fights, like always."

He flicked on the set. A well-rifled Sears catalog lay atop it. He picked it up and flung it at the living room wall. Damned spendthrift! Her middle name ought to be Gimme. Gimme this and gimme that. He stomped over and shut the connecting door between them.

"Hey!" she yelled. "What'd you do that for?"

"Can't hear thunder," he called back.

She opened the door, leaving soapsuds running down its face. "Well, you'll just have to turn up the sound. It's too hot in here with the door closed."

Frowning, he got up and squatted squarely in front of the television. There was a knot along the line of his jaw where it always was when he'd got a crawful of Ada Sue. He ought to pop her one but it just wasn't worth the wrangle.

Seemed like life was just one big boil that had almost festered to a head. All these aggravations: Ada Sue with her constant demands, Doris Jean with hers. And the unnamed unrest churning inside him which had, somehow, to do with the bright woman he had plucked out of the lake. Envy, maybe, that she was passing so effortlessly. Compulsion, almost, to bring her down, expose her, put her in her place.

Eventually the banging stopped and Ada Sue scuffed into the front room and flopped into the recliner, her long arms flailing out over the chair arms like a rag doll's. Perry didn't take his eyes off the set, but he couldn't seem to concentrate.

"You could of shut that door behind you," he said. "It'd keep out the heat of the kitchen."

"Shut it yourself. I'm too tired to move."

Obediently he got up and shut the door then returned to the couch, leaning forward stiffly, elbows on his knees. Silently they watched television for some fifty minutes. Suddenly the woman snorted and roused herself, got up, clumped over and switched off the set.

"What'd you do that for?" he cried.

"Ain't nothing on but the wrap-up," she said. "You don't care nothing about it and neither do I. We might's well go to bed."

He shrugged and sighed, but got up, locked the door, switched out the lights and followed her into their tiny bedroom. Other than the bathroom, it was the only other room in the house.

She was pulling her housedress off over her head. "Ain't you going to tell me what that phone call was about? I heard it ring whilst I took out the trash, but you never said nothing about it all night."

He skinned off his pants and hung them on a peg behind

the door. "It was the boss. Folks coming up tomorrow. Going to spend the night. That means I'll likely be out to all hours. So you'll probably want to go over to your mother's."

She sighed. "Might's well. I sure ain't going to stay in this creepy place all alone. What I want to know is, why in hell do you have to stay out all night?"

"Got to help with trotlines. That kind of stuff." He went into the bathroom and shut her out.

It wouldn't do to get into a hassle with her tonight. He was resolved to keep peace, and it wasn't just because of the bite, either. Sometimes he was afraid he really would hurt her bad, if he didn't watch himself. He fingered his healing chest gingerly and thought about the woman who had first dressed it at the doctor's office.

"Well, it's funny to me about this job," she hollered. "You told me it would be a soft touch, but seems like every time I turn around they show up, and you wind up practically living over there!"

He came out and she stood before him the way she always slept, bone-bare, her hipbones protruding at right angles from her torso. Usually he avoided looking at her like this, but tonight he took a certain perverse gratification in studying the scaly skin which hung loosely from her angular skeleton. In her stringy, brittle red hair. The too-large feet, the knobby knees. The crepey look of her chicken neck. The space in her mouth where her canine tooth ought to be. He didn't know why, but always on the eve of a rendezvous with Doris Jean, he took a certain pleasure in his wife's complete, total and utter ugliness.

"You know well as I do," he told her. "Most days I don't have to work more'n a couple of hours. Only once in a while is all. Once in a while I have to be out late."

"Oh yeah? Then why you always carting me off to Mama's and leaving me stranded all day?"

210

He didn't answer. Maybe he'd take a bath.

She was turning back the covers, turning her slack rump on him, her sagging breasts dangling loosely over the bed. "Sometimes I think you got some woman, maybe ten different ones."

"Quit your bitching," he retorted. "You got nothing to complain about. You got a nice house and good clothes and a good car to run around in."

She brightened. "You going to let me take the car tomorrow?"

Perry squirmed. "I hadn't figured to. Figured to take you over in the morning and come get you Sunday."

"Why'n't you let me take the car?" she wheedled. "Mama don't never get to town, and I could take her and stay for the church singing Saturday night."

Perry thought about this. Little chance that she would return unexpectedly. "All right. Just so you don't bring it home empty."

She was like a little child, a skinny, ugly, grotesque, hideous child. "I won't," she promised happily. "Guess I'll pack. We got a box?"

He shook his head. He couldn't look at her, skipping around like a damn nitwit. "Why'n't you use a sack?" Yes, maybe he'd better take a bath. He went in and turned on the bathwater. As he stepped into the tub, he thought about Buck's words, "Talk about smellin' like white trash, you the one!" And he scrubbed himself vigorously.

He was still scouring himself fanatically when Ada Sue stormed in on him, her sallow face discolored by two bright flushed spots on her rawboned cheeks. "Somebody taken that five dollars out of the tin box! It was there yesterday mornin', I know, because I looked to see. What'd you do with it?"

He busied himself with his washing. "Why do I have to answer to you?" he asked, not looking up. He wished she would put on some clothes. "It's my money. I earned it, and I can spend a little now and then—"

"A *little*?" she screamed.

"—without having to account to you. Besides," now he looked at her squarely, "what were you figuring to do? Blow it in town tomorrow behind my back?"

"I wasn't going to blow it, no. But I did think it'd be nice to have a little change along." Her eyes narrowed as she tried to recollect the day before. "Where'd you go yesterday afternoon, anyways? What'd you do with that money?"

Perry splashed noisily but ignored her. He was through with talking. Ada Sue glared at him exasperated, knowing better than to press him. She didn't care to wear any bruises to town and he knew it. Presently she turned and stalked out of the bathroom, leaving him to deal with the tempest within himself.

Goddam bitch got no right to ask how he spent his money. Ought to slap her around a little. Would, too, if she wasn't going over to her folks tomorrow. Old man Otho Carnes see them bruises, he'd come up here with a shotgun, hotheaded old bastard.

When he came into the bedroom some minutes later, she was searching through drawers, in purses, pockets, everywhere, snuffling noisily. Scratching in corners for a penny, a dime, anything. Guilt clutched him just below the Adam's apple, constricting his throat. She wouldn't be so pitiful if she'd just put on some clothes.

"I—I shouldn't of took it," he confessed. "Don't you look no more, Suckey. I'll get you some money to spend."

Frustrated, defeated, she shook her stringy red head. "Where'bouts? Every extra cent's got to go for car payments or air-conditioner payments or TV payments or something. Never any to spare. I know that."

"I'll get some," he insisted. "I'll get it tomorrow. Before you leave. I'll—ask—the boss for an advance."

She padded over and placed a hand, falteringly, on his arm. "You ain't never done nothing like that before," she said softly.

They got into bed without another word, and she gave herself to him for the first time in months. It was an awkward act which afforded neither of them much pleasure. Afterward, when Perry was almost asleep, Ada Sue said, "What *did* you do with the money, anyways?"

Perry thought for a long time before answering. Finally he said, "You know I ain't never complained about you helping your folks."

"I know," she agreed. "You been real nice about it."

"Well, yesterday I used that money to help my people."

She hitched herself up on one elbow and tried to see his face in the dark. "You ain't never said nothing about no people. Where'bouts you got people? I thought you come from up around Kingston."

"That's where they're at. Daddy's dead, and Momma's too old to work anymore. I just got to feeling bad about not helping her out. So yesterday I took the money to town and mailed it to her."

Ada Sue pondered this while Perry burrowed deeper beneath the blasted hot covers. "I still don't see why you ain't never told me nothing about your mother before."

He punched his pillow up under his cheek. "Just wasn't no reason to. When I left home, I left for good. Kinfolks don't mean nothing to me no more, and I don't mean nothing to them."

She was going to pester him all night. Right now she was leaning there on her bony elbow thinking about something else to ask him. Lordy, lordy, wouldn't he never learn?

"Anyhow," he said, "if you don't shut up and leave me get some sleep, I ain't getting you no money, ain't giving you no car, and what's more, you can go to town bare-assed, for all I care."

She settled down and lay there staring up in the dark, wondering, a smug sense of satisfaction growing within her.

"Anyways," she murmured, "have I got something to tell my daddy now!"

Leah looked at the luminous face of the clock. Three thirty. Now who could be calling at this hour? Jennings, who had been snoozing peacefully for hours while she tried hard not to flip and flop, struggled to reach the jangling telephone.

"Sheriff Gunn? What've you got?" His voice was groggy with sleep. Leah sucked in her breath and waited.

Jennings threw off the covers and sat up. "Good Lord! I'll get right over!" He jammed the phone on its hook and was halfway to the bathroom before she could flip on the lamp.

"Coy's hurt," he said. "Multiple knife wounds."

She actually breathed a sigh of relief. "What happened?"

"Fight with a colored boy. One of Cousin Frank's boys. Leroy, that sorry bastard!"

She lay back and dismissed it from her mind. She hardly heard Jennings leave. She turned out the lamp and stared at the patterns made by the streetlight on the ceiling.

God, what a mess! What a fouled-up, mucked-up mess!

She wouldn't even have known what a mess she'd made if she hadn't been gloating. Driving home from the Tollivers', patting herself on the back for her triumph, she couldn't resist projecting in her imagination what was going to happen. How Joe Billy was going to grab himself in pain, how he would fall over and writhe on the floor and maybe vomit blood. She wished she knew for sure how it would be. She guessed he would hemorrhage to death. There would be an autopsy and

214

they would find a big hole where the lye had eaten away his stomach, and they would call it, "death caused by a perforated ulcer." She wondered how long it would take.

She had to know. That's why she had asked. "Jennings, don't you worry about your patients leaving town like that?"

"Hm? You mean Doris Jean? She's not really my patient. I'm just the flunky she calls for head colds and bellyaches."

Jennings was scrupulous about not discussing his patients at home. This was his first mention of Doris Jean's being his patient. Funny how it just slipped out.

"I mean Joe Billy," she said. "He's leaving town early in the morning. What if he got to feeling worse?"

"What do you mean? There's nothing wrong with Joe Billy."

A tiny cold fear began to sting in her throat and in her chest. "He's got an ulcer; everybody knows that," she insisted.

"Correction. He *had* an ulcer. For about six weeks, years ago. He's fine now, although he drags it out when the occasion warrants."

She sat there letting the roar of the engine beat in on her, and she thought. And thought. And realized that her sweaty palms were sticking to her patent leather purse.

"Jennings? Didn't you just write him a prescription last week?"

"Who? Oh, you mean Joe Billy. No. Why?"

"I *know* I saw a bottle of pills in the bathroom," she persisted. "For his nausea. I'm—sure it was very recent."

He was quiet for a moment. He seemed reluctant to answer. At length he sighed. "I don't make a practice of doing things like this," he said. "But Doris Jean backed me in a corner. I did it as a friend." He laughed wryly. "See, I told you: she doesn't trust me to deliver her baby, but she'll let me prescribe for her nausea. And then she'll put me on the spot and ask me to give Joe Billy's name to the pharmacist, so the

215

whole town won't know about her baby before she surprises Joe Billy."

Her baby. Jennings could have told her that at least.

"What you did—that was wrong!" she cried.

"It was a small thing," he said. "Doris Jean wouldn't have understood if I had refused. I'm having enough trouble staying on their good side right now, anyway, with Joe Billy breathing down my neck about this personal injury suit."

There was an inevitability about her failure, so that she wasn't very surprised that things were going wrong. Just like always, she reminded herself. Even Jennings, the infallible, had let her down. So the pills in the overnight case weren't for Joe Billy at all. It was Doris Jean's case, and she would be out at the lake house alone.

So what to do, what to do? Nothing, maybe. Maybe it's just as well this way. Hurt him a little, anyway. Shake him up. They would get in touch with him and tell him his wife had died—no, no one would find her. For days. Joe Billy would come back from St. Louis and get to wondering and drive out there and find her. Give him a terrible shock. They would all think she had a miscarriage or something, like as not. But that didn't solve the problem of what to do about Joe Billy. Still there was Joe Billy.

She flopped over and stared at the wall. So many things to consider. It would kill her family, the Peavys. Not Joe Billy, though, most likely. He'd just wait a decent time and marry some rich bitch. She might even be doing him a favor. She flipped back over on her back.

For another hour she stared at the ceiling, almost in a trance. Finally, by degrees, the terribleness of what she had done began to seep in. Restlessly, she began to toss again, to escape the awfulness of it all. But there was no respite, no deliverance for her. Eventually she must face it. She sat

216

straight up in bed and cried aloud, "My God, I must be insane!"

Get up, turn on the light, look in the mirror if you dare. Murderer. Casual murderer. No target, even. Just scattering your shot around. Monster, heinous monstrous criminal. Killing an unborn baby, completely innocent.

Stamping up and down, wringing her hands, searching the darkened sky for hints of dawn, wishing for the day, she talked aloud, trying to fetch herself from the brink. "What am I doing? What have I done? What kind of maniac have I become, dear Lord?"

Eventually she stumbled into the kitchen and mechanically filled the coffeepot. It gave her something to do to fill the time.

Where is that thin line between sanity and insanity? she wondered. And exactly when did she cross over? She hadn't even known it. Drowning must be like that.

After a cup of coffee, she could think more clearly. Must do something, take some action. Undo the thing. The thing couldn't happen. She must get over to Doris Jean's early, make some excuse, get that bottle. Even if Doris Jean has to know, she thought. She must tell her, if necessary. Tell Jennings, too. Get the whole thing out in the open. Then Joe Billy won't matter, she thought. Even if I have to go to jail, lose all this—

"No," she said resolutely. "There must be some other way left."

24

Saturday, June 18, 1960

PERRY JOHNSON was standing at the kitchen window, watching the spume of dawn shoot fingerlets over the lake when he heard the roar of Doris Jean's Cadillac.

"Be back directly with the five dollars," he hollered over his shoulder to his wife.

He bounded off through the brush around the lake's edge, hitting an even stride. His thoughts caught the rhythm of his gait.

"Bring her down—, bring her down—, bring her down—"

He didn't ask himself whether he meant Ada Sue, Doris Jean or Leah.

Or maybe, all three.

Leah had been dressed for hours and was preparing to leave the house when the phone rang. It was Monica, Jennings' receptionist.

"Mrs. Palmer, has the doctor left yet?"

"Dr. Palmer hasn't been home yet," Leah corrected her. "He went in after midnight for an emergency, and I haven't seen him since."

She got rid of Monica quickly and slammed out the door before the phone could ring again. The sun had already gathered a daylight brilliance; time was wasting. The old Chrysler balked at starting, and she almost flooded it. It seemed that she couldn't get going fast enough, couldn't maneuver the big old boat quickly enough through unexpectedly heavy early-morning Saturday traffic. She hit every red light, had to yield at every intersection.

When she reached the Tollivers' driveway, her heart sank. The garage was empty, except for the Tolliver jeep. Both Cadillacs were gone. She jumped out of the car and ran up on the porch. She rang the bell, heard its hollowness somewhere inside, pounded on the door just to make sure. A cardinal chirped in the redbud nearby. She peeked through the window of the mute house. The place was deserted, there was no doubt about it: they were both gone. She had missed them.

Just to make sure, she went around to the back, but the side gate was even locked. She felt listless, tired. It was just like always. There was nothing for it now but to tell Doris Jean, phone her at the lake house and just tell her.

There was a phone booth two blocks away. She left the motor idling while she called the operator.

"Information for the Tollivers' lake house. It's out on route seven."

Interminable wait. "I'm sorry. I find no listing for Tollivers' lake house."

Of course the number would be unlisted. She should have figured it, with her luck. Then she remembered the caretaker, Perry Johnson. She asked the operator for his number and tried to think of something besides his bare chest with the bite wound, and his breath on her. Strange thing to come to her mind at a time like this.

She dialed the number and found herself stammering when a woman answered on the first ring.

"Mrs. Johnson? This is Mrs.—a friend of Mrs. Tolliver's. I'm trying to reach her. Do you have her number?"

There was a long pause. "You mean the Tollivers' lake house number?" came the voice over the wire finally. "I sure don't have it here handy, and my husband ain't here. He may know . . . but I don't think Mrs. Tolliver came, though."

Leah was puzzled. "She didn't come?"

"I don't think so. Mr. Tolliver's already there, but I don't think the lady was planning to come. Why'n't you check in town? Who'd you say this is?"

Leah mumbled something and hung up quickly. It didn't make sense, what Mrs. Johnson said. Maybe she should have asked her a few more questions, instead of hanging up so suddenly.

She couldn't know that her telephone call planted a seed of doubt in the mind of Ada Sue Johnson which would seal her fate forever.

Leah dialed the office and waited for Monica to answer.

"Doctor's still holed up at the hospital, Mrs. Palmer. I called to check, and he's assisting Dr. Grainger in surgery right now."

Leah had no time to dwell on it. A plan of desperation presented itself. "In that case, tell the doctor I may not be home to fix his lunch. I—think I might be needed at the Moseleys' house, or at the hospital, to—be with Mrs. Moseley. Tell him to eat at the hospital."

She replaced the receiver without really hearing Monica's reply. Coy Moseley's injury provided her with an excuse to go to the lake. To tell Doris about her brother-in-law. Leah could

220

ask to use the bathroom, same routine, get the pills back, go home. Then start all over, figuring out what to do about Joe Billy.

It was just a block over to the highway, but she began to have doubts even before she reached the city limits. What if she couldn't find the place? Why hadn't she paid better attention when they were going out to the lake house? What if she took the wrong cutoff road, got to the lake house too late and found her already dead? Who could she ask for directions? She didn't dare ask anyone.

Frank Ramsey drove up into Buck and Pearlene's yard and honked his horn. It occurred to him that old habits were hard to break, that he should have gone to the door. But anyhow, the place stunk.

Pearlene waddled out onto the porch and waved. She didn't want to come down the steps unless she had to. Frank hollered out the window.

"Is Buck around?"

"Wellum no sir. He be in town. Everybody be in town but me and Dorothy and the babies."

Frank studied his sculptor's hands on the wheel and tried to decide what to do. "Well, send Dorothy out, then."

Pearlene did not immediately go inside but seemed to be trying to choose the right words. "She—she be real disappointed if she have to work today, Mist. Frank. She be gussied up for a date. It's Eve of Juneteenth, yessir." It was a long speech for Pearlene.

"I don't want her to work," said Frank. "Just want to talk."

Pearlene still didn't move off the porch. "Wellum yessir. It—it ain't about Leroy, is it? He ain't been home all night."

"Just send her out, Pearlene. I'm in a hurry."

Reluctantly the old woman disappeared into the house, and

in several long minutes Dorothy shambled slowly out to the pickup. Frank jerked his shaggy head at the seat beside him and she obediently climbed in. Frank drove off down the winding lane about half a mile without speaking. Then he parked the truck and turned off the motor.

"Dorothy, I just didn't have the heart to tell your mother. Leroy's in trouble. He got in a fight last night with a white man, Mr. Moseley, and he knifed him. The sheriff's locked him up."

"Wellum yessir."

"They let him call me this morning, and I've already been in town to see him. But they wouldn't let him out on bail, so that gives you an idea how serious it is."

As yet, Dorothy's narrow, sensitive face had remained impassive. Now she turned big, frightened eyes on him.

"What they going to do to him, Mist. Frank?"

Frank shook his head. No need to speculate on Leroy's fate if Coy Moseley didn't make it. Big tears splashed down Dorothy's cheeks, and she snuffled noisily. It occurred to Frank that Dorothy could easily become hysterical.

"Dorothy, your mother will have to be told. Think she can stand it?"

Dorothy shook her head vigorously. "No sir, No way. It'd kill Momma, and Buck not be home."

Buck was in town for Juneteenth doings. Like as not, he'd be hearing about it, and maybe he would come home to be with Pearlene. Frank was worried about the old woman, who had been like a second mother to him. He knew Jennings had put them both in the hospital because of the graveness of their conditions. He wished someone would come along to take this burden from him.

"I tried to call Perry," he said, "but nobody's home."

She looked at him incredulously. "You know where Perry stay?"

He was astonished to realize that Perry hadn't told them, that he had kept it a secret, even from his family. He hesitated now, weighing Dorothy's stability. "Dorothy, can I rely on you not to cause him any trouble or tell anyone?" She nodded. "Perry lives out east of town on Tolliver's Lake. I think he—has a white wife."

She regarded him dumbly, trying to take it in. He could see the light dawning.

"I called his house, but nobody's home. And his in-laws don't have a phone."

"Her people," she said, "what's their name?"

The sculptor hand cupped the mouth, as if to recover words already spoken, as if to prevent any more foolish disclosures. She read the gesture correctly.

"Lord knows, Mist. Frank, I wouldn't mess nothin' up for Perry. But if I knew their name, I could maybe look for him, and bring him back here. My boyfriend got a good car. We could find him. Perry can be with Momma and she be all right, Mist. Frank."

She looked at him so pleadingly out of her enormous black eyes that at length Frank had to believe her. "All right, Dorothy. I'm going to let you find Perry. God knows we need him here now. But so help me, if I *ever* find out you've given him away, I *promise* you, I'll tear your tail to shreds!"

"Wellum no sir."

He sighed. "Perry's married to Otho Carnes' daughter. Ada Mae or Ada Sue—something like that. The Carnes place is south of Tolliver's Lake on Farm Road 69, I think. Perry might be over there, but if he is, be careful what you say in front of the Carneses. All those Carneses have volatile tempers, and they'd crucify Perry if they knew the truth—you, too, maybe."

She shuddered.

"And now I'll take you back to tell your momma you're going into town, and then I'll run you into town to find your boyfriend and his car."

And Frank Ramsey started the motor to take Dorothy on the first leg of her last journey.

25

Doris Jean lay on the couch and listened to the clock tick. As soon as she'd handed Perry the five dollars he'd asked for, he took off through the woods like a shot. That seemed like ages ago. Maybe he was just baiting her again. Talk about cocksure!

Then she heard his foot upon the steps. She sprang up to unlatch the front screen door. He hardly looked at her, just sauntered past her and made directly for the kitchen. He got out a glass and poured himself a drink.

Doris Jean padded along behind. "What kept you so long? Did you have trouble getting rid of—her?"

He drained his glass, never looked up at her in her new shorts and halter. "Who?"

It was going to be one of those days. "Who do you think? Your wife!"

He poured himself another bourbon, this time adding ice. He still hadn't so much as glanced her way. "I'm here, ain't I?"

She shrugged and sauntered to the bar which divided the two rooms. She took the clips from her blond hair and shook it out so that it fell glittering about her bare shoulders. "I gather, the way you're putting that stuff away this morning, that you've had your breakfast."

He nodded and let his eyes travel over to her bare midriff. She was winning. She leaned over the bar, fingering the string at the neck of her halter, purring at the hunger in his eyes.

"Well, I haven't," she confessed. "Soon as Joe Billy pulled out I took off. Maybe after a while you'll have somethin' with me?"

"Maybe." He came around the bar, set his glass down and kissed her soundly. She was astonished. In all this time he had rarely just kissed her.

She drew back, chuckling. "What was that for?"

"Maybe it was for the money," he said.

"Maybe I ought to give you money more often," she said, twining her arms around his neck and kissing the V of his shirt front.

"Or maybe it was because this is a special day, and you have something to tell me."

She was caught off guard. "You know?" Utterly trusting.

"That you're pregnant?" He reached for his glass and his hand trembled only slightly. "I've known for a month." Then he scooped her up in his arms and matter-of-factly carted her off to the bedroom, where he undressed her idly, indolently, preparing her for her mauling.

But she wished he would say something about the baby. Anything.

Bumping along Farm Road 69. Got to be the right road. All so familiar, but all so alike. Turnoff somewhere along here. Maybe I passed it. Maybe I should have taken that left fork back there. Even though it looked no more than ruts.

226

She was coming up on a little gray shack on the right. Maybe she should take the time to stop and ask the way. The name on the mailbox said Carnes. There were barking dogs all over the place. No one would ever sneak up on this place.

A battered pickup shot out of the yard directly in her path. Luckily, she had already braked the car. She recognized the Carnes beak through the cab window. It must be Blackie's Uncle Otho. She remembered seeing him at the funeral of old Molesworth Carnes.

A gaunt and faded red-haired woman stepped out on the porch and tossed the contents of a slop jar across the yard. She took one hard look at Leah and went back into the house. On the other side of the house, an old blue Buick had apparently just driven up and parked, because the brake lights went off and a vaguely familiar woman got out of the car. She was a younger version of the woman in the house, hair a shade brighter, frame a bit leaner. Leah recognized her as the wife of the caretaker at the lake. I can't be far from it now, she thought.

She scooted over to the right-side window and called out: "Hello! Remember me? I'm looking for Tolliver's Lake. Am I headed right?" She instantly regretted identifying herself to anyone. What if Doris Jean were already dead?

Ada Sue Johnson crept toward Leah's car with the stealth of a cat, squinting into the interior as if she hoped to fathom some mystery. "You goin' up there fishin'?" Derisively.

"No. Not really going there at all. I mean—I just want to stop by and—tell Mrs. Tolliver something."

The woman obviously didn't believe her. "*Mrs.* Tolliver?"

"Am I on the right road?" Leah was wasting too much time with this wretch. Why was she looking like that?

The Johnson woman studied her a minute, then shrugged. "Turn off two mile on the left. . . . Say, did you call earlier?"

But Leah had flung a thanks over her shoulder, slid across

the seat and shifted into gear, glad to leave the woman and the yelping dogs.

Frank Ramsey let Dorothy out in front of the courthouse, the usual Saturday gathering place for Clarington's colored community. There was always at least one Saturday rummage sale sponsored by a church or club group, but today there were three on separate corners of the square. Signs read, Juneteenth Specials and Get Your Juneteenth Togs Here and, democratically, Best Wishes to Our Colored Neighbors on Emancipation Day.

The town had a bustling, festive air. As usual on Juneteenth, there were few white faces on Main Square. Of course, Emancipation Day was not really on Saturday this year, but always when it fell on a Sunday, the celebration began on Saturday. Today, over on the back side of the square, what everybody called the far corner of the square, over in front of the jailhouse, a group of white men were clustered, but nobody else paid them any mind. Except Malcolm Gunn, who, with his deputy Fen Ledbetter, circled the square in his squad car about every fifteen minutes, then returned to his post in the jailhouse.

Dorothy hurried past groups of noisy friends—and there were no strangers—and waved absently, but she was looking for her boyfriend. "Seen Otis?"

Everybody knew Otis, too. The younger girls all considered him the best catch in town. He stopped in regularly at the rummage sales to pick up pieces of jewelry which he passed out freely. He was a natty dresser, and he had a souped-up 1946 Chevy with a silver streak painted down each side. Everybody knew Otis, all right.

Otis made a good living as a furniture mover. He was a good hand, and he knew it. He was proud of his strength, of his powerful build, of his reputation with the women. Nobody

228

messed with Otis. Or with Otis' girl. For the past few weeks that had been Dorothy.

Dorothy could tell that word hadn't got around about Leroy yet, and she was glad. Maybe Buck hadn't heard. She caught sight of Buck leaning heavily against a tree, his round head sweating profusely, talking to an animated trio of older men. He detached himself from them and ambled over to meet her.

"Where your momma? Decide not to come?"

She nodded. "She say she too old to get out in the heat of the day." She pulled him close and lowered her voice. "You ain't heard about Leroy?"

The old man wiped the sweat off his upper lip and glowered. "I know he done took the pickup last night and never come home, that's what I know. I know I had to walk most of the way to town before somebody picked me up, that's what I know."

"Leroy in bad trouble," she told him. "He done got in a fight and cut a white man. The law done got him locked up. Mist. Frank's done been over to the jailhouse, but they wouldn't turn him loose."

Buck looked stricken. "Where's my pickup?"

Dorothy shook her head.

"Your momma know?"

She shook her head again, vigorously. "No, and I ain't going to tell her else we all gets home. . . . Is Otis hereabouts?"

"Your brother's bound for the penitentiary and all you can think about is your boyfriend?" His voice was rising. She shushed him.

"Hush up, Daddy. Mist. Frank say they might be trouble if everybody know. I want Otis to help me find Perry. Perry's got brains. He know what to do."

Buck had turned and was straining to see down to the jailhouse parking area, hoping to spot his pickup. "You know where to find Perry?"

"I think so. Mist. Frank done told me. He stay out south-east of town about twenty mile."

Buck shook his head. "I can't help you, then. Got no pickup."

"Then help me find Otis," she pleaded. "You go thisaway and I'll go around on the other side. . . . And, Daddy, if you gets drunk, please don't say nothin' about this to nobody."

It was a few minutes past ten when Leah stopped at the mailbox marked Tolliver. The drive into the lake was paved with caliche and was better than the main road. It was a half-mile down to the lake and another half-mile following a ragged line of brush around to the Tolliver house. She knew her way now. She would drive slowly so as not to kick up dust or make noise. There was a good chance, if Doris Jean were down on the pier sunbathing, that Leah could enter by the front door, pick up the pills and be gone without being seen— because of the thick underbrush that grew almost down to the water's edge.

Inside, Doris Jean raised up on one elbow. Instinctively, she drew the sheet up under her chin. "I thought I heard a car!"

Perry raised up and looked out the window. "Sounded like it was clear up on the main road. Probably the postman. Now kick that damn sheet off! It's hot enough as it is!"

Leah left the car behind a clump of youpon beyond a rise which screened it from the house. She walked the rest of the way, picking her way carefully, but trying not to look as if she were skulking, in case anyone was looking. Ever so cautiously, she stepped up on the front porch and tried the screen. It was locked.

Have to risk going around to the back. May run right into her. May have to dredge up my story . . . let's see: Coy's been hurt I tried to call and tell you but there was no number I knew you would want to know your sister-in-law needs you won't you come home by the way may I use your bathroom . . . Some good comes from everything. Thank you, Coy, for your abominable temper.

Warily she picked her way around the side of the house to the back door. Doris Jean's Cadillac was pulled up near the back and screened her view of the pier area. All to the good: if Doris were down sunning, she couldn't see the back door, either. Leah tried the back screen. It was unlocked. The door was ajar. Should she call out or push her luck further? She pushed the door open cautiously and stepped into the kitchen. Still the decision, to call or not to call. Groceries still sitting in a box on the cabinet. Nothing unpacked yet. Bags probably still unopened in the bedroom. Might as well chance it.

Leah started down the hall, but she froze midway, completely dumbfounded, too astonished to move.

The bed was clearly visible from the hallway door, as was the thrashing tangle of naked flesh emitting intermittent growls, gasps, squeals, grunts and groans. Leah had seen it all, heard it all before, cowering in the corner of the room she and Mama had shared, bedded down for the occasion on a pallet on the floor. Pulling the cover tight over her ears, trying to drown out the awful animal sounds and willing that they could not be her mama's. Decreeing that when she opened her squinted eyes, this nightmare would have ended and Mama would be sleeping alone on the cot.

Leah would have turned and fled, but she must have sucked in her breath audibly, because Perry stopped in midthrust and jumped to his feet. Doris Jean sat up, the initial fear on her face immediately supplanted by outrage which blazed from red-rimmed eyes when she recognized her apprehender.

"Leah Palmer! What—what in the maggoty goddam hell are you doing in my house?" She scrambled out of the bed and snatched a robe. Leah blushed fiercely. Her knees had turned to jelly.

Somehow her defense mechanism had failed. She'd had no warning. Now she was a momentary blank. Helpless, the way she'd been long ago. There were no words, not even any thoughts, anywhere in Leah's head. She couldn't even have remembered why she came to be here. The woman who lurched at her was a madwoman, and belatedly the lights and the sirens went on: danger! danger!

"You goddam sneaky little two-bit bitch!" Doris Jean was screaming as she covered the ten or fifteen feet between them. "You breathe a word of this and I'll make you sorry you ever came to this town!"

Leah didn't even know this person. This disheveled tramp with the streaked mascara and the smeared lipstick, eyes flaming hatred, mouth spewing obscenities—this wasn't the hostess who'd sported a corsage from her Sunday-school class. Leah recovered her composure at the realization. Life suddenly took on new meaning.

"Now, Doris." She held up a restraining hand and enjoyed the taste of malice, sweet as sorghum on her tongue. She felt totally collected and serene. Holding the reins. "I hardly think you're in a position to bargain—about anything except the price of your services." She chuckled and glanced at the man who still stood rooted by the bed. She didn't fear him, but couldn't he put on something?

But Doris Jean couldn't hear her, for she had never stopped ranting. She was livid, almost incoherent, babbling her thoughts almost before she had them. "Who's going to believe

232

Doris Jean Tolliver would play around with this—this half-breed? Especially from you, who'd believe it? Bitch! Maybe you're a damn half-breed yourself!"

Leah felt herself consumed with rage, and it didn't all have to do with Doris Jean or the here and now. There was a pent-up quality about her rage, and it seemed to call to mind Cleon and even some others whom she didn't know, never knew. Her black eyes were narrow slits, slicing past Doris Jean and burying their darts in the flesh of the man who stood beside the bed. Why do I have to look at the man? Why does he have to look at me? He knows. Their eyes met, but his gaze wavered. He seemed to be trying to come to a decision.

Before she realized it, her fist flew up and crashed into Doris Jean's face. At the same moment Doris Jean leaped at her and gouged her fingernails deep into the flesh of the right side of her face. In that moment Leah realized that Doris Jean meant business, that she was striking to kill.

"I ought to get the shotgun and blow you away! Goddam trespasser! Sneaking in my house—spying! I'll get you—you—"

There was no chance to answer. Leah fought frantically against the larger woman, but she was quickly, easily thrown to the floor with a crushing thud, and Doris Jean was on top of her, pummeling her with hammer blows to the head, the breast, the midsection. The pain was piercing, unbearable, and she shrieked, screamed, cried out for mercy in spite of herself. She knew then for a certainty that she was going to die, there on the floor in Doris' hallway. With Doris Jean's knee in her chest, crushing her heart, with Doris Jean's fists in her face and the dark man looking on.

It seemed appropriate, somehow, that she should die this way, in the hiatus of what seemed to her a sexual orgy. She used to wonder if she would really ever die—she could hardly believe it was possible. But when she reconciled herself to the

233

fact that she would someday die, she used to wonder how it would happen. Several times she had willed it, had longed for it while her mama wrestled and panted with Cleon, had prayed for it when she was abandoned to the sisters at Saint Agnes, had deemed it her due when she had waked on the morning after Christmas and too much wine to find that she had thrown away her carefully guarded virginity so casually upon a man she hardly knew. But she had always envisioned an easy death—just a falling to sleep from which she never wakened. Just like always. She was even muffing her death.

Abruptly, just as she had resigned herself to losing consciousness, the blows stopped, and she opened her eyes to see that the naked man had dragged Doris Jean off and was struggling to hold her back.

"Get out of here!" he growled.

With a surge of strength she didn't know she had left, she scrambled painfully up and fled, stumbling out the back door. She was panting and sobbing hysterically when she reached the car. Spared, dear Jesus. Alive. For what? Why, Lord?

Somehow she got the motor started, after ripping her torn sleeve free, and she drove blindly down the road. She wasn't sure that she wasn't going to faint. She wasn't sure that she cared.

Time to think later. Get out now. Get back to sanity. Dear God, where is sanity?

26

DOROTHY SNUGGLED down smugly in Otis's front seat feeling very special and cherished. No doubt about it: she *was* special to Otis, else he'd never have been persuaded to leave the fun to drive her out to the Carnes place. It had taken more than a little cajoling, but Dorothy was good at that. It had taken a promise to go to the bushes on the way home, too, but Dorothy was equally good at that. Still, he'd been grumpy when they started out, but several pulls on the bottle in the seat between them had put them both in a warmer mood.

Sometimes Otis's driving made her edgy. She knew he could do anything, but sometimes she got to thinking that he might make a mistake. Might get to cutting up so much that he'd run off into a ditch or something. But you didn't criticize Otis, even when he weaved dangerously close to the road's edge.

"You sure you know where you going, you crazy thing?" Dorothy's laugh was thin and shrill and, she hoped, not too frantic.

"Man, I mean!" The big stud reached over and gouged her knee, making her squeal. "Ain't no place in this county Otis Wyatt don't know. Even know that sorry Carnes bunch, and I know why you be going, too."

She wasn't even amazed. Not at Otis. "You do?"

"Man, I mean! You think I don't know about Perry? I been knowing about Perry for a long time."

It seemed to her important that he should understand about Perry, the way she thought she understood about him. "It was what my momma wanted," she said. "When we was little, they had a school out in the country by us. Momma never wanted him to go to it, but he did, anyhow. Then, when I was six and Perry was fifteen, they done closed that school and run a bus there to carry us into town to the colored school. But Momma, she put her foot down and say Perry couldn't go. And one day after that Perry disappeared. Buck, he cussed, but my momma didn't cry. She know what he was up to, and it made her proud."

She thought about it a minute and added, "Maybe Momma even helped Perry. Wouldn't surprise me none."

Otis nodded and pulled again at the bottle. She settled back, satisfied.

"I know about Leroy, too," he said, swiping a shirt-sleeve across his mouth.

"How come you know then don't nobody else know?"

Otis laughed, throwing his head back and showing his abundance of beautiful white teeth—and veering clear across onto the left side of the road. "Got it straight from Lincoln. Him and some of the boys was still out in front of the Red Roof last night when it happened."

She said a little silent prayer for their safety, her feet planted rigidly against the floorboard. Eventually he steered back over to the right and she relaxed. "Then how come the whole town don't know?"

236

"Maybe they scared. But not me!"

They bumped along in silence. Dorothy knew that Otis was savoring the moment, that he would continue in his own good time. "Seem Leroy been cuttin' in on Mist. Moseley's territory pretty good," he said at length, with a chuckle. "Mist. Moseley come wheeling up at the Red Roof about one thirty this morning. He called over Lincoln—who was outside puking at the time—and he say, 'Boy, run in there and tell that sonofabitch Leroy I wants to see him out here right now!' Well," he cackled and stomped the floorboard with glee, "old Lincoln look up and he throw up all over Mist. Moseley's shoe!"

Dorothy was convulsed, and Otis laughed so hard his eyes watered.

"Anyway," he said, "Leroy come out about then, feeling no pain, and Mist. Moseley jump out and grab him by the shirt. And he say, 'Nigger, I ain't going tell you again: stay out of my territory or they's going to be one dead jaybird!' And Leroy, he be just tight enough not to be scared, and he say, 'Wellum yes*sir*, but you better watch it: you messing up my shirt.'"

Dorothy sucked in her breath. It was a wonder Leroy hadn't been shot right then.

Otis was enjoying himself. "Man, I mean! Mist. Moseley got so mad, he flat knocked the dung out of old Leroy! By then the other boys move in to help, but Leroy, he got up and brushed them away. 'Step away,' he say. 'This one's mine. Just step away,' and they did.

"Anyways, from then on, it was just a ordinary fight, only Mist. Moseley outweighed him about forty pounds. And when things commenced looking bad for Leroy, he done pulled his knife and stob Mist. Moseley a few times, that's all."

Dorothy was living the fight, the blood pumping fast through her temples. Otis was still talking.

"About that time Sheriff Gunn come cruising by sniffing around and that was it for Leroy."

Dorothy sighed. "Things don't look good for Leroy."

Otis swigged on the bottle. "Ain't no honor in 'em. Two colored boys gets in a fight, one of them gets stobbed, he don't tell. He wait till he heal up, and he settle it himself, honorable. You can't fight with a white bastard."

They bumped around a curve and Otis pointed. "Up yonder's the Carnes place."

"And there's Perry's car!" she said.

Otis stopped the Chevy some twenty yards from the house. The dogs ran wildly in circles, barking furiously, but they didn't come near the car.

"You walk from here," he told her. "Dogs don't bite girls."

Dorothy didn't feel his confidence, but obediently she opened the door and got out, anyway. She could see a tall thin red-haired woman standing on the porch.

"What you want around here?" called Ada Sue Johnson. "Move along. We don't want nothin' and my daddy don't allow niggers on the property."

Dorothy stopped a moment and looked around. Perry must be in the house. She continued to advance. The dogs sniffed at her heels and the hem of her dress. Dorothy was used to dogs. She knew to pay them no mind. One by one they returned to the shade of the porch.

"Did you hear what I said?" cried Ada Sue. "My daddy don't allow niggers on the place. Now what you want?"

"You Mrs. Carnes?" Dorothy called pleasantly.

Ada Sue relaxed a little. "No, I ain't. She's back at the privy. She don't have time to see you today. Fixin' to go to town."

"Wellum yes ma'am. You Mrs. Johnson?" By now, Dorothy was standing well in the yard, very near the porch.

The white woman eyed her narrowly. "Yes, I am. What you want?"

"I'm lookin' for Mist. Perry. Would you send him out, please ma'am?"

Ada Sue sized her up warily. "He ain't here. What business you got with my husband?" She tapped her foot on the porch.

"I—works for his family," she faltered. "Somethin' come up he need to know."

"You mean you come all the way from Kingston in *that?*" Ada Sue asked incredulously, motioning to the steaming Chevy.

"No ma'am. Oh. Kingston, you say. Yes ma'am. That's where we come from. Yes ma'am."

Ada Sue studied the car, shading her squinting eyes with both hands so that Dorothy could see the wet red hair under her arms. "I seen that car with them stripes in town. Got Clarington plates, too. Seems like I seen that nigger before, too."

"Wellum yes ma'am. He—live in town," Dorothy stammered. "He just brung me out here. He don't live in Kingston, no ma'am." She smiled and bobbed at the red-haired woman who was still tapping her foot on the rotting porch boards.

"You got a name, blackbird?"

Dorothy could feel the blood rising in her cheeks. "Yes ma'am. Dorothy." She took a deep breath and plunged on. "Mist. Frank say stand up for ourselves when people call us names."

The foot tapping stopped. Ada Sue now stood with feet planted apart, both hands in tight fists on her hips. "Mr. *who?*"

"Mist.—I mean Mist. *Johnson.* Mist. Perry's daddy." Dorothy took a step backward. One of the lazing dogs let out a low, throaty growl. The sun seemed to hesitate overhead.

The foot tapping began again. "You know my husband's daddy? You seen him lately?"

Dorothy was beginning to believe that Perry really wasn't about. Surely he'd have heard her by now. She took another step backwards, and the dog growled again. "Wellum yes ma'am. I seen him while ago."

The red-haired woman's red-rimmed eyes blazed, and she pointed a spindly accusing finger at Dorothy. "Now I *know* you're lying, jigaboo! Perry's daddy is dead!"

Dorothy was stunned and, for the first time, really scared. She looked around to measure the distance back to the car, where Otis waited, slouched down low in the seat.

"Wellum yes ma'am. Maybe I done made a mistake."

She turned to head back to the Chevy, but the white woman leaped off the porch and stepped in front of her, and her sudden action frightened the dogs so that they scurried out of her way and farther under the porch.

"You're lying!" she screeched. "You done called me Mrs. Carnes at first! You knew where you was coming and you know where you're at right now! Look at me!" She almost grabbed the black woman, almost touched her, then she recoiled.

Dorothy's temples throbbed. She could feel her lips curl up and quiver in a sort of smirk. "What's the matter, Mrs. Johnson? Almost forget and get your hands dirty?" She was getting dangerously out of control. What was the matter with her? She knew better.

Ada Sue looked around, but there was no one to come to her aid. She assessed the man in the waiting car then spit out at Dorothy, "Don't talk to me like that, nigger girl! You ever had a hex put on you, huh?"

Otis honked the horn and motioned for Dorothy to come on. Ada Sue took another step in front of her.

"Don't walk away from me, you black bitch! I want answers, and I want 'em now! What do you want with my husband?"

Dorothy took a step backwards and felt her foot brush

against an old tire casing. She kicked it aside and stepped back again. Otis honked another time.

"If you don't say something quick, I'm going to pick up that jack handle and whack you over the head with it!" Ada Sue screamed.

Dorothy felt something against her back. She started and put her hand behind her. She felt the rough surface of a pine tree trunk. Ada Sue, never taking her eyes off Dorothy, leaned over and picked up the rusty jack handle and held it menacingly in front of her. Otis honked frantically.

Ada Sue whistled. "Pup! Here, boy! Sic 'em, boy! Get her!"

The dog called Pup seemed reluctant to venture from under the cool porch at the beck of a woman with a weapon in her hand. But one of the younger dogs, who hadn't been around long enough to be afraid of people with weapons in their hands, leaped out and growled threateningly.

"Sic 'em, boy, sic 'em."

The dog lunged forward and caught the girl on the thigh with his fangs. The other three dogs, hating to miss the fun, jumped up to join the fray. At the same time, Ada Sue struck at her with the jack handle, landing a solid blow on her left shoulder. Dorothy sank to her knees with a yelp of pain. The dogs, seeing the blow coming, had scattered in terror.

Otis had seen the attack coming, too, and had covered the twenty yards between them in seconds. Before Ada Sue could bring the weapon down upon her victim a second time, he was upon her from behind. He wrenched the jack handle from her and brought it soundly down against her skull. The sound that it made was like splitting an oak stump. It was a sound that meant business, a final sound. Then Otis turned on the dogs with a fury, with kicks and flails that sent them howling for the safety of the house.

"Give me that!" Dorothy sobbed, jerking the jack handle

241

from him with her good hand. Then, still on her knees, she bashed the writhing white woman again and again in the face. Each time she struck, she felt a lightning pain shooting from her searing left shoulder down her limp and useless arm, and this only increased her frenzy. Again and again she pounded the metal bar into the spurting skull until, gasping and completely spent, she couldn't raise the weapon for another blow. She let it fall and dropped down moaning upon the ground.

Otis, after his one moment of rage, had realized with panicky alarm what they had done. He ran gasping back to the car and drove it up into the yard near the groaning girl and the still twitching spewing corpse, jumped out and scooped up the jack handle.

"Can't leave this lying around," he panted. He threw the dripping tool into the window of the Chevy. "Get in the car! Got to get out of here!"

"I—can't move," Dorothy sobbed. "I think my shoulder's broke."

He hurried back and lifted her awkwardly and dumped her into the passenger seat. She screamed in agony, then slumped back, only half conscious.

They sped off down the road in a cloud of pebbles and barely missed a car on the curve. Otis hoped he wasn't recognized by the car's occupant. He thought he recognized her.

It was the doctor's wife.

27

"LET GO of me, you—"

Doris Jean struggled against the man, who still gripped her arms from behind. With each vain attempt to free herself, he tightened his grasp.

"Go ahead," he challenged, "say it!"

She kicked him on the shin and only bruised her bare heel. "Let me go, I say!"

He clamped down so hard that she cried out in agony. "Say it! What were you about to call me?"

"All right!" she screamed. "Nigger! Jig! Coon! Is that what you want to hear?"

Perry wheeled her around and slapped her with such force she was sure it dislocated her jaw. The force of the blow sent her reeling against the wall of the hallway. She grabbed her raw cheek with both hands, stunned beyond pain. Then her eyes narrowed and flamed with hatred. She allowed herself a lopsided contemptuous smile.

"You can't stand it, can you?" she sneered. "You can't take the truth! Well, I don't care how white you are or how well you talk or how—how pretty you are, you're nothing but a nigger! It sticks out all over you—always has. It even sticks out in the way you—"

Perry turned and stalked into the bedroom and began drawing on his jeans. Doris Jean felt her stomach drawn in knots. She stepped into the bathroom and opened her makeup case which sat on the counter. There she found her Miltown, her nausea capsules and the aspirin tablets. She took one of each of the first two and three aspirin. As she stood before the mirror, she was shocked at the swelling face, the smeared makeup, the wild hair. Ignoring the pain, she rummaged around for her hairbrush and lipstick and repaired herself hurriedly. Then she returned to the bedroom and leaned against the door facing. Perry was sitting on the edge of the bed putting on his shoes. She was not through with him. With Leah gone, she vented all her animosity on him.

"Hurry up and get out of here," she said. "I can't stand the sight of you another minute!"

Perry said nothing, but he seemed in no hurry to go. He was sitting with his back to her, so she couldn't see his face. Couldn't see his look of expectation.

"You're the cause of all my trouble," she said, gingerly touching her face. "If you only knew how much I loathe you at this minute, you'd get the hell out of here."

Still he did not move.

Doris Jean was incensed by the way he seemed to be ignoring her. She was on the verge of attacking him from behind, pulling his hair, scratching, biting—when a cold fear clutched her.

"Wh-why are you just sitting there?" she faltered. "Why don't you say something?"

244

Still he was silent. She scarcely breathed. Finally he began to speak, although he didn't turn around.

"You've taken every kind of ravishment from me," he said quietly. "Why?"

Doris Jean didn't know what to say. He turned sideways on the bed so that he could see her. She was terrified by the look of cold despite in his eyes. He looked like an animal, ready to spring and rip her to shreds.

"I asked you somethin'," he rasped. "Why, if you loathe me so, have you taken every kind of abuse from me?"

"Abuse!" she whispered. "I thought you—were—making love to me!"

"But you didn't loathe me," he said. "You loved me. Else you wouldn't want to bear my son."

She had forgotten for a time about the seed she bore within her which had warmed her, spilling over joy just by being there. "No, that's not true. It was a baby I wanted."

There was a vast sadness in his eyes and his big shoulders sagged, a certain inevitableness about his whole manner. "Enough to have one by a man who's part Negro?"

Doris Jean shuddered. Her whole body convulsed. "All right! I loved you! Even though I have always suspected what —what you were, I loved you enough to overlook it!"

The sadness had changed to cold contempt. "You mean my unpardonable sin? How generous you are!"

Tears were streaming down her cheeks. Her whole moon-white body quivered with the need to be comforted, to be cherished, nurtured. She longed to take the few steps between them, to throw herself into his arms, to be absurdly grateful for a pat on the shoulder. Anything. "Why?" she sobbed. "Why are you torturing me this way? All right! You've got me down to your level now. Groveling. I do love you. I've never loved any other man the way I have always loved you.

245

I'm carrying your child inside me right now. I've given you myself completely. You know—you've known all along how much I care about you. Why, if you don't love me, have you —have you—"

He leaped up and covered the distance between them in three steps, grabbing her savagely by the arms. "Look at me! Look close! What do you see?"

She shook her head, bewildered. "I—I see the man I love," she said frantically. "Perry, Perry don't do this to us! Whatever it is you're doing to us, don't—don't ruin what we have! I—I'm sorry I was cruel. I don't care what you are. I love you, Perry. Don't leave me! Don't destroy this! It—it's the most important thing I have. More important than money or prestige or position or . . . Perry," she flung herself against him, "I'll—leave Joe Billy. We'll go away. We'll make a good life together—"

He loosened her arms from around his waist. "I'm afraid that's not possible," he said, a funny, thin, sardonic smile playing at one corner of his mouth.

She was panicky. There was nothing else to offer. "Don't say that! I'll have a little money . . . Even if you don't care for me the way I care for you, you can have a good life. We—"

Grasping her arm, he jerked her over to the dresser mirror. "I told you to look at me!" He stood beside her, still gripping her arm. "Look at me! Look at you! There's your reason! Don't you recognize your own brother?"

Doris Jean gaped wonderstruck into the mirror. She opened her mouth, but no sound came out.

"Look at John Peavy's daughter," he jeered. "And look at John Peavy's son!"

She faced him, searching his eyes, his mouth, his chin, her arm aching under his grip. "No! You're lying!"

"Look at me!" he yelled again. "Take a good long look! Then tell me I'm lying!"

Through the tears, she tried to see him, tried to deny the resemblance. Why hadn't she ever noticed before? The high forehead, the flat ears, the same cleft chin which both she and her father had. She felt herself sinking. He pushed her roughly to the bed and stood over her. He was breathing heavily.

"I watched you grow up, always from the outside. I saw them pushing you, saw you worming your way into the right circles. I watched John Peavy borrowing and stealing to scratch up enough money to put on a big show! I watched Wanda Peavy drive around town in a fine car and good clothes while my mother walked to work wearing flour-sack dresses. I saw your picture in the paper when you graduated from that fancy college, while my mother worked on her hands and knees to keep me in school through the sixth grade. John Peavy could have worked; he could have, once in a while, provided something for his son, but he never did."

His voice softened. "I don't know how I got mixed up with you. It wasn't on purpose. But you kept throwing yourself at me like the goddam bitch that you are, and I couldn't resist."

Her stomach was churning. Her world was flying apart. She was gasping, sobbing, choking. "You—you knew this even way back then? All the time I thought you were making love to me, but you were—you despised me! You were waiting for this day, when you could confront me with—with incest!"

He stood over her, smiling a mocking smile. "You thought you could hold me by tricking me," he said, "by getting pregnant. The baby is your problem."

She thought of the many times when his violent lovemaking had been almost too painful to bear. She had taken his primitiveness for passion, a sign of his lust for her.

She felt acutely sick and lunged for the bathroom, throwing up all over the floor, terrible bloody stuff. He made no move

247

to follow her. She felt utterly feeble and weak, given over completely to gagging and heaving.

He sauntered to the door holding a freshly lit cigarette. He gazed at the mess impassively but made no move to help her. Instead, feeling a new, sudden pride, he stepped over the mess and walked out, hitting the back door with a bang.

George Bob Carnes whipped his Ford into the driveway beside his sister-in-law's Cadillac. Blanche had seen him coming, but she had been unable to avoid him. She hated Saturdays. George Bob and his bunch always descended like a swarm of grasshoppers and picked them clean. But it wasn't her place to deal with them.

George Bob sprinted around to Blanche's car window. "Hey, wait a minute! We heard about old Coy! Is he going to make it?"

Blanche, unable to leave without backing over her brother-in-law's foot, gave up. "He's hurt real bad. They operated most of the night—or early morning, at least." She looked over George Bob's shoulder to see John Tom and his friend Rudy emerging from the car. She sighed.

"Man, that's bad news," said George Bob. "The last of the by God Moseleys. Goddam nigger! I hope they give him the chair for this!" He said this more to his two friends, who came to lean on Blanche's windows, than to Blanche.

Blanche made a wry face. "They never punish them much anymore. He'll probably get off with twenty years."

George Bob shook his greasy head. "They ain't a by God thimbleful of justice anymore!" The others murmured agreement.

"Blackie at the hospital?" he asked. She nodded.

George Bob slapped the side of the car, a signal of dismissal. "Well, I think we'll hang around here awhile and see if he don't show up."

248

The other boys sauntered off toward the back door.

"Listen, George Bob Carnes," she warned, "if I come back and find out you thugs have cleaned out our liquor supply again, so help me, you'll never set foot in my house again!"

He turned from her and marched into the house, slamming the back screen loudly to drown out her further admonitions. With satisfaction, he heard her roar out the driveway. He found the others in the kitchen, having pushed the remonstrating maid aside, mixing themselves generous drinks from Blackie's well-stocked liquor supply.

Sedalia, the dried-up little colored woman, fidgeted a moment in the corner where she had been shucked, then came out fighting. "You boys get out my kitchen! How you expect me to get dinner and you mess up everything? And me tryin' to get away early today!"

"Oh that's right!" George Bob exclaimed in mock distress. "This is Sedalia's big day! Juneteenth Eve! *Beg* your by God pardon!" He bowed grandly in her direction, then led his snickering companions up to the front of the house, to Blackie's small, secluded den. He shut the door behind them.

"Hey, don't you know they're really celebrating today?" John Tom said as they settled themselves in comfortable easy chairs. "One of their boys done knifed one of ours!"

George Bob drained his glass and slapped it down on the end table with a crash. "Yeah. They're probably toastin' that sonofabitch in every jig gatherin' for miles!"

"You know what, Georgie?" said Rudy, reaching for the bottle. "Maybe we just ought to turn up at some of them gatherings. Give them coons somethin' to think about!"

"You crazy or somethin'?" cried George Bob. "You ain't going to catch George Bob Carnes messin' with no crowd of by God drunk niggers! I'm just as brave as the next fellow, but I ain't going to commit by God suicide!"

"He's right," John Tom put in. "But there ain't no reason why we couldn't have a little fun of *some* kind."

Whiskey loosened George Bob's mind. He jumped to his feet, slapping his fist into his other palm. "Hey! I got it! I got just the caper! And the best part is, we can be miles away before they ever know what hit 'em!"

The boys leaned forward eagerly. George Bob tiptoed over to the door and made sure it was shut tight, then put his finger to his lips. He loved the drama. It was no wonder he was their leader, he thought.

He spoke quietly. "Tomorrow where will every coon in the county be?" Nobody answered. "At that colored park donated by the chemical plant."

"Oh yeah," said Rudy. "Down yonder behind the factory."

"Right! Now anybody got any ideas? No? Well, how's this: what if, when old Attaway Jackson steps up to light the barbecue fire, what if somebody has poured a little gasoline around, or somethin'? Or gunpowder! And what if somebody made a trail with gunpowder all around the park, so that when old Attaway struck a match, the whole place was to turn into one great big by God nigger-chaser—like we used to get on the Fourth of July, you know? Man, I can see them niggers scattering now!"

He was whispering and tittering and shushing the others as they concurred gleefully with his plan. They were getting carried away, their voices rising dangerously close to loud. George Bob made the rounds, biffing and bopping each one into silence, settling them down. He knew how impetuous they could be if he didn't keep them in line. But they were bright boys, once you got them to thinking. They always embroidered on his plans, gave them a certain twist he'd never have thought of. They made a good team.

250

"Only thing is, we wouldn't get to see it," said John Tom in a whisper. "We can sneak up yonder tonight and doctor up the place, but it wouldn't be smart for us to be hangin' around tomorrow when the by God fireworks commence!"

"Well now, I don't know," Rudy injected. "We might could get us a good grandstand seat somewheres. What about climbing the water tower to the factory? We could see them fine from up there, but they wouldn't be lookin' for us up there."

John Tom was usually the wet blanket, the pessimistic one. "O.K., tell me somethin'," he said. "Where we going to get all the stuff we need? We ain't going to *buy* it, that's for sure. And after old man Davis done put a burglar alarm on his hardware store, I don't aim to go messing around there no more. . . . Where we going to get what we need?"

George Bob walked to the window and gestured grandly toward the garage. "Where else, my friends, but from my generous brother Blackie! He's got gasoline and a big can of cleaning fluid out there, and some turpentine, and"—he turned to the built-in cabinets which occupied the wall on either side of the window—"there must be a lifetime supply of gunpowder right here!"

He flung open a door to reveal gun racks and shelves lined with boxes of shells.

John Tom, ever doubtful, asked, "Yeah, but Georgie, how's he going to take us copping all his stuff?"

George Bob returned to his chair and poured the last of the liquor into his glass. "You think, after what happened to Coy, that he's going to mind us shooting up a few niggers?" He sloshed his drink around and held it aloft in a toast. "Drink up, y'all, and let's go home and sack out awhile. It appears like we might be up most of the night. And we don't want to be home sleeping tomorrow, either! Besides, I don't aim to be

251

around here when my by God-fartin' Cousin Ada Sue pops in for her usual Saturday visit."

But what remained of Ada Sue Johnson was already growing cold on the blood-soaked ground of the front yard of Otho Carnes' place. And overhead, buzzards circled.

Otis' Chevy rocked and careened over the winding back road. Occasionally it hit a chuck-hole that sent them flying out of their seats, their skulls banging the top of the car. Dorothy leaned over sidewise in her seat, drawn up in pain from the wounded left shoulder. Occasionally she let out a wavering moan, and in between her lips parted in a perpetual raw whimper as she drifted in and out of consciousness.

Soon they reached a fork in the road, the left, a well-delineated set of ruts, the right, hardly more than a cow trail. Otis veered to the right. The jostling rallied Dorothy, who could think of nothing but reaching town and Dr. Palmer.

"Where we goin'? This ain't the road to town."

Otis mopped the sweat from his cheek with a shrug of his shoulder across it. "You think I'm goin' to town?" he growled.

Saliva oozed from the corner of her mouth, and she fought to stay conscious. "Where we goin' then? Got to get to a doctor fast. My shoulder must be broke."

"You ain't goin' to need no doctor," he said grimly. "You think any doctor can save you from the hex? I heard what that old witch said!"

Dorothy fell back limply against the seat, her head lolling forward like a rag doll's. "You think we're done for?"

"I know you is," he said.

They bumped along and he thought about it. Biggest mistake he ever made, getting mixed up with Dorothy. Getting talked into coming out here in the country in broad daylight. For years and years he'd worked to better himself, got himself some nice threads, money in his pocket, first-class job, nice place to live. Then Dorothy comes along. Brought him nothing but misery, and for what? Nothing he couldn't get ten other places, better.

She winced as he hit a particularly vicious bump. "You the one what cracked her head open first," she said weakly.

He felt around for the bottle, which had bounced off under the seat. "Don't say that! You the one that kept on a'hittin' her until they weren't no hope of her ever liftin' that there hex off. You doomed, gal, and I ain't goin' to be around when the Devil comes after you, neither!"

"Where you goin'?" she asked, hardly caring, her eyes squinched tight as her whole side throbbed with the pain.

Groping down between his feet, he located the bottle and, uncapping it with his teeth, drained the last of it. "It don't matter to you none."

The road petered out at the banks of a swampy bayou. Otis stopped the car and got out. He surveyed the landscape for an instant, then went around the car and opened the other door. Grabbing the girl by her right arm, he jerked her roughly from the car. She shrieked feebly once before losing consciousness. He dragged her limp body by the arm through the mud to a clump of swamp grass ten yards away. Dropping her facedown, he stepped back a few steps, looking from side to side as if he expected to see the Devil himself rush out to claim her then and there.

On his last backward step, he lost his footing. The ground beneath him seemed to slide away. He floundered waist-deep in the mire, tried to right himself, felt himself sinking in the bog. He scrambled, he struggled, he fought for solid footing; he was up to his shoulders in it now. His legs pumped, his arms treaded the awful stuff. He arched his back; he made great, gross movements with his whole body.

"Dorothy!" he screamed. "For God's sake, help me!"

He invoked the gods, fighting now as he had never fought before. Every movement seemed only to suck him in farther.

"Not me!" he screamed. "Not me, you stupid Devil! She's the one, not me!"

Panic left him momentarily and he began to rationalize the futility of trying to work himself upward. Instead, he would try to move his body forward, toward the bank, toward solid footing. All he needed was one rock. He must work fast, but he must remain calm. Each movement must count, because movement only seemed to suck him in deeper. He felt the warm thick stuff oozing down his collar. He lunged toward the bank . . . why wouldn't his feet come? He felt the stuff in his mouth. Pursing his lips, he tried to right himself, to bring his feet to a position directly under his torso. He was making headway; he knew he was. He would make it, only three or four or five steps. He lunged again. The silt slapped him in the face, forced itself into his nostrils. Don't give up, he told himself. One last effort to get a breath of air. He strained upward. The ooze was a weight holding his arms its prisoners. He held his head back and gulped for air.

It was all mud.

Perry had, he realized, just walked out on his job. By the time he was off the Tollivers' back steps he was running—

through the brush, across country laced with sloughs, taking the shortest route to the main gate and the road that led to the Carnes place. Maybe if he was lucky, he could catch Ada Sue before she and her mother took off for town in his car. Got to have his car now. Got to get out, get away. Figure out what to do.

It was a sultry, muggy Saturday midday. With no breeze, the dust from a passing car—probably Leah Palmer's—still hung heavy in the air. Maybe she wasn't too far ahead. If he got near enough to the road and saw her, he'd ask for a ride. She might even say yes. He licked his dry mouth as he remembered her standing there in Doris Jean's hallway gaping, her skin gone pink with rushing blood. A nymph she was, he felt it. Knew it by the insinuating curve of her thigh beneath the wet, misshapen sunsuit that time he had pulled her out of the water. Yes, she might even say yes.

He sprinted along easily, his anger carrying him along at a faster pace than usual. The road was winding; he knew a shortcut or two through the woods. It was two miles by the road, but only half that distance through the woods, across Scruggs Slough and over the lip of a shallow escarpment which hid the Carnes place from his view.

He came upon the Carnes place from the back, but he could see sunshine flickering through the lace of a sweet gum, splashing against the fender of his old blue Buick at the corner of the house. Good. He was in time. But what was that god-awful wailing? Part of it was the dogs, but he could also make out a banshee screech that must be human. Panting, he rounded the house and saw Juanita Carnes standing over a mass of something which he couldn't make out because of the circling dogs—but which caused him to catch his breath in awful premonition. And then he was aware of what had not consciously registered before now. Just above eye level, he had been heading toward an ever-growing circle of buzzards.

256

Juanita turned, still screaming, and saw him. Pointing a trembling finger and backing away, she screeched, "Monster! You! I knew it was you! Don't touch me, monster! Murderer! Mur-der-er!"

And she ran down the road, arms flying, still screaming. The dogs, undecided at first what to do, eventually decided to take out after her to safety.

He saw it then.

The gruesome corpse lay facedown, the spindly legs, still twitching, drawn up under it, the blood-covered hands reaching for the mushy nub that had once been the head of his wife. Several big green flies swarmed and buzzed noisily around the exposed brains.

Strange that no shock wave hit him. It was as if the scene before him could not possibly be reality. He walked over to the car and looked in. The keys were still in the ignition. He got in, backed up and drove out of the yard, being careful not to drive over the body.

Doris Jean pulled herself to her knees and dragged herself to the telephone. "Find Dr. Grainger or Dr. Palmer and get him out here," she told the operator. "I think I'm dying!"

Her windpipe was burning. Much worse than usual when she threw up. She limped into the bathroom, trying to dam the flow of tears with her hands as she went. She had done nothing, nothing at all to deserve this. It was her daddy's fault, bringing that black bastard around all the time she was growing up. Oh, she would make John Peavy pay, and she would make Perry Johnson pay, and she would ruin, completely destroy Leah Palmer before she spread this all over town.

And Joe Billy? What would he say? He'd never believe it, that's what. "Me, shacking up with a colored man? Leah Palmer must be out of her mind!"

Opening her makeup case, she took out another capsule. As she filled her water glass, she opened the medicine cabinet to see what other relief she might find—and she saw the bottle. How long had it been there? She forgot now why they bought the castor oil . . . seems like it was to bait a trap, maybe. Now it was an answer to prayer. She had to get rid of this child she carried. Wouldn't castor oil do it? Seemed she'd heard . . .

It was too vile to swallow. Clutching the bottle against her burning diaphragm, she tottered into the bedroom. On the bed table stood Perry's half-empty glass. She doused in the whole bottle of oil and then drained the glass, shuddering as she forced herself to swallow. Then she dropped exhausted onto the bed and waited for help to come.

29

IT MUST'VE been the whisky. Otherwise Leah'd never have left the house. She had intended to sit by quietly until the one o'clock news, to see if anyone had discovered the Carnes woman's body—or Doris Jean's. Instead, she found herself out on the streets again, milling with the Saturday afternoon crowd on Main Square.

Head buzzing, tortured, tormented, she crossed to the courthouse green, where hordes of people jostled her—her people. But they looked at her as if she were a stranger, as if Leah Palmer didn't belong in this Juneteenth celebration. They turned from her, went on with their carnival, their boisterous good fun that she should have been a part of. She staggered from one knot of laughing, riotous revelers to another, only to have them ignore her, turn and move away. On and on she went, weaving through the crowd, searching, searching for someone—maybe just a friendly face.

She wasn't aware that she'd worked her way around to the jailhouse. If she'd known where she was, she'd probably have run. But the Scotch was having its way with her, and she saw only her immediate surroundings.

The man came out of the jailhouse and passed very near her. Through bleary eyes she saw his black shirt, his clerical collar. Doggedly she followed him, reaching out urgent hands.

"Father," she cried, catching him by the sleeve. "I must talk to you. I have sinned, Father. I was not married in the Church." Was there more she was forgetting?

The man thrust her from himself and continued to walk toward the street. But she must make him hear her confession. Again she grabbed his sleeve, attaching to it like a cocklebur.

"Father, please hear me! I have sinned!"

The man looked with mocking, questioning eyes and pried her fingers from his sleeve coldly. "Ma'am, I don't know you. I am an Episcopal minister, not a Catholic priest. And you, lady, are very, very drunk and sick. Turn me loose."

Turn me loose.

She tried to follow him, holding out supplicating arms, the anguished tears streaming down her cheeks. But then someone took her gently but firmly by the shoulders and led her away, put her in his pickup and took her home. She slept on Frank's shoulder all the way home, and after he carried her into her house and laid her on her bed, she clung to him, tried to make him stay. But he, too, pried her fingers loose and left her alone. There was no one to caress and comfort her, to tell her that everything was going to be all right.

She drifted into an uneasy sleep, taunted by Joe Billy groping for her, clutching at her the way she had clutched at the priest. The body—was it Doris Jean's body?—would divert Joe Billy, make him loose his clutch for a while so that she could breathe. Unless Perry Johnson talked. But Perry shouldn't have been there. He wouldn't talk. He wouldn't hurt her. Hadn't he rescued her? Hadn't she lain against his chest when he pulled her out of the water so long ago? The chest that she had laved and bandaged, wondering all the time about the bite wound, wondering what it would be like to bite a man. Did the corpse who had been his wife bite him, or was it Doris Jean, tussling and cavorting with him in their love nest? Leah flipped and turned, pushing Perry out of her mind, trying to push him out of her dreams. Trying to hold him at arm's length in her dreams. So that she could dream about something else. Besides the way the hair grew in his groin.

It must have been the whisky, finally. She didn't sleep, exactly, but she must have passed out, for she knew, when she came to, that the doorbell had been ringing for a long time. It was Frank Ramsey, looking more disheveled than usual, his deep-set, feeling gaze boring into hers.

"Leah? Are you all right now?"

"Come in, Frank. I'm fine. What a stupid thing to do."

He patted her on the shoulder and moved past her into the entrance hall. "Jennings not home yet?" She shook her head. He laughed nervously. "I—really came by to use the phone, anyway. Harriett must think I've fallen in a hole."

She motioned toward the telephone in the den and excused herself to freshen up as he talked. But she could hear something about "Sheriff Gunn" and "bail." Her heart was pounding when she returned to the den. He replaced the receiver and rose hesitantly, expectantly.

"Have some coffee with me, Frank?"

He took a step or two toward her, still not certain. "Do you—do you mean coffee, or—"

She couldn't believe what she was hearing. Amused, exasperated, disheartened, she threw back her head and laughed. "Oh God, what a day! I mean coffee, Frank! Nothing more."

He looked relieved. "Am I glad you asked! I think I even forgot to eat lunch."

She went into the kitchen and rummaged around in the bread box for some pound cake. He followed her in and turned on the burner under the leftover coffee. Together they examined the contents of the refrigerator and came up with some cheese and apples. It was good to feel comfortable with someone again.

"Did you leave home early today?" she asked, not wanting to ask him that at all.

He shrugged and pulled out a cigarette, lighting it and drawing slowly before he answered. "I'm playing feudal lord today. I swore to God I'd never do it; I'd pay my help a living wage and let them fight their own battles. But here I am, drawn into this mess in spite of myself."

She poured him a cup of warmed-over coffee and sat down at the kitchen table opposite him. She could hear her heartbeat throbbing in her ears. "What are you talking about? What's happened?"

He turned, eyebrows raised, the misty, ethereal look which he perpetually wore altered by surprise. "You don't know? About Coy Moseley? About one of my boys stabbing him last night?"

She had forgotten all about Coy. The pounding subsided.

"Feelings in Clarington rise to a frightful pitch when a colored boy is involved with a white man," he said. "And now, with two of those Johnson boys in jail—"

It struck her. "Two of those Johnson boys!"

"Sure," he said. "Dorothy still works for you, doesn't she? Well, it's her two brothers. Leroy is in for stabbing Coy, and they picked up Perry early this afternoon . . ."

Her temples were pulsating again, and now she was seeing gray. Now that she thought about it, she wasn't even surprised. "Perry Johnson," she murmured. "Dorothy's brother . . ."

Frank slurped his coffee and chomped down on a crisp apple, not noticing her agitation. "They found his wife beaten to death," he said around a mouthful of food. "No way I can help the poor fool. He had a white wife. If Gunn turns him loose, they'll tie him to the fender of a car and drag him around town until he's dead."

The world was buzzing, and it wasn't the whisky. She shuddered. "You—seem so sure, Frank."

"Sure I'm sure. I've seen it done many times. Used to haunt my dreams as a kid."

She tried to think as Frank talked on. Did no one else know that Perry was innocent? That he could not possibly have committed that murder? The murderer knew, of course—but was there no one else besides her?

Pretending to notice for the first time that it was so late, she apologized for having to rush Frank off, claiming a prior appointment. At the door she laid a hand on his arm and said, "Frank? I'm grateful to you for not mentioning my conduct earlier this afternoon. What can I say? I'm not used to drinking; it just hit me hard. And thank you for bringing me home."

He accepted that and took her to town to pick up her car where she had left it on the square earlier. As she drove away, she circled the square and looked up at the jailhouse windows, but no one was there. Her fluttering, uncertain heart leaped to feel him so near.

Why doesn't he tell them he is innocent? That he was with Doris Jean at the time his wife was killed. Why have they locked him up? Doris knows. Doris could help him. But Doris never would have. She'd have gone to her grave denying Perry was with her.

Back home, she called the hospital to check on Jennings' whereabouts, learned that he was out on a country call and decided that she had bought herself another hour or so. She went into the bathroom and conjured up a sleeping pill out of

263

the nest of drug samples that Jennings had tossed carelessly into a box on the top shelf.

Got to knock myself out before I do something stupid and crazy. Like confessing.

She made herself go to her room. Made herself lie flat. Made herself quit asking why. Why is it all so complicated? Just like always. Waited for sleep to suck her under.

Maybe she dreamed that Jennings came home. Told her that Doris Jean was in the hospital gravely ill. Miscarriage and esophageal burns, probably caused by something she took trying to abort. They pumped her stomach, in any case; may have to remove burn scar tissue later. They were trying to get hold of Joe Billy. It could have been a drugged wishful fancy...

Maybe, too, she dreamed her own hysteria. The story blurted out about the body she saw kicking there in the Carnes's yard. Maybe the heaving, rambling confession was part of the dream, the prick of Jennings' hypodermic needle before she'd finished, Jennings' voice: "Please. I am able to overlook what I don't know."

It was Perry who dominated her narcotic stupor from that time on. Perry who enfolded her, consoled her, caressed her, made love to her, transporting her to such rapture that she awakened with a start, flooded with guilt.

She woke in her own room in the house on Redbud Street, the streetlight blinking through the domestic curtains she had made and splattering the pinkish ceiling with light and shadows. She lay perfectly still, trying to sort out her dreams from reality, until she heard the turning of a magazine page. Jennings sat beside her in the half-lit darkness.

"Jennings? What time is it?"

He put down the magazine and reached for her pulse, looking at her in a detached way that told her he was counting.

Then he smiled and leaned over to kiss her lightly on the forehead. "It's after midnight. I've been worried. Even after the tranquilizer I gave you, you've been so restless."

The grim black thing grabbed at her chest, and she reached for her bandaged cheek. "Oh, then it wasn't just a bad dream after all."

He raised a finger of admonition. "Now, Leah, if you get hysterical again, I'll have to give you another sedative."

She swallowed with difficulty—her mouth tasted as if it were stuffed with cotton—and let her head drop limply to the pillow. "No, don't do that. I—I've been escaping all day."

"Good. You need to get your thoughts together. The sheriff's been waiting all evening to talk to you."

"Dear Jesus!" She raised herself on one wobbly elbow. "He doesn't think *I* did it!"

Jennings gave a short laugh. "Of course not."

He was a little out of focus. She was so confused, so destitute of assurance. "But, Jennings, do you suppose I *did?* Maybe I did kill that woman."

He pushed her back to the pillow and arranged the covers around her shoulders with a touch of finality.

"That's enough dramatics for one night! Now, I've already given the sheriff all the details just as you told them to me. How you talked to the woman, drove up to the lake, saw the man—but I didn't say where—how you drove back and found the woman dead. Gunn has it all down. He just wants you to sign a statement."

Relief rushed over her in a warm gush. She let herself go limp into the pillows. "Then they'll let Perry—the caretaker—go."

"Who knows?" he said blandly. "Might be better for him if they didn't."

She was holding him in jail. She must get down to the jail now—tonight—so that he could get away while it was still dark. Otherwise— She threw back the covers and got unsteadily to her feet.

"I should go on down there now," she said.

"Leah!" His sharp tone shot a chill stinging along her limbs. She stopped on her way to the closet and searched his face, the face of a stranger. His square jaw was set; his steel-blue eyes were oblique, impassive. He caught her by the hand and pulled her down beside him on the foot of the bed.

"Leah, the sheriff wants a statement from you. About the time you found the body. There are other witnesses. You are not *involved* in these people's problems, do you understand?"

She did not. What she did understand was that person with a solicitous arm around her shoulder was a stranger—or maybe not. Maybe she was the alien. She nodded as if she did understand, and he let her go, got up and began undressing himself for bed. She went to her dressing table, fumbled in the bottom of her lingerie drawer.

Jennings had laughed at her because she could never go to bed with him unless she was wearing her wedding ring. Sometimes, when she saw him coming, she had to get up and run to the kitchen drainboard to find it. It was just a quirk of hers.

Tonight she felt the same, except tonight, lying with this stranger, being an alien in a foreign bed, she needed a buffer. It must still be there where she dropped it: the cross Sister Fain gave her years ago. Her hand closed over it and she drew it out, her totem against the world.

It was a large enameled cross with an initial *L* painted on it. On the back was inscribed, "I have called thee by thy name and thou art mine. Isaiah 43:1."

She palmed the cross and went back to bed, slipping it under her pillow and gripping it tightly, lying wakeful and remorseful, unable to understand the aching breasts and the insidious fire aborning in her flesh but knowing that it must be part of God's punishment.

30

OTHO CARNES was a man alive, a man with a cause, a goal, something to strive for: to wreak justice upon Perry Johnson, the man who'd brought shame and degradation upon his house. He would make Perry's pretty face look like a dime's worth of dog meat, just for starters.

Otho was among the last to learn of his daughter's murder. For after Otho had made a stop for gas and Red Man, he'd paid a call on his nephew Blackie and his plain as cornmeal wife, Blanche—it seemed to Otho every woman in his life, from his mother forward, was nine ways uglier than turkey droppings. But there was no help for it. Life is full of blisters.

Blackie wasn't at home, to his disappointment, for he'd brought along a dog tied in the back of the truck that he thought Blackie ought to have. Blanche only sniffed at the idea, so Otho decided not to press the matter until he could get his nephew alone. He still thought he might get a nice price for his dog from Blackie.

Otho'd left home without breakfast; by ten thirty he was so hungry his belly thought his throat'd been cut. But Blanche was bustling around the kitchen hell-bent on getting out of there to take a covered dish up to the Moseleys' place, and that colored girl of hers was busy as a pack rat in a bucket of tar, so there was nothing for it but to go on. He'd be back later, he told Blanche, for Juanita and Ada Sue planned to drop by. There. He'd given her fair warning; surely she would feed them when they returned. He set off for greener pastures; the panting, whimpering dog still tied in the skillet-hot truck bed.

He drove back out on the highway to Shorty's Bait Shop to get a bite to eat and maybe a game of dominoes with one of the sitters in the back. That was where Blackie found him several hours later.

They escorted him out to his old house, Blackie driving Otho's pickup and Blanche following in the Cadillac. The yard was filled with cars. Otho was stunned. The preacher from Pine Hill Community Church was standing on the porch.

Otho stepped over the blood-soaked ground where his daughter had breathed her last and was helped onto the porch by his nephew Blackie. The preacher extended his hand.

"Brother Carnes, my deepest sympathy," he said.

Otho looked at the outstretched hand as if it were a foreign body. He wiped his hand on his overalls and shook the preacher's hand, mumbling something unintelligible. Otho didn't know what to make of this.

Inside, he found that someone had put Juanita to bed and that his sister-in-law, Molesworth's widow, had taken over the kitchen. Several men and women from the surrounding hills were standing around in his front room. Otho didn't know what to do. He sat down on the couch and tried to think. But the people kept talking, kept expecting him to make replies.

Kept asking about arrangements. Otho was not given to introspection, but he had to think. He excused himself and went out to the outhouse and sat down with the door open, so he could look out at the sky.

Should have had more kids. But times was so hard back during the Depression, and who could know they'd get any better?

Should have had more. Now there was no one to take care of him. He couldn't depend on Perry; he'd probably hang, anyway. He'd just have to be careful about cultivating Blackie; there was no one else except George Bob. And so far, George Bob had done a passel of stirring and no gravy.

Somebody was leaving. Otho strained to be sure they didn't walk off with something. He never did trust that preacher. It was coming onto dark. He could hardly see.

It set him to thinking about Perry. Maybe he ought to go up there and check out the place. Somebody might turn Perry loose, post bail or whatever. Maybe he ought to head on up there and see what he left. After all, whatever Ada Sue had, it belonged to him now.

Otho sneaked across the yard and got into his truck. Somebody had untied the dog and let him go. He eased the truck out of the yard without turning on the lights, and soon he was jouncing over the road to Tolliver's Lake.

The lights on his old pickup were dim and uncertain, projecting only a few feet past the nose of the truck. But he knew the road by heart. Had known it all his fifty years.

She was a scrawny mite of a babe, ugly as hog jowls from the day she was birthed. Otho couldn't believe his misfortune that she was not a boy. There was not a day that she lived when she was not a disgrace to him out in public, at fiddle festivals and the like. Maybe it was one reason that Otho gave up playing the mandolin so long ago: Juanita always insisted on coming along when he played, and she always dragged

269

that vulture of hers along with her. That was how Otho always thought of Ada Sue: as Juanita's child. Howsomever, there was enough of himself in her, in the lay of her ears and the set of her eyes, to assure himself that Juanita had not been unfaithful to him.

It set him wondering about Perry. Nobody had been as shocked as Otho when Ada Sue'd turned up with a suitor. Except that was not exactly the way it came about. There was no courting that he was ever aware of. Ada Sue just clumped in one day and announced she was getting married.

Otho was at the table at the time, sopping the last of his red squirrel stew up into a biscuit when she dropped the news. He must have looked awful silly, his biscuit poised in midair, dripping stew all over his front, his mouth, wide open in expectancy, dropping even wider in astonishment. Until that moment he'd figured to have to support her until his dying day.

"Close your mouth, Daddy." Ada Sue was giggling. "You're slobbering on your shirt."

Otho began to put two and two together. It made him mad. He shoved the biscuit in his mouth and talked around it. "You're in a family way, ain't you, by God?"

Her eyes blazed in indignation. "I ain't hardly ever been kissed, much less anything worse, you dirty-minded old man!"

"Watch how you talk to your daddy!" Juanita warned. Until now she had stood over by the stove with her back turned. Otho could always count on Juanita. Nearly always.

"Who is this ninny, then," Otho said, "Simp Wilkins?"

Simp was the joke of the Pine Hill community, being dull and dim and always forgetting to zip his trousers. But he could pick a mean "Foggy Mountain Breakdown," which made up for a lot. It wouldn't be so bad having Simp in the family, except that he'd hate to have to feed him, ever. Simp must weigh in at about three hundred pounds, most of it right

270

square in front. Which, come to think of it, might be the reason he couldn't see to zip his pants.

Ada Sue drew herself up haughtily. "Don't even speak of Simp Wilkins and me in the same breath." Then she could no longer contain her glee. "His name is Perry Johnson, and he's right outside. I'll go fetch him."

She came back leading a good-looking specimen all nicely dressed in a plaid sport coat and one of those Hawaiian shirts that were so popular. He filled up the whole kitchen, standing there, clasping and unclasping his fists, waiting for the inspection to be over.

Otho looked him over in relieved disbelief. "Where you come from, boy?"

A slight hesitation. "Kingston."

Otho's eyes narrowed. "You in trouble with the law? Escaped from jail, is that it?"

Perry shook his head.

"You a foreigner?"

Again Perry shook his head.

Otho motioned at the women. "You all get on out in the yard somewheres. Get on off away from the house. I got to talk to this boy in private."

The women did as they were told and Otho motioned to Perry to sit down, rising as he did so and circling behind Perry, looking him over from all angles.

"How come you want to marry Ada Sue?" he asked finally.

Johnson shrugged. "I need me a wife."

Otho thought about this. It made sense. Everybody needs somebody around the house to do the work.

"Where do you know my girl from?"

"Met her on the road a few weeks back," Perry said. "I stopped to ask directions to Tolliver's Lake. We got to talking—"

"You know Tolliver?" Otho asked.

Johnson nodded. Otho was impressed. "You going to take Ada Sue up to Kingston to live?"

"No, we'll be living right close by," Perry said.

Otho's face fell. "How you planning to support her?" he asked. "Because I'm warning you right now that if you think I'm going to take you in, you're way yonder off. I ain't no by God dunghill gentleman!"

Perry stood up, drew himself up in pride. "I got me a road-work job now, but soon as Mr. Tolliver gets my house fixed up, I'm going to be the overseer of Tolliver's Lake. Now is that enough to satisfy you?"

Otho turned him loose and spent the rest of the night grinning like a hound with a coon treed. It was like he'd always figured. Life didn't treat you half bad if you lived right.

He pulled in at Perry's house and couldn't believe his bad luck. The place was locked tighter than the head on a tenor banjo. Well, there was nothing for it but to break in.

The house was just as Juanita had promised: nice big television set, pretty good couch—better than his, anyhow—good cooler in the window. He wished he'd brought Blackie and some of the boys along to help.

As if in answer to his wish, his nephew George Bob pulled up in front. He brought with him that overgrown ox, John Tom Bacon, the fellow who wasn't supposed to be seen about just now, for some reason, according to George Bob. But Otho was mighty glad to see him now. He beckoned them inside.

"You boys get in here and take ahold of this here daveno," he said. "I think we can load it in back and tie the television on the seat to protect it."

George Bob sauntered in and surveyed the room with amusement. "Never thought I'd see the day my Uncle Otho'd be napping on a by God nigger's sofa," he chuckled.

Otho's ire was kindled. "He ain't no more colored nor you or me!" he said stoutly, imitating Juanita.

272

John Tom and George Bob exchanged glances and burst out laughing. George Bob walked past them and into the bedroom. "The hell you say! Blackie even recognized him at Daddy's funeral. He's one of the Ramseys' niggers. You're the only one in town don't know."

Otho felt his blood rising. Women set such store in things around the house. And here he was about to overlook who they'd belonged to, just because of her. Been the laughingstock of Pine Hill, he would've, and even of his own kin. What would Blackie have thought?

Savagely he kicked in the front of the television set. The sound brought George Bob into the room, grinning ear to ear.

"Change your mind? Need some help?"

George Bob and John Tom set about systematically destroying things, not like Otho, who was so goddam mad he was doing a haphazard job of it. In a few moments, however, he felt a sharp pain in his chest, had to sit down, scared. He sank to the sofa, gasping.

"One of you boys take me home," he said. "I'm having a by God spell."

Reluctantly the boys returned to stand around and gawk at him, but they sure didn't look very worried.

"Hey, how about if we spread a little cheer around the Ramseys' niggers' place later on tonight?" George Bob asked in sudden inspiration. "We're going to be out that way, anyhow."

John Tom was dubious. "What you got in mind?"

George Bob shrugged. "Whatever. Spread a little gasoline and gunpowder around, maybe somewheres close to where they burn their trash. And we could trail gunpowder all the way around the house . . ." He was getting gleeful, just talking about it.

"I don't know," John Tom said. "We might kill somebody."

George Bob looked at him hard. "How many by God nig-gers have you ever killed?"

"Not any."

"Then don't knock it until you've tried it," George Bob said mockingly. But Otho knew he was only talking smart. George Bob was by God cram-ass full of smart talk.

"You boys take me home," he said again. "Then do what-ever you by God please. I wash my hands of the whole by God mess. Just like Pontius Pilate, by God!"

31

June 19, 1960, Emancipation Day

THE BEDSIDE telephone jangled before dawn. Jennings, ordinarily a light sleeper, was deep in exhausted slumber and didn't move. Leah leaned across him to reach it, but his square antiseptic hand closed over hers.

"This is Dr. Palmer. Oh!" He sat up, instantly alert, and his aseptic professional tone changed abruptly to one of concern and a certain degree of intimacy.

She left him alone and stumbled weakly into the bathroom, surprised all over again at her sallow reflection with its foreign bandage. She splashed water on her face and drank copiously from her cupped hands. Her mouth was dry, and she was husked of feeling.

"Leah?" He tapped on the door facing, and with a sudden display of modesty she fumbled with the bodice of her gown. "Leah, I must go. Ernestine is pretty upset. Coy seems to have reached a crisis—"

Coy. She'd forgotten all about him.

"It wouldn't do not to be in church today," he said.

It was a command.

"Even if I don't make it, it's best that you put in an appearance. And, Leah if you insist on speaking to Sheriff Gunn, I wish you'd wait until I can be with you."

She was standing behind the half-opened door, watching his profile in the basin mirror. Now she understood what he was really worried about. She stepped out and ran her hands under the thin piped lapels of his striped pajamas.

"Don't fret, Hippocrates, I'll protect your precious Doris Jean—" His mouth closed perfunctorily on hers and she could pretend for a brief moment that the light hadn't gone out between them.

She supposed she would go to church; he expected her to be there. But there would be plenty of time to go to the jailhouse first. She didn't, after all, promise Jennings that she would wait until he could go with her. After a cup of coffee, she had a bath and took meticulous care with her grooming. Considering how gray she looked, she was able to camouflage it well. By eight o'clock she was dressed in her Easter outfit, her broad-brimmed Easter straw disguising her still disheveled hair. Around her neck, just for luck, she wanted to wear the cross which had kept her company during the night, but remembering how Methodists felt about wearing crosses, she dropped it into her purse instead, and she put on the eye amulet of Frank's, hoping it had as much magic.

As an afterthought, she went to the armoire where Jennings kept the zippered money pouch which he always brought home from the office over the weekends. She had no specific plans for the money, but intuition compelled her to take it.

The clouds hung heavy on this humid morning, and somewhere off in the distance she heard a faint ominous rumble. The streets were empty, and there was an oppressive quiet downtown. A gaunt and seedy pariah dog trotted sideways onto the courthouse square, stopping to lift its leg at an iron hitching post. He reminded her of the Carnes dogs, and she shivered, remembering.

She recognized Malcolm Gunn's squad car parked at the curb in front of the jailhouse. In the tiny asphalt square behind the jailhouse sat an ancient pickup which she recognized as Buck Johnson's. Beside it was an old blue Buick, the one she'd last seen Ada Sue Johnson getting out of at Otho Carnes's place. For reasons of her own, she stifled her revulsion and pulled in beside the Buick.

There was no back door to the jailhouse, and even the windows were obscured by rampant honeysuckle vines. She made her way around to the front through dawn-damp grass, wondering exactly why she was bothering and what in the devil she was going to say. Overhead, the low-hanging clouds thrummed in subtle warning.

Gunn was alone in the front room. His amused, condescending smile rankled her, but she blustered ahead with her story, which Gunn dutifully recorded on an ancient typewriter. After she had a signed her statement, she asked, "Will you be releasing Perry now, Sheriff?"

"Not likely, ma'am. He isn't formally charged with anything, anyhow. I just took him into protective custody because I didn't want any premature nigger lynchings."

"But isn't he here against his will?"

Gunn shrugged. Leah was getting the picture. She opened her bag and drew out the money pouch and tossed it on the desk.

"How much, Mr. Gunn?"

He managed a pained expression, but he couldn't quite disguise a small smile of disdain. He probably imagined the worst between her and Perry, and she really didn't care. A funny catch, a quick thrilling shot through her groin at the

277

thought, even. Reminiscent of a feeling, certain stirrings from long ago. Something to do with Father Richard, who knew her and accepted her just the same.

Eventually he relented, as she knew he would, and accepted a little more than half the contents of the cash pouch, which he folded and put directly into his pocket, as she also knew he would. Then there was the eternal wait while he fished around in a desk drawer for the keys to Perry's Buick. Another wait while he located the large manila envelope containing Perry's few belongings: a wallet, obviously empty, a comb, a few coins. At last he led the way back down the narrow wooden hall to Perry's cell. The key clanked noisily in the lock. She stood behind Gunn and wiped the sweat off her upper lip. Perry didn't look surprised to see her.

"What kept you?" he said. It was as if they'd always known each other. He passed her up and strode down the hall, his leather soles clicking against the plank floor, his prideful, measured movements flaunting a sinuous rhythm. She hurried to catch up with him.

"I—I'm sorry about your wife," she said breathlessly.

He was signing for the manila envelope, checking the contents. He shrugged, nodded, but didn't look at her. Then, turning to the front door without a word to Gunn, he held the door open and waited for her to go out.

Once outside, she said, "What will you do?"

He was looking off somewhere, somewhere to the west. "Help my brother Leroy, I guess," he said.

"Perry—" She almost laid a hand on his arm, thought better of it and clasped her arms awkwardly over her chest. "Frank Ramsey said they—they'll drag you through town."

He thought this over, a thin veil of melancholia falling down before his eyes so that some of the dark spark went out. "They catch me first," he said, and she knew that he was accustomed to running. He headed slowly for his car around

278

at the back of the building, his massive shoulders slumping ever so slightly, she thought. She tagged along a few steps behind.

"Will I—ever see you again?" she asked. Wild poundings, the catch, the stirrings. Everything was getting out of hand.

They were at the back corner of the jailhouse when he turned in solemn deliberation and looked all the way down into her soul. A brittle breeze whipped between them.

"Not likely, little sister," he said, and he took her hand, and he kissed her palm. In broad, glooming daylight. Then he walked away.

Her palm burned, branded forever. She put it to her throat, felt the eye amulet, felt the carved letters on the back with the nebulous message: "This above all . . ."

He was standing between their two cars unlocking the old blue Buick. The wind was beginning to kick up dust from the parking lot. She didn't run after him this time, but took her time, walked quietly up behind him. He was still bent over the lock, waiting.

She could think of nothing else to say. She stood looking at his back, her fist guarding her branded palm. The sky was a fomenting gray mass. She looked up and thought that it was a hangover morning. When she lowered her gaze, he was facing her, one hand resting lightly on the door handle. He was very close.

"Today is Emancipation Day." She reached a timid finger out and timorously stroked the forefinger of the hand on the handle. The contact was electrifying, intoxicating.

He tore off her Easter straw and sent it sailing into the wind, then grasped the back of her head and pulled her gently up to meet his mouth. Oblivious of the gathering elements, of everything else, she gave herself to her pent-up cravings, her free-roving hands groping for ways to get to him, finding the opening to his trousers shamelessly. With his free hand he had gathered up the hem of her Easter dress, had pushed aside the supporter strap of her garter belt and, with one deft snap, ripped the panel from her undergarment. Then he lifted her easily, impaling her upon himself.

The wind whipped up a scrap of paper from the parking lot, and overhead the clouds rolled upon themselves and thundered like distant Congo drums. But Leah was riding upon the wind, free at last, a flower blooming upon his stalk, writhing in desperate frenzy, her world now revolving upon this magnificent stob that she had known all her life, gyrating upon this pulsating axis, this fomenting spindle which had become her whole universe. Life had become so simple. It was Sunday morning on the square, but that held no reality for her. His mouth had released hers and was searching her throat when the most extraordinary shudder seized her, and she knew, for possibly ten seconds, an ecstasy that must never end—and yet if it did not end quickly, she would die. He remained with her throughout, although she somehow sensed that he was not the cause, and when she was subsiding, her ears ringing from the sudden surge of blood away from her head, he reached behind her and opened her Chrysler. He bent her backward so that she dropped gently onto the front seat, and after tucking her legs into the car and shutting the door, he left her.

"Happy Juneteenth, little sister," he seemed to say, but the wind swallowed his words. She heard his car door slam, heard the motor grind reluctantly, the Buick roar away. In the enormous stifling emptiness she was left alone, lying in their mingled juices, awash in her own tears.

But the air in the closed car soon became suffocating, and she was forced to sit up and open a window. It was a different world she faced. It was not possible to go to church, not even possible to go back to the house on Redbud. Not possible to care about Joe Billy or Jennings. She had no friends save

Frank and Harriett. Instinctively, but with no plan at all, she pulled out and headed westward, toward the Ramsey place.

The sky was dark all around, but the blackness was tinged with pink northwest of town. She wondered idly what caused the unnatural glow. She never thought of fire.

32

PERRY DIDN'T want to go back to the lake; he never wanted to venture onto that side of town again. But his clothes were there, and his fishing gear, and he wanted to take the television set to Buck and Momma. For all he cared, Otho and Juanita Carnes could have everything else.

He knew, before he set foot on the cabin's front porch, that someone had been there. The front screen had been cut. The blood rushed, raging to his head.

"Damn sheriff!" he muttered. He kicked open the front door with a fury and stalked over the threshold. Glass from the bashed-in television was scattered all the way to the door. Chairs were overturned; table legs had been axed off. The contents of the kitchen were strewn all over the house; cornflakes and cleanser and sugar and milk covered the worn rug. In the bedroom, a knife had been drawn down the center of the mattress, and cotton spewed out. Even as much as he hated Gunn, he couldn't attribute such destruction to him. Even his clothing was rent into a hundred pieces. The dresser mirror was smashed, but across one small unbroken portion was scrawled in lipstick, "Dirty SOB By God Nigger Murderer."

Blood thundered in his ears and he cursed to the top of his lungs. "Goddam white bastard! George Bob Carnes!" He stood in the middle of the bedroom shaking with rage, unable to rationalize, unable to plan, trying only to hold back tears . . . Until finally, when all logical reasoning power was spent and he was operating entirely on instinct, his senses were frozen on a horror of urgency—urgency to reach his mother's home forty miles away on the other side of town. A new rush of energy propelled him out of the house. Gone was the rage, replaced by cold fear.

His old blue Buick was so unwieldy. He drove like a madman, avoiding the town and traveling over back roads he'd known as a child. The overcast sky was threatening, and when a burst of lightning lit the dusky midmorning, he took it as an omen, a sign of impending calamity. Gripping the wheel tighter, he bore down on the accelerator, willing the old car to move faster. It wasn't designed for sharp curves on hilly country roads, and he had to brake often to slue around sharp turns. Rain began to pelt him through the open window of the steaming car, but each drop which stung his face only seemed to scald.

A summer rain can come on very quickly and bury one field in a hoary wash, leaving an adjacent piece of land parched and dry. He was driving through the downpour now. The road became slippery, but he held the Buick on track with animal instinct, often swerving, wheels churning, just in time to avoid sliding into the rapidly filling brown ditches. The lightning set up a yellow glow to the north, but it quickly faded. To the west, a constant pinkish glow seemed to grow larger and shade to orange as he neared it. Something reflecting off the low-hanging clouds, he supposed, if he thought about it at all. At times it was obliterated by the drumming rain, but gradually he ran out from under the worst of the storm. Now great yellowish-gray billows rose and hovered over the road, but the original pink glow appeared to be fading, dying down.

From far off, he had assumed the billows originated at the chemical plant, whose farthermost western boundary bordered the northeastern edge of the Ramseys' place. But as he entered the Ramsey lane, he saw with alarm that the smoke was much closer than he supposed. And now a great roar rose from the woods to the north, behind where Buck and Pearlene lived.

As he saw the smoking house, he half slung on the brakes and flung himself out of the car before it stopped rolling. He fell forward in the mud, but caught himself on his hands and saw, fleetingly, his Buick slide to a stop against a tree. He ran for the crackling house, but there was little left. The flames had subsided, beat back temporarily by the short-lived downpour, and there was only smoke. And heat. Snapping floorboards, so hot that they scorched his feet through the soles of his shoes, crumbled beneath him. Thick, stifling smoke hovered a foot or two above the floor, making it impossible to see. Choking, coughing, he covered his nose and mouth and felt his way forward instinctively until he stumbled against the hulk which was his mother's body. He fell beside her and wrapped his great arms around her, stifling the bottled grief which threatened to spill from his smoke-stung eyes.

"Momma, hang on." He tried to lift her, sobbing inwardly.

She raised a plump hand and patted him feebly, patted him as she always did. But no sound escaped from the burn-peeled lips.

With herculean effort he half dragged, half carried his gross burden into the open until, slipping in the mud, he collapsed with her body upon him. Weeping openly now, he tried to right himself and lift her from the mud, denying that she was dying.

"It's all right, Momma. I should of never leave you." His tone was soothing, singsong, hiding the convulsive catches of breath. He tried again to lift her from the mud, but she winced in pain.

"No, baby. Can't take the blame for the Devil's meanness." She was growing weaker. Her voice was hardly more than a shallow rattle.

His arms ached with the weight of her. He sat on his knees and bundled her great scorched body against himself, rocking back and forth and moaning, chanting, "Momma, I done this. Lord, have mercy." Her only answer was a single wordless gurgle.

It was a long time before, completely spent, wept dry, he came to accept that she was gone, and he let her head rest leaden upon the soggy ground. In the distance he heard the wail of sirens, and from all sides now, he recognized the moans and wails of his kin—and of Buck, standing in the clearing in a circle behind him. He realized now that Frank Ramsey was at his side, and with him Leah, and they were taking him by the arms, talking, soothing, leading him away. Leading him away from the smell of his mother's burnt flesh. He'd scarcely noticed the smell before now. He looked back once more at her body and saw something he hadn't noticed before.

In her right hand she clutched something wrapped in newspaper. He knew what it was. He went back and put the red sofa pillow under her head.

Epilogue

THERE WAS no extra of the *Clarington Sentinel*, the local weekly which had, on several occasions, won awards for "best news story" or "best feature story" among the papers in its class. Fact to tell, there was no more *Clarington Sentinel* for almost eight months.

But the catastrophe at Clarington got statewide, even nationwide, coverage. The *Kingston Herald/Reporter* devoted a whole section to the calamity. Folks could pull it out and keep it, tuck it away with the others, the ones announcing, JAPANESE ATTACK PEARL HARBOR, PRESIDENT ROOSEVELT IS DEAD; TRUMAN SWORN IN AS SUCCESSOR, INVASION IS ON D-DAY, V-E PROCLAMATIONS AWAITED TODAY, ATOMIC BOMB USED ON JAPS; EQUALS 20,000 TONS OF TNT, PEACE, EXPLOSION, FIRES ROCK TEXAS CITY. The Clarington holocaust was said to be second only to the 1947 Texas City disaster, not in number of lives lost, but in property destroyed.

Not many Clarington residents ever saw that newspaper

account. Those who were left and were able were busy for days, digging through the wreckage, looking for bodies, ministering to the casualties, salvaging the salvageable, ignoring stray gobbets of flesh which clung to stark treetops.

According to best accounts, a fire of undetermined origin, probably from a trash fire behind a colored shanty on the property owned by Mrs. Rade Ramsey and her son Frank Ramsey, had spread northward through the unseasonably matchstick-dry timber, which even a local summer shower could not dampen. The fire had reached mammoth proportions by the time it reached the boundaries of the cleared land owned by Justice Chemical Plant. Speculation was that heat of the fire might have ignited the first storage tank. Other speculation centered around a series of miniexplosions in the area of the colored picnic grounds adjoining the plant proper on the west. It was theorized that, despite company regulations forbidding the use of fireworks in the colored park, which was donated by the plant, someone may have smuggled in a large cache of fireworks for the Juneteenth picnic, scheduled to be held that afternoon. At any rate, there, at about high noon, a series of explosions rocked the entire area.

Nearby residential areas, which were predominately colored, were obliterated. Fortunately, most of the residents were attending church at the time at the Mount Ebenezer Baptist Church, where a sudden violent summer rainstorm had forced the congregation into the storm cellar. The entire congregation escaped unscathed by the blasts, and, in fact, was not aware of them at all until the conclusion of the service at nearly 2:30 P.M.

Damage to the downtown section of the town was extensive. The hundred-year-old stucco jailhouse just collapsed from implosion, and the roof of the courthouse, a sheet metal one placed there after the 1949 cyclone lifted the other off,

287

simply rolled up from the impact. Walls of numerous business establishments crumbled, but, because it was Sunday, a number of shopowners escaped serious disaster. One prominent businessman, Grady Tolliver, owner of Tolliver Bros. Dry Goods, escaped serious disaster by only a short time. He had planned to spend the day in his store, inventorying following a Juneteenth sale, but he was called to the side of his daughter, whose husband passed away. His department store, a landmark in downtown Clarington for twenty-five years, was flattened.

Compiling a list of the dead took weeks. Colored dead were not listed, and so the names of Leroy Johnson, at the jailhouse, Pearlene Johnson, at home, and Dorothy Johnson and Otis Wyatt, at the bog east of town, were not missed. Bodies of white dead were, in many cases, unrecognizable, but, in the area of the chemical plant water tower, the body of one George Bob Carnes had been identified. Apparently, when the water tower collapsed, the water put out fire on Carnes's body, but the weight of the tower crushed him. Authorities were still checking on identification of possible companions, since parts of bodies scattered in the area suggested the presence of other persons.

The sheriff and his deputy, Fen Ledbetter, incidentally, escaped injury when the jailhouse collapsed. At the time of the explosions they had driven out to pay their respects to an old school chum, Otho Carnes, whose daughter had died the previous day.

Listed among the missing and presumed dead was one Perry Johnson, husband of Ada Sue Carnes Johnson, whose brutally mutilated body had been found only the previous day. According to Sheriff Gunn, Johnson was still in "protective custody" in the jailhouse at the time it collapsed, nobody having come forward to pay his bail. Also missing and presumed dead was one Leah Marie Palmer, wife of a prominent

Clarington physician, who usually sang in the choir of the First Methodist Church but who was absent that morning. According to her husband, Mrs. Palmer apparently left the house dressed for church and just never arrived.

A touching human interest sideline to the news was the story of how Dr. Palmer, although overcome with grief over the apparent loss of his wife, had worked tirelessly in the emergency room of the Clarington Memorial Hospital—and how Mrs. Ernestine Moseley, whose husband Colton Z. Moseley had only hours earlier succumbed to fatal injuries received from a crazed Negro, had cast her own grief aside and had returned to the hospital to assist Dr. Palmer, never leaving his side for a moment.

One other interesting anecdote concerned the showplace home of Mr. and Mrs. Joe William Tolliver, a palatial ranch-style home set on two acres of immaculate grounds only one-half mile due east of the plant. This Clarington landmark was completely gutted by fire, but fortunately, the house was empty at the time. Mr. Tolliver was out of the city on business and Mrs. Tolliver had been rushed to the hospital the evening before, suffering a miscarriage. The near disaster so unnerved Tolliver that he vowed to sell the property, electing to move his wife permanently to their home on Tolliver's Lake.

Some months after the event Dr. Palmer's old Chrysler turned up near Half Moon Bay, California. Police had seen it parked down near the water for several days before they investigated. They contacted Jennings Palmer about it, posing the speculation that his wife may have been kidnapped rather than having perished in the fire. However, Dr. Palmer preferred not to speculate. He told them not to bother to return it.

And on Decoration Day the following year, Dr. and the new Mrs. Palmer visited the grave of her first husband in the

Moseley family plot, and then they dedicated a monument to the memory of his first wife, Leah, although, of course, there was no grave, since her remains could never be identified. All their friends were present for the occasion except the Frank Ramseys, who were out of town at the time, having gone to San Francisco, where Frank was sponsoring a showing of the work of a new watercolorist. Common name it was, according to Aunt Ida. Johnson, seems like.